Dear Reader:

   In HarperPaperbacks's continuing effort to publish the best romantic fiction at the best value, we have taken the unusual step of pricing nine of our summer Monogram titles at the affordable cost of $3.99. Written by some of the most popular and bestselling romance writers today, these are magical and exciting stories that we hope you will take to your hearts and treasure for a long time.

   Open the pages of these wonderful books and give yourself the gift of a reading experience like no other. HarperPaperbacks is delighted to present nine extraordinary novels—at a very attractive price—by favorite authors who can bring the world of love alive for you.

Sincerely,

Carolyn Marino

Carolyn Marino

PRAISE FOR **JILL LIMBER** AND **MONTANA MORNING**

"Brimming with heart and the spirit of the Old West, *Montana Morning* is a wonderful debut novel."

—Sharon Ihle,
Author of *The Marrying Kind*

"A gem of a love story, vibrant with historical detail and wonderful characters."

—Lynn Kerstan,
Author of *Raven's Bride*

"Vibrant characters and a powerfully charged, emotional plot make this a treat that should be savored over and over again. One of the brightest new stars on the horizon is Jill Limber."

—*Rendezvous*

Harper
Monogram

Montana
Morning

⊰ JILL LIMBER ⊱

HarperPaperbacks
A Division of HarperCollinsPublishers

HarperPaperbacks   *A Division of* HarperCollins*Publishers*
10 East 53rd Street, New York, N.Y. 10022

Cover illustration by Rick Johnson

First printing: June 1996

Printed in the United States of America

HarperPaperbacks, HarperMonogram, and colophon are trademarks of HarperCollins*Publishers*

❖ 10 9 8 7 6 5 4 3 2 1

To my mother Peggy, the most romantic of us all!

A special thanks to the people of Miles City,
especially David Riviens,
who keep the spirit of the west alive.

1

Late August, 1882

In the Montana territory, people took pride in the swiftness of their justice, especially when it came to a gang of rustlers, the lowest vermin of all. The trial wasn't over yet, but no one waiting at the gallows doubted the outcome. The outlaws had been caught red-handed.

Katherine Adora Holman stood alone in the crowd milling at the base of the scaffold. People wandered around her in groups, speaking in hushed tones. A macabre reverence held the gathering in awe. She knew a few of the townsfolk watched her, curious about a stranger in their midst. Someone new in a place like Dennison always caused comment, but the hangings took precedence today. The bells in the church steeple rang out eleven times. The whole town would be in the square by noon.

The dust of summer swirled around her feet, clinging to her black riding boots and split suede skirt. Relentlessly the sun beat down upon her brown felt hat, the heat penetrating her thick dark hair through to her scalp. She pulled the brim low, shading her brown eyes, and stared at the scaffold, waiting. In all her twenty-three years, she'd never seen one built with five nooses.

She glanced around. At the back of the crowd, a photographer and his assistant worked to set up a heavy-looking tripod topped with a big black camera. Katherine rubbed her sweating palms down the sides of her skirt and wondered who would want to buy pictures of a hanging.

A sweating, stocky man in a wool suit jostled her. Nerves on edge, she started, and her hand slid into her pocket and touched the cold metal of the derringer she always carried. When he lifted his hat politely and apologized, she merely nodded at him.

A shout rose from the front porch of the dance hall where the trial was coming to a close, and the crowd turned as one. The jury had reached a verdict. Katherine decided she was too nervous to wait for the sheriff to bring the condemned men out, and she pushed through the crowd. No one else moved. She guessed they didn't want to give up their front row spaces at the scaffold when they already knew the outcome of the trial. But her reason for coming to Dennison today was to stop one of the hangings.

Katherine stamped the dust off her boots when she reached the boardwalk and took off her hat as she hesitated in the doorway of the dance hall. She'd never before set foot inside such an establishment. The dirty windows allowed little sunshine into the dim room. The stale smell of tobacco and beer lingered in a haze over the expectant crowd.

The jury filed down the stairs at the back of the room and took their seats on two long benches set along the wall.

The accused sat chained to their chairs, up on a raised platform that probably served as a stage. An old man dressed in a black suit sat facing the prisoners at a table on the platform. A cane with a fancy gold knob lay on the scarred surface of the table.

The first prisoner looked to be at least sixty. No, she thought, too old.

The next man, who looked inches shorter than her own slight height, sported filthy clothes and a beard stained by tobacco juice. She imagined she could smell the rankness of him from where she stood. No, not him.

Chains rattling, the third man lunged toward the judge, nearly upsetting his own chair. His ugly face contorted with rage and he screamed a string of obscenities. One of the deputies stepped behind the prisoner and tied a gag in his mouth. Definitely not him, Katherine thought.

The fourth man wasn't a man at all. He couldn't have been more than fifteen. He cried openly, and Katherine felt her heart go out to him, then braced herself against her tender feelings as she recalled the article about the gang in the Miles City newspaper that had brought her here to Dennison and these hangings. Besides being part of a gang of rustlers, the boy was the one they said had done the cold-blooded killing of a woman in Wyoming. He'd never stand trial for that crime. All his sins would be paid for today. Feelings aside, he was too young to be considered.

Katherine couldn't see the face of the last prisoner. He appeared to be a big man. His head hung down, his bearded chin resting on his broad chest. Along with the shackles and chains, a rope around his ribs tied him to the chair. It looked like the only thing keeping him upright. With apparent effort he raised his head and she caught a glimpse of his battered, bruised face before he slumped back down. She shuddered at the sight of him. A sympathetic murmur went up from the onlookers.

How odd, she thought. The crowd felt sorry for him because he was hurt, but at the same time they'd come here to see him sentenced to die.

A man slipped into the room and brushed past her as he found a seat in the last row. He pointed to the last prisoner and made a questioning gesture to the man beside him. His companion explained in a loud whisper.

"Poor bastard." He spat onto the floor to punctuate his comment. "Probably don't even know what day it is. They carried him into the courtroom like that, and tied him to a chair so he could be at his own trial. He's been senseless for the whole two hours."

Katherine shuddered and wondered briefly what he had done to get himself beaten, and then turned her attention to the little white-haired man with a cane who stood and addressed the jury. He must be Judge Casey.

"Have you reached a verdict?" He squinted at the juror who stood to face him, a portly whiskered man dressed in a gray suit.

The juror glanced nervously at the prisoners. "We have, your honor."

Judge Casey waited for a moment before he spoke, then pounded his cane against the floorboards. "Well, tell me what it is. I can't read your mind."

The man swallowed before he spoke. "Guilty."

"All of them?"

The juror nodded. "Yup."

"You're excused." Judge Casey waved the jury away as if they were pesky insects. He peered at the prisoners as he handed down his verdict. "You've been found guilty. At noon today, you will each be hanged by the neck until dead." The crowd erupted with noise.

People streamed past Katherine and out the door, intent on finding a spot to watch the hangings.

The judge stood up and, using his cane like a gavel, he pounded on the tabletop. "Sheriff, do your duty." Amazingly spry for a man his age, the judge then hopped down off the stage and left through a back door.

The sheriff directed his deputies to unlock the prisoners and remove the chains from their chairs, then shackle each man to the other.

Katherine had to make her final decision. Time was running out. Eyes closed, she thought about each of the five men, feeling as if she really had very little choice at all. It had to be the last man. He was certainly grown, but he showed no gray in his hair or beard, so his age shouldn't present a problem. She considered the fact that his condition could be a plus. He certainly didn't appear to be in any shape to be a physical threat to her until she could get him to the ranch.

Her attention shifted to the sheriff. He went through the formality of standing in front of each prisoner, reading the charges and findings to the nearly empty room. Sweat ran freely off the condemned men's faces.

A tall, thin minister, dressed in black and looking like a giant crow clutching a bible, moved to the front of the room and followed the sheriff, offering words of comfort to each man. All of them ignored the preacher except the boy, who sobbed uncontrollably.

Katherine moved forward and listened carefully to the charges against the last man.

"Wesley Austin Merrick, you have been charged and found guilty of the crime of rustling. The sentence is hanging. Do you have anything to say?" The sheriff finished his dramatic little speech and looked out over the room, obviously not expecting a response from the prisoner.

A good decision, Katherine thought wryly. Two deputies, one on each side, struggled to keep Merrick's long, lean frame propped upright. If they put the noose around his neck right now and let go of him, he'd probably hang himself.

Merrick, she thought, trying to recall what the newspaper had said about him. All of the others in the gang had been on various wanted posters all over the territory. Little had been written about the one named Merrick.

Before she could lose her courage, Katherine moved down the center aisle. She put her hand on the stage and felt the rough wood under her sweaty palm.

"Sheriff?" The hum and murmur in the room stopped, leaving an awesome silence. She hesitated for a brief moment, as the paunchy middle-aged man with the badge on his chest turned to face her.

"Sheriff, I want to claim Mr. Merrick under the laws of the township of Dennison." With an effort, she kept her voice steady and looked him in the eye. The town still had an old English law on its books allowing a female to claim a condemned man for her husband. The idea was that a woman's love and good influence would save him from his wickedness, although Katherine's motives were more urgent. She had to keep her head now.

At first he just stared at her. Then his face turned a mottled red and he shouted. *"Are you loco!?"*

She kept her back to the rising din of speculation from those few remaining in the room, and spoke up so the sheriff could hear her. "No sir. It's my right as an unmarried woman, and I want to claim him." She put her hand over the nervous flutter in her middle.

The sheriff's face went purple and he sputtered, seeming at a temporary loss for words. Katherine supposed she'd spoiled his show. He looked ready to explode when he pointed a stubby finger at her and yelled. "Wait for me in my office!"

She clasped her trembling hands together in front of her and drew herself up to her full height, making her voice as stern as she could manage. "I will. But don't you hang him. I claimed him and he's mine."

Katherine turned away from the sheriff and hurried out into the sunlight into a crowd that had come alive with speculation. She refused to look at anyone, knowing she would see disapproval in their eyes. Brace yourself, she thought. Once again she would find herself at the center of a scandal.

She crossed the dusty street and ducked into the sheriff's office. The smell of stale tobacco, old coffee, and sweat hit her as she walked through the door. A hot breeze swirled dust across the rough wooden floor and ruffled the mess of papers on the scarred desk that dominated the middle of the place. The back half of the building was constructed of stone, partitioned off from the main room by metal bars into three cells. Judging the distance from the stove to the prisoners' cots, she decided the jail would be a sorry place to spend a winter night.

Moments later the sheriff burst through the door. She turned and saw the deputies behind him, dragging

Merrick along with them. At the sight of the prisoner, she didn't know whether to feel relief or dread.

The sheriff had regained his self-control. He motioned to the deputies to put their prisoner in the cell. They dumped Merrick on a cot and didn't even bother to close the door of iron bars.

"Now, Missy, would you kindly explain to me exactly what you were doing back there?" The bark in his tone reminded her of her late father when he was angry.

"According to the law of this town, I can claim him." Katherine wiped her sweating palms on her riding skirt.

"I know what you did. I want to know why." He eyed her with suspicion. "Where are you from?"

"East of here. I own a ranch near Miles City." What she said was nearly correct. She almost owned the ranch.

"So you don't live in Dennison." He had a hopeful look she didn't like one bit.

Had she made a fool of herself all for nothing? Frantically she searched her mind for what she had heard about the law. "Does that make a difference?"

"Well, I don't rightly know. J. P., go get Judge Casey." One of the deputies bolted from the office. The sheriff turned back to her. "Want a cup of coffee?"

The gesture of hospitality struck her as ludicrous, given the situation. Her stomach was so riled at this point that she knew she could not swallow anything just now, especially the evil-smelling brew she had noticed when she walked through the door. "No, thank you, I don't think so."

The sheriff shrugged and sat at his desk, motioning her to a chair. She sat for a moment, and then rose to her feet and began to pace, too nervous to stay still. The one deputy left in the room did not meet her eye when she glanced at him, but she felt him watching her. The sheriff studied some papers on his desk with great interest, muttering something she didn't catch. The deputy covered a snicker with a cough and turned away.

Merrick moaned and rolled on the narrow cot. If he moved any more, he would end up on the floor. Katherine spoke up, directing her comment to the deputy. "Put him on the floor before he can do any more damage to himself." The deputy hesitated for a moment, then at a nod from the sheriff he entered the cell and lowered the outlaw none too gently onto the filthy floor.

The outside door opened and the judge, looking cranky, came hobbling in on a cane.

"What the hell is going on in here?" he demanded, whacking the side of the sheriff's desk with his stick. The sound of wood smacking wood made Katherine jump.

"Judge Casey." The sheriff lumbered to his feet and came around to stand by Katherine. She wondered if he would protect her if the judge took a swing at her.

"This here deputy said you weren't going to hang one of them because of a woman." He waved his cane around as if he were looking for something else that needed hitting.

The sheriff stepped out of range and pointed to Katherine. "This woman claimed him. Can she do that?"

The judge waved one fist in the air, as if threatening the sheriff, and yelled at him in a high, thin voice. "Course she can. I tried to tell the city aldermen to change a bunch of those silly laws, but they never got around to it. Too busy making up new ones. It's still on the books." His expression told everyone what he thought of the men who ran Dennison.

The sheriff looked like a man trying to hide a good poker hand. "But she's not from here."

"Don't matter," the judge came up close and gave her a quick once over. "Don't say she has to be. She just can't know him is all." He turned on his heel and stomped around the office, muttering about stupid laws, and stupider women. His cane made a rhythmic tapping on the wooden floor until he stopped at a shelf containing books and pulled down a black leather volume.

A quiet descended on the group. He held the book out to her. It was a copy of the Holy Bible. "Raise your right hand."

Obediently Katherine followed his directions, then placed her left hand on the bible that he thrust at her.

"Do you know him? What's his name? Merrick? Ever seen him before today?" The book trembled in his gnarled old hand.

"No sir." She did know the law. A woman could only claim a stranger, and she had never laid eyes on the outlaw named Merrick before today.

"Do you know what you have to do now?" The judge tossed the bible onto the sheriff's desk and ran his fingers through his wispy white hair.

Unwavering, she looked the little man straight in the eye. They were of like height. "Yes sir."

The hard part: she had to marry the man. The solution to her dilemma might turn out to be her worst nightmare. She took a deep breath and prayed that her breakfast would remain just where it was, despite its quivery dance in her stomach.

The judge pointed at a deputy with his cane. "J. P., get the preacher. We're going to do this right." When the deputy opened the door, the street outside was full of people.

The judge looked out the open door and turned back to her. "Looks like you all got plenty of guests for your wedding."

Katherine didn't care if the entire territory witnessed the ceremony. She needed a marriage certificate, and unfortunately a husband came along with it. She never intended to marry again after this, so what difference did it make to her if there were witnesses?

The sheriff, who had been standing quietly by, spoke to the remaining deputy in a resigned voice. "Let's get the prisoner on his feet."

The tall, thin clergyman came puffing through the door, and stopped in his tracks. His gaze swept the room and he blinked in confusion, his Adam's apple bobbing in his skinny neck. "What's going on? I got prayers to say over the hanged men while the photographer takes pictures."

The sheriff interrupted him. "That can wait. You got words to say over a live one."

Judge Casey waved his cane and yelled at the minister. "Hurry up and marry them, Alonzo. Mrs. Casey's waiting dinner on me."

The minister nodded and shuffled his feet, his glances darting around the room like a nervous bird. He pulled a small volume out of his coat pocket, opened the book, and started the ceremony.

Katherine turned her back on the crowd outside and tried to concentrate on the words the clergyman spoke.

"We are gathered here today to witness . . ." his voice droned.

She had a strange feeling of detachment, as if everything were happening to someone else and she was only a spectator. When prompted, she repeated the appropriate words. Chin on his chest, Merrick swayed on his feet between the sheriff and a deputy. His grunts of reply seemed more a response to pokes in the ribs from the deputy than to the words spoken by the minister. Katherine couldn't tell if his eyes were closed, or swollen shut.

The minister held up his bony hand. "Judge Casey, I can't tell what he's saying when I ask him the questions."

The judge pounded the floor with his cane. "Get on with it, Alonzo. He's saying yes. Any sane man would choose marriage over hanging."

Katherine signed the marriage certificate with a shaking hand. "I'll get my wagon," she told them, and fled the office, making her way through the crowd to the general store to pay for her supplies. Expertly she brought the wagon around to the back of the sheriff's office. The deputies loaded the outlaw in the wagon bed and laid him out like a sack of grain.

Twice Katherine stopped on the lonely ride home and climbed in the back to wedge some of her purchases around Merrick. He lay senseless, and despite her efforts, he continued to bounce around in the old buckboard like a loose sack of potatoes. The boxes and bags shifted on the rough road, and his limp body rolled like a rag doll. Good thing he slept, she thought. Considering his condition, the trip could have been a misery for him if he had been awake.

Katherine knew exactly when her wagon crossed onto her land. The rolling prairie welcomed her with its late summer shades of green turning to gold, looking fair and fertile. Fat, white-faced cattle took their last graze before they settled down for the night. Their gentle lowing soothed her.

Something tight inside her relaxed, like a spring unwinding. The calm feeling grew as she approached the entrance to the shallow valley that sheltered her home. She paused on a small rise to drink in the sight of the two-story rambling stone and wood house and the surrounding outbuildings in the distance, nestled against the low hills.

Her father had built the house to replace the original homesteader's cabin now occupied by the ranch's foreman. The main house had four bedrooms upstairs. Julius Holman had come here with his wife, two children, and a dream. He had expected to fill those airy rooms with more babies, but his vision that his name would live on in the Montana territory would never come true. None of the children born after Katherine had lived, and now she was the only Holman left.

The ranch had been her home for so long that the land was a part of her. She would do almost anything to avoid losing it, including marrying the outlaw who lay senseless in the back of her wagon. This was the only place she felt truly safe, the place she intended to raise her daughter.

Merrick was simply a necessary but temporary fly in her ointment. She would send him packing as soon as he had served his purpose. Perhaps she could give him some money to get a fresh start and make him promise to mend his outlaw ways before she sent him away. She didn't like the thought of being responsible for putting an intractable rustler back out on the range.

The sun slipped behind the horizon, throwing long shadows against the hills as she pulled up in front of the bunkhouse and tied the reins to the brake lever.

She yelled at the open door, "Gibby, come out and give me a hand." Gibson Sawyer lived in the homesteader's cabin he and Katherine's father had built over twenty years ago, but at this time of the evening she knew she would find him in the bunkhouse with the hands.

The wiry old foreman strolled out and tipped his hat. "Evenin' Miss Kate. You want the boys to take the wagon to the cookshack and unload them supplies for you?"

She stood on the seat and climbed over into the wagon bed. "Is there an empty lower bunk?"

His seamed old face showed his puzzlement for a moment. "I think so. Why?"

"Get a few of the boys to get this man out of here and put him to bed." She pulled a sack of flour away from Merrick's prone body.

Gibby peered into the wagon and then looked questioningly at her. She ignored his gaze. She had no intention of offering him an explanation.

After a moment he shrugged. "Yes ma'am." He lowered the tailgate.

"Then see to the supplies. The small box goes up to the house." Katherine jumped down out of the wagon and headed across the yard to the big house. Dusk gave its rock walls a forbidding appearance, but the light shining from the windows invited her home.

At the sound of a mournful howl from behind the bunkhouse she added over her shoulder, "And you can untie Hamlet."

Before she got to the porch, the huge brown mutt almost knocked her off her feet. "Ham, down!" He backed up three paces and she readied herself for another charge. Adroitly she sidestepped the dog and then called him to her, scratching him behind the ears as he calmed down. "Good boy." Hamlet waited until she straightened up, then took off across the yard in pursuit of a rabbit.

She had placed her foot on the lowest step of her wide front porch when the door opened. A chubby five year old, dressed in a short calico dress and pinafore, ran across the porch, down two steps, then launched herself fearlessly into Katherine's arms. The child was getting too big to catch, but that was exactly the reason Katherine did not put a stop to it. Hannah was her only child and was growing up far too fast.

"Mama, Mama." She held Katherine's face between her dimpled hands and gave her a noisy smack on the cheek.

Katherine hugged the child and murmured into her sweet-smelling curls as she climbed the steps, "Missed you, Hannah," and carried her into the house, loving the feel of her sturdy little body.

"Me too," the girl hugged her again. "What did you bring me?"

She laughed at her daughter's response and set her on the floor. "Were you a good girl?" She tried her best stern mother look.

Big brown eyes blinked solemnly as she nodded, "Like always, Mama."

Katherine groaned to herself. She'd better have a word with her housekeeper if Hannah had behaved like always today.

"Where's Consuela?" She watched her daughter hop around the room on one foot.

"In the *cocina*." Hannah's vocabulary was an interesting blend of English and Spanish.

"Let's go ask her how you behaved today."

The child tried to switch her hopping to the other foot and promptly fell down. A frown crossed her face. "Maybe later."

"Maybe now," Katherine insisted. She took the reluctant child by the hand and led her to the kitchen.

Consuela greeted her, her round old brown face breaking into a smile. She wiped the flour off her hands, poured Katherine a cup of coffee, then returned to kneading her bread dough.

When questioned, Consuela insisted Hannah had been an angel the whole day, even eating all her supper. Although Consuela had a different concept of what constituted angelic behavior than Katherine did, she pulled a sugar stick from her skirt pocket, unwrapped it, and handed it to the delighted child.

"Hurry and eat, *mija*," Consuela encouraged, "it is almost your bedtime."

Outside, someone banged on the kitchen door. Motioning for Consuela to go on with her work, Katherine answered the door herself.

Gibby stood on the enclosed porch, holding the box of supplies. "I ain't sure why you brung me that busted up cowpuncher, but I got a question. You attached to him in any special way?"

Katherine sucked in a breath. She stepped out onto the porch and closed the door behind her. What had the outlaw said to Gibby? She had hoped to keep the marriage a secret for as long as possible. "Why?"

He handed her the box. "'Cause he's got a busted arm and he's puking up blood."

2

Katherine clutched at the supplies and stared at Gibby. If Merrick died, her plan died with him. What was she going to do? George Anderson, the executor of her father's estate, had always been a man who paid a great deal of attention to details. She had no doubt that he would challenge the legality of a marriage that had only lasted a few hours before the groom died.

"Well, Miss Kate? What do you want me to do with him?"

She shifted her weight, resting the box against her hip as she took a deep breath. She hadn't planned on this. Marrying a rustler was one thing, but she certainly didn't want him in her house. After a moment's thought, she realized she didn't have a choice. "I guess you better bring him up here."

Gibby shrugged, his weathered face unreadable. "If you want." He reached past her and opened the door to the kitchen.

Katherine stepped back inside, kicked the door closed with her foot, and sighed as she leaned against the solid wood for a moment, deciding what to do. Consuela and Hannah stared at her as she set the box down on the table. She ignored their puzzled expressions.

"Consuela, please open up Father's room. Are there linens on the bed?"

"Si senora." The housekeeper wiped her hands and untied her apron.

Katherine thought quickly, deciding what needed doing first. "Put down the oil cloth and one of the old sheets over that." It would be foolish to ruin her good bedding on a rustler. "And build up the fire."

With a nod the housekeeper left to do her bidding. Consuela never asked questions, and never offered opinions. Their long relationship had always suited Katherine perfectly.

Her daughter never failed to ask questions. Hannah climbed up on a chair and watched Consuela leave, then turned to her mother. "What, Mama?"

Katherine considered telling the child to be quiet, but she knew putting her off would only inflame Hannah's curiosity. "One of the men is sick, and he'll stay in the house for a while so I can take care of him."

Hannah pulled the half-eaten candy stick out of her mouth. "Who, Mama?"

"He's new, he just came today." Hannah accepted the explanation and turned her attention back to the candy.

Katherine had never anticipated having the outlaw in her home. Anxious to have her curious daughter out of the way before the hands brought Merrick into the house, Katherine thought for a moment. Eyeing the filthy youngster, she decided on an obvious ploy she knew would work. "Hannah, have you had a bath?" She hid a smile when her daughter made a face. The child hated soap and water almost as much as she hated green vegetables.

"It's getting late. You can skip it until tomorrow night." Hannah readily agreed. "Come on, I'll take you up."

Taking her daughter by the hand, Katherine retrieved a wooden box of medical supplies from her office, then climbed the stairs. She left the box outside her father's bedroom door and took Hannah to her room.

Keeping an ear open to hear Gibby, she whisked the child out of her dirty pinafore and dress, into her night-clothes, and wiped her sticky hands and face.

Together they knelt by the small bed while Hannah said her prayers. After blessing everyone she knew, she picked up a small porcelain figurine of a cat from her nightstand.

"And God bless Papa and Grandpa in heaven." She kissed the top of the kitten's head and handed the figurine to Katherine.

As Katherine held the cold painted ceramic in her hand, it began to warm with the heat of her body. The little likeness of the cat was the only thing she had to remind her of Gerald, besides Hannah. He had given it to Katherine the last time she had seen him. Their daughter loved to hear stories about her father, and insisted the cat must sit on her night table to watch over her while she slept.

After replacing the figurine in its ritual spot, Katherine tried to remember Gerald's face. She could not readily recall his image in her mind, and once again she wished she had a photograph of him.

"Good night, darling girl. Mama loves you." She gave her daughter a big hug and tucked the covers around her sturdy little body.

"Me too," Hannah answered with the smug certainty of a child who held no doubts about her mother's feelings.

Katherine kissed her child on the forehead, then closed the door as she left the room. She paused in the hall to listen for the sound of small feet hitting the floor.

After a moment's silence, Katherine went down the hall to see whether Consuela needed any help. Standing in the open doorway of her father's room she was stung by the memories of the many sad hours spent there as he lay dying. She hadn't been back inside in the months since she had buried him on the hill behind the house. Everything stood just as it had then, but without the awful odor of illness. A shout from downstairs jolted her from her thoughts.

She walked down the hallway to the landing and called softly down to Gibby in the front room, "Bring him up here."

The foreman and his men struggled to get Merrick up the stairs. The cowpunchers had the outlaw suspended in a blanket, carrying him like pallbearers. The narrow stairway made maneuvering difficult. All she could see of the rustler were the tips of his boots sticking out the end of the blanket.

Katherine stepped aside to let them pass and pointed down the hall. "Put him in Father's room."

The hands lowered him onto the bed, blanket and all. Gibby stood back, hands on hips. "He stopped puking, and I set his arm. Don't know how well it will heal."

The man's sleeve had been cut away from his right forearm. Strips of faded plaid flannel held wooden splints in place.

Gibby tipped his hat. The others did likewise, then followed the foremen silently out of the room. One thing for sure about cowboys, they didn't waste time talking.

Consuela brought two lamps and placed them on the small tables beside the bed.

Katherine stared down at the man. Swelling and bruising marred his face, but with all of the dirt and dried blood, she couldn't tell what needed to be done for him. She was relieved to hear he had stopped vomiting.

"Consuela, get me a couple of buckets of hot water and some rags. He smells terrible. And some old linen we can use for bandages."

When the housekeeper left, Katherine perched uneasily on the side of the bed. She reminded herself she had chosen this man because he was in no condition to hurt her. The outlaw looked big and strong, and if he had been healthy, he would have scared her to death.

"Mr. Merrick, wake up." She poked his arm with her forefinger. He didn't stir. Reluctantly she reached to unfasten Merrick's filthy shirt. Several of the buttons were gone. When she finished, she carefully spread the tattered fabric open, revealing his wide chest. She gasped at the sight. Ugly purple and black bruising marred the flesh over his abdomen and ribs.

Katherine felt an unexpected rush of rage toward the sheriff of Dennison and his deputies. She wondered briefly how Merrick might have provoked them, then she pushed the thought from her mind. It didn't matter what he had done, no prisoner deserved such brutal treatment.

She felt herself relax a bit. He was in no shape to do anyone any harm. What mattered now was seeing to his injuries and making him as comfortable as possible. No wonder he had been spitting up blood. Some of his ribs had to be broken. She couldn't tell how far up the bruises went, because a thick dark mat of hair covered the upper part of his chest.

"*Dios mio*," Consuela breathed from behind Katherine, making her jump, "who would do such a thing?" She set the buckets beside the bed.

"I don't know." Katherine wasn't going to alarm the older woman by telling her who Merrick was. "Consuela, hand me that pillow." She cradled his head in her hand as she slid the pillow under him. When she lowered him down and pulled her hand away, it was covered with fresh blood. She looked away until a wave of nausea passed. A wound on the back of his head must have broken open while he rolled around in the back of her wagon on the trip from Dennison.

Katherine's hands shook as she rinsed them in the bucket, and this time she had to force herself to relax. She studied the man on the bed while deciding what they needed to do for him. "We're going to have to cut away what's left of his shirt. I don't want to move him any more than we have to."

"Si." Consuela deftly cut the shirt off in pieces. Even relaxed, the muscles in Merrick's arms looked strong.

Katherine fingered the dirty blanket her men had used as a sling to carry him. "I think we can pull this blanket out from under him."

After they slid the blanket away they washed his chest and arms. It occurred to Katherine while she bathed one of his big square hands that Merrick hadn't fought back with whoever had beaten him. There wasn't a mark on his knuckles. Either they hit him from behind and beat him while he was senseless, or someone had held him down. In any case, the treatment they had given him hadn't been fair.

While Katherine dried him off, Consuela tore wide strips from an old sheet. He had a series of bruises, about three inches across, along his ribs on both sides of his body. The flat toe of a boot would leave a mark like that, Katherine thought. If he had been kicked hard enough to bruise, she had to assume some of his ribs must be broken, even though she couldn't feel any obvious breaks. Together the two women bound his ribs, no small task considering how heavy he was. Every time Katherine pushed the roll of bandage under him, she noticed how firm and warm the flesh on his back felt. She had to shove her hand under him quite a few times to wrap him from his armpits to just above his waist.

When they finished with his ribs, Katherine's arms ached. She stood back from the bed and shook her limbs out, trying to relieve the fatigue. She rubbed her hand across the crick in her neck, and smiled at Consuela.

"I think that was the hard part," Katherine said to the quiet old Mexican woman who had taken care of her since she was a baby. Consuela must be getting tired too.

They cleaned and wrapped the wound on his head. Every time they moved or jostled him now he moaned. Katherine supposed that meant he was waking up. Good news, from a medical point of view.

Consuela leaned over to rinse out a cloth in the bucket. When she turned back to the bed, her wrinkled brown hands froze in midair. Katherine had unbuckled his belt and unbuttoned the waistband of his denim trousers.

Consuela hesitated, then spoke, "Do you think we need to undress him any more?" The housekeeper's hands fluttered in front of her like a timid virgin's might at the thought of seeing a man without his pants on.

The denims he wore showed patches of blood and dirt. Katherine considered the question, along with the older woman's obvious discomfort, and made a decision. "Consuela, I can do this. You go and make me some supper. I'm very hungry." She had to check the rest of him for injuries, but she could accomplish the task by herself. There was no need to upset Consuela.

Apparently Consuela didn't need any coaxing. Maybe the woman had never seen a naked man. Katherine had taken care of her father's personal needs when he could no longer see to them himself. She had never considered what Consuela's experiences in that area might be, and chuckled to herself when the woman left quickly, carrying the soiled linens and the smelly blanket.

Katherine trimmed the sputtering wick on one of the lamps and moved the light closer to the edge of the table.

One at a time she worked off his boots. The fine leather looked to be in good shape, and the quality of the workmanship impressed her. They looked to be custom made, and she wondered where he had gotten them. She doubted a rustler would stay in one place long enough to order boots. She peeled off his stockings and dropped them on the floor beside the footwear. Unlike his shirt, his underthings were reasonably clean and in good repair.

She unfastened the rest of the buttons down the front of his trousers. He was wearing cotton underdrawers. Good. She would leave those on to preserve some sense of propriety. She tried to pull his pants down over his hips, and found they were firmly anchored by his weight. She sat down on the mattress for a moment and pondered the problem. There was no way she could lift him by herself, but perhaps if she rolled him from side to side as she pulled, she could ease the trousers down.

Kneeling beside him on the bed, she braced one hand against his hip, and with her other hand she gripped his waistband. She pushed and tugged at the same time. The pants moved down a few inches. Encouraged, Katherine moved to the other side of the bed and repeated the process. After several turns, she tired of climbing on and off the bed, so she straddled his knees, tucked her hands inside his waist band as far around his sides as she could reach, and threw her weight into a backwards heave.

His pants slid the rest of the way over his hips, tumbling Katherine back onto the bed. She sat up, delighted that her plan had worked, and came face to face with the fact that his underdrawers had slid off with his pants. She stared with fascination at his naked body, then she averted her eyes, scolding herself for looking.

It was wicked, she muttered, wicked to look at him like that. But she didn't feel wicked, she felt keenly curious.

Katherine fought with her conscience, and told herself again she shouldn't look, not at *that* part of him, but curiosity got the better of her. Her eyes strayed up his bruised, strongly built thighs to his hips. Oh my, she thought, as she picked up a piece of toweling with trembling hands and tossed it over his maleness.

Katherine climbed off the bed and put her hands on her hot cheeks. She took a moment to compose herself, then moved to the end of the bed where his bare feet hung over the mattress. She tugged at the legs of his pants, sliding them the rest of the way down his limbs.

Starting with his feet, she bathed him gently, avoiding the bruising and trying to concentrate her thoughts on the task at hand. As she reached his thighs, Katherine felt herself flush anew. She dropped the wet rag into the bucket and tossed an old quilt over him. That was as clean as Mr. W. A. Merrick was going to get. Gingerly she reached up under the quilt and snatched away the piece of toweling she had used to cover him.

Consuela arrived and glanced at the man in the bed. "You go, senora, and eat. I will sit with him."

Katherine picked up the remaining bucket and went downstairs to the kitchen. By the glow of the fire she lit a lamp. The huge reservoir on the back of the stove held hot water. She made herself a cup of tea and looked at the plate of food in the warming oven, but found she wasn't particularly hungry. When she sat down at the wooden table, she sighed with fatigue. Her day had started long before dawn, but her exhaustion was as much emotional as physical.

If Merrick died, all Katherine could do would be to bury him on the hill above the house alongside her family, then try to convince Mr. Anderson that the marriage had been legitimate. She guessed that that would be easier said than done. Frustration that her father had not thought she could manage the ranch alone welled up inside of her. She remembered how she had been mortified in Mr. Anderson's office the day after the funeral, when he read her the clause in the will. Father had even had the attorney write in some requirements for what type of husband she must have. Thankful that no one else had been there to hear the will, she had reminded her father's attorney that he had a duty to keep silent on the matter.

Katherine knew exactly why father had had Mr. Anderson put that clause in the will. He had always disliked Gerald, Hannah's father, and thought he was a weak man. Gerald loved writing poetry and refused to handle a weapon of any kind, even to hunt. He had thought it was wrong for men to end a life, even that of an animal, and Katherine had respected his feelings, knowing all the while they weren't practical in a place like Montana.

When Gerald had finally summoned the courage to ask for her hand, her father had refused. Katherine wondered now if part of the reason she had been drawn to Gerald had been because her father disliked him so.

The couple had planned to be married in secret, despite her father's feelings. Katherine was sure her father would change his mind, once the marriage became a fact.

The night they made their plans to run away was the night Katherine had given herself to Gerald. He insisted that if she was serious about defying her father, she would allow him the privileges of a husband now that they were betrothed. What a fool she had been. Because of that night, her father blamed her for being completely irresponsible, and he had added that hateful clause to his will.

Her father had viewed Gerald's sudden death from cholera a month later as the ultimate desertion, as if Gerald had chosen to die rather than live up to his responsibilities and marry her. When he died, Gerald hadn't even known she was carrying his child, but her father didn't want to hear what he called "excuses for that weakling's cowardice."

She put the thoughts from her mind. No good would come of getting angry all over again. She had let bitterness eat away at her over the last four months since her father died, and her tirades at his controlling ways had accomplished nothing. Now with only two months left she must put the past behind her and go forward with a plan to keep possession of the ranch.

If Merrick lived, Katherine would have Anderson declare the rustler her legal husband, and get the deed to the ranch transferred to her name. She pushed her chair away from the table and went back upstairs.

Consuela had moved a lamp to the dresser, leaving the bed in shadow. Katherine made out the stark white of the bandage on the man's head against the dark shape of his face. He lay very still under the quilt.

Consuela spoke softly. "Senora, I will sit with him. You go to bed."

Katherine didn't like that idea. She took full responsibility for the outlaw being in her home, and she knew the Mexican woman had already worked all day taking care of Hannah and the house. She waved her out of the room. "I'll stay. If I need you, I'll wake you."

Consuela stood her ground for a moment and looked as if she might argue, then wished her a quiet *buenos noches* and left.

Katherine pulled the rocking chair over beside the bed, and settled into the padded seat. She rested her head against the high back, and pushed gently with her feet, starting the rhythmic, soothing motion.

She watched Merrick's battered face as he lay still as death on her father's bed. She needed him around to prove to Mr. Anderson that she had a husband. Later, she could give him enough money to get him to leave the territory. Perhaps he would think being saved from

the gallows was enough payment. As soon as she had
the thought she discarded it. An outlaw would never be
so honorable.

Quietly she rose and took the lamp, holding it high
above the bed. He looked reasonably peaceful. Maybe
he wasn't hurt as badly as she had thought.

She stepped out into the hall and went downstairs to
the big desk in the room she used as the ranch office,
and unlocked the top drawer. The last will and testa-
ment of Julius Bernard Holman lay in the middle of the
drawer. She carried the document upstairs and once
more settled herself in the rocker. Finding the section
that had haunted her since her father's death, she read
it again.

> *The property owned by me, known as the Rocking
> H and comprised of about one thousand acres,
> located SE of the settlement of Dennison,
> Montana territory, may pass to my daughter
> Katherine Adora Holman on the condition she,
> within six months of my death, is married to a
> man with knowledge of the cattle business.
> Otherwise the property shall be sold and the
> money placed in trust, to be paid to my daughter
> in a monthly sum to cover her necessary
> expenses.*

Her father had taken care of every angle. If she was
forced to sell the ranch, but had control of the trust
fund, at least she might have a chance to buy the property back. But he clearly did not trust her to use her
own money wisely. Katherine glanced over the document at the outlaw in her father's bed. A rustler certainly was not what her father had had in mind, but

Merrick did know the cattle business. She didn't do this to spite her father, but he hadn't left her any choice. The will forced her to marry within six months of her father's death or lose the ranch, but it said nothing about *keeping* the husband.

If she had wanted a permanent husband she could have found one around Miles City, but she refused to humble herself the way the men in town seemed to think a fallen woman should. After Gerald's death she had considered entering into a real marriage until the time one suitor had called Hannah her bastard daughter, and she realized that no man would accept another man's child born out of wedlock. She might be willing to make exceptions with her own feelings, but not where her child was concerned.

Katherine tried to put her animosity toward her father aside and understand that he had done what he thought would be best for her when she was all alone with a daughter to raise. Several years ago, when her older brother, Farley, had died falling from his horse during a stampede, Julius Holman's hopes of carrying on his name along with the land died too. Farley's death had taken the spirit out of Julius.

She took the marriage certificate out of her pocket and folded it around the will, then closed her eyes and leaned her head back against the chair. Father would never have considered the possibility of her running the Rocking H alone, even though he had known what the ranch meant to her. For the last year of his life she had taken care of everything, from the books to the roundups and stock sales, but his stubborn pride had stood in her way, and he had refused to acknowledge her contribution. At the end he had been too sick to notice.

If she got lucky and Merrick healed fast enough, he could go along with her drovers when they took steers to market next month. Then he could just keep on going, out of the territory, and out of her life. Heaven knew, she could use a little luck.

Alert to possible danger, Wes Merrick lay still against the pain and listened. Wherever he was, it was too quiet to be in a town, and it smelled too good to be a whorehouse.

The female voices he had heard earlier were gone now and he wondered if they had been part of a dream. He didn't know how long it had been since he'd found the band of rustlers, but this was the most comfortable he'd been in a while. The time between then and now was a curious blank in his mind, and he didn't like the feeling one bit.

Wes tried to open his eyes, but for all the luck he had, they might as well have been glued shut. Damn. He was helpless as a newborn calf and twice as vulnerable. He wondered where he was, who had brought him here, and even why he was still alive. He smelled clean linen, and felt a soft down bed under him. When he tried to move, every inch of his body ached and throbbed. The hurt went deep, as if he'd been thrown into a cactus patch and stomped.

His arm no longer burned with pain. Someone must have set the broken bone. Unable to move, he had to content himself with the thought that he had a sense of being safe, but why he should feel that way he couldn't say. Fighting to stay awake for even so short a time exhausted him, and he relaxed and welcomed the blessed relief of sleep.

*   *   *

The early morning sun filtered through the crisp kitchen curtains and warmed Katherine as she sat and drank her coffee and watched her daughter finish her porridge. She had dressed with care in a conservative soft gray traveling suit adorned with black braid and a small matching hat.

After finishing her coffee, she rose to place the cup on the dry sink. Consuela came in the back door carrying a ham. "I'm going into town," Katherine told her. "Do you need anything?"

Consuela shook her head and took Hannah upstairs to dress the little girl for the day. Katherine went through the back door and stopped on the big porch to get her driving gloves.

Outside the barn she called to one of the wranglers to hitch up the buggy, and by the time she had tied Hamlet behind the bunkhouse, the trap stood ready. The mutt, who wanted to follow her everywhere, howled when he saw her leave. He was not welcome in Miles City, due to several previous lapses in manners on his part.

The prairie flattened out as Katherine drove north, and she could tell by the dry smell of the early morning air that the heat wouldn't break today. This time of the day was always her favorite. Dew still clung to the short grasses, and the smell of the earth rose up from the hooves of her horse. In the distance, two mule deer stood motionless, heads raised, looking in her direction. She lifted her hand to shade her eyes, and the deer, seeing the movement, turned and bounded gracefully away. Above her, a falcon circled and soared, resting on the gentle wind currents while searching the land below for prey.

Katherine paused to take in the scene around her, wondering if she might still lose this land she held so dear. The thought seemed to squeeze her heart in an uncomfortable grip.

She patted the pocket of her skirt to reassure herself the marriage document was safely tucked away. The paper had not been out of her possession since she had signed it. She had even slipped it under her pillow last night before she finally went to sleep.

Silently Katherine rehearsed what she would say to Mr. Anderson when she reached town. She had to convince him that she was legally married; her future depended on him accepting her marriage.

She hoped word of what she had done yesterday in Dennison had not yet reached Miles City, and Mr. Anderson's ears. The story of the actual events, told by her, would likely be quite different from the rumors that would circulate. She knew firsthand how vitriolic her neighbors could be.

Within the hour she arrived outside the bank where Anderson kept his office. The wide main road through the middle of town was more than just a thoroughfare. Along the north side of the street where Katherine tied her buggy one could find shops, a restaurant, the church, and a general store. Behind the businesses sat a tidy neighborhood where the good folks of Miles City resided. The south side of the street was lined with saloons, gambling dens, a pawn shop, and "social clubs" where the soiled doves lived and worked. Behind these unsavory businesses that catered to the baser instincts of the cowboys were some of the first dwellings built in the town, little better than shacks, along with a number of canvas tents. Respectable women never went across that wide dusty boulevard and ventured into what they called "that part of town," when they spoke of it at all.

Directly across from the bank, a group of buffalo hunters lounged along some benches in front of a saloon. She could smell them from forty feet away, their shaggy buffalo coats giving off the odor of badly tanned hides. She had never seen a more despicable looking bunch. Wild hair and beards looked no cleaner than the filthy clothes they wore. Nervously she climbed onto the boardwalk. She smoothed her hair and dusted off her jacket before entering the brick bank building, ignoring the cat calls from across the street.

Pausing just inside the door to allow her eyes to adjust to the dimness inside after the bright sunshine, she spotted her banker, Mr. Moody.

The bank manager hurried to greet her, "Good morning, Miss Holman. What may I do for you?" The gold watch chain across his ample brocade waistcoat winked at her in a shaft of sunlight.

She smiled at his round, earnest face, "Good morning, Mr. Moody. I'm here to see Mr. Anderson. Is he in yet?" She nodded to the closed door across the lobby. Her mouth felt dry. She'd never been very good at lying, and she was about to tell George Anderson a real whopper.

"I'm sorry, Miss Holman, but he left town five days ago for Boston. Got a telegram. His father is ill." The banker managed a proper look of concern. The very conservative Mr. Moody never did anything that didn't appear proper.

Gone? How could he! What was she going to do with Merrick, if he survived and tried to leave before the attorney came back? Tie him to the bed? Katherine immediately felt contrite. How selfish of her to think only of her own predicament. Of course Mr. Anderson had had to go to his family's home.

"Miss Holman, are you all right?" The banker's concern sounded genuine. His hands fluttered toward her, but never made contact with her person.

Katherine made an effort to drag her attention back to the banker. "Do you have any idea when he might be back?" She realized as soon as the words were out of her mouth it was a silly question. How would he know?

He shrugged, and his demeanor in no way indicated he thought it a frivolous question. "Can't say that I do. I could send a message to your ranch if I hear from him."

"That would be most kind of you. Please, as soon as you hear." Katherine waited only for him to nod in assent, then patted the paper in her pocket and, her thoughts whirling, walked out the door.

Dazed by her bad timing, she nearly collided with Sheriff Martin Denty's considerable bulk outside on the boardwalk.

He tipped his hat in greeting, his thin hair plastered to his pink scalp. "Katherine, I thought that was your buggy. It's good to see you." He looked at her with the usual flat expression in his small light blue eyes.

She had hoped to get out of town before he spotted her. "Martin, hello."

He didn't indicate by his expression that he noticed any lack of enthusiasm in her greeting. He drew a pocket watch out of his stained leather vest and flipped open the engraved cover. "Come. Have an early dinner with me. The hotel dining room opens in ten minutes." He grabbed her elbow in a proprietary hold.

She didn't want to spend any time with him. She had lost count of the number of times he had proposed to her, and she had turned him down. Now, when he found out about Merrick, at least that would stop.

"Thank you, Martin, but I really should be getting back to the ranch." She hid her annoyance with a polite smile and wrenched her elbow out of his grasp. He had doggedly courted Katherine since he had come to Miles City. She'd given him no encouragement, and had the distinct feeling that he didn't really like her personally, but the ranch made her attractive to him. He pointedly ignored Hannah's existence, never speaking of the child. She kept her daughter out of sight when he visited, refusing to subject her to that kind of shabby treatment.

He dismissed her statement about being busy the way he always dismissed anything he didn't care to hear. "Nonsense. You have time for a quick meal." From the tone of his voice she knew he wouldn't take no for an answer graciously.

Martin Denty was single-minded, rigid in his views, overbearing, and used to getting his own way. He had upheld the law in Miles City with an iron fist, and most of the residents thought him wonderful for keeping the peace in a wild cow town. Well, he might be a good sheriff, but Katherine didn't think much of him as a human being. She had seen a cruel streak in him surface more than once. If Merrick had been his prisoner, she wouldn't have been the least bit surprised at his injuries. Maybe the sheriff of Dennison was cut from the same cloth as Martin Denty.

Swallowing a retort, she decided to avoid making a scene and have her noonday meal with him. The last thing she wanted was to draw attention to herself. "Thank you, Martin. I am a bit hungry."

"Good. We'll have time for some conversation." That's right, she thought, I can spend the entire meal listening to him talk. Conversation with Martin Denty tended to be a very one-sided affair.

She nodded to people she knew as they walked down the boardwalk. She wondered how they would greet her when they found out she had married a rustler. They would find out soon enough, gossip being what it was. The entire town would be abuzz when they heard what she had done in Dennison.

She supposed it would be a reasonable idea to keep on the sheriff's good side, if that was possible now that she had married someone else. Who knew what would happen with Merrick?

Perhaps if she had this meal with Denty today in town, he would not call at the ranch for a while. She didn't want him nosing around now, but she might need to ask for his help later, if Merrick healed up enough to become a physical threat to her before she got him off her property.

Katherine shot a sideways glance at Denty as they entered the hotel. Perhaps she could find an excuse to go into his office before she went back to the ranch. She would feel better if she checked the rogues' gallery on the wall behind his desk for a wanted poster on Merrick. What if he was wanted for crimes other than rustling? What would she do if there was a poster there accusing him of murder?

3

Lying tense and still, Wes listened to the quiet, trying to assess his safety. He ran his dry tongue over a deep split in his lip. Last thing he remembered, he had been sneaking up on the band of rustlers to get the drop on them. Now he had no idea where he was, or who had brought him here, or if he could trust them. He hated feeling defenseless, and worse yet, busted up as he was, there wasn't much he could do about it.

The unsettling sensation that he had lost a chunk of his life had stayed with him. He hadn't yet had the strength to ask the women who came in to care for him what had happened, or even what day it was.

At last, able to pry his swollen eyelids open enough to squint, he could see sunlight flooding through a window. His brief moments of consciousness had come more often lately, and he became more aware of his surroundings, in spite of the incessant pounding pain in his head. He saw nothing at hand he might use to defend himself, no weapon he might improvise.

From the light, he judged that the room faced west, and that it was afternoon. The windows lacked any curtains or coverings, just the way he preferred, open to the outside. A simple dresser, a wardrobe, and tables by the bed were the only pieces of furniture in the room, along with a couple of overstuffed chairs. His clothes were nowhere in sight. Whoever took care of him was tidy. His mother would have approved.

He did not know the women who came to tend to him. One had sounded familiar at first only because she had a Mexican accent, so common in his native Texas. But he wasn't in Texas, he was in the Montana territory. The other woman was young and pretty and smelled like lavender. Even with his eyes closed he knew her by her gentle touch, her quiet voice. Her cool smooth hands had soothed his forehead.

The next time one of them came to take care of him, he vowed to get some answers. He closed his eyes to rest and wait. Despite his efforts to stay awake, exhaustion overtook him and he slept.

When he woke, he heard voices in the room, speaking so low and soft he couldn't make out what they said. He felt the mattress dip slightly by his hip. A face floated into his line of vision. The woman leaned over and studied him with large, dark, concerned-looking eyes set in a pale oval face, framed by a mass of brown hair.

He had questions, but he doubted he could do more than mumble through his swollen, damaged lips. If he could get her to come closer, she could hear him. Blindly he reached for her, his callused hand coming in contact with soft skin. She gasped and jerked away from his touch, jostling the bed. He heard himself groan as he floated on waves of throbbing pain.

Katherine dropped the jar of ointment she held as she jumped up from the bed. She watched him, his face contorted with pain, as she rubbed her arm where he had grabbed her. Slowly her heartbeat slowed to normal.

Goodness, he had given her a fright, waking up like that. She had wanted to get a look at how his face was healing, and she thought he had been asleep. All of a sudden she had been looking into eyes the color of cobalt and had felt a surprisingly firm grip on her arm. She chided herself for being so jumpy. There were other people around and she could always call for help if she felt any real danger from the outlaw. A little hint of guilt niggled at her. Cowardice had caused her to jump from his bed, and she knew by his moan her sudden movement had hurt him. Katherine decided to let him rest for a while. The ointment could wait. She scooped the jar off the floor.

Consuela followed Katherine out of the room with a handful of dirty linen and closed the door behind her. Together the two woman walked down the hallway, stopping at the landing.

The housekeeper hesitated before she spoke. "Senora, are you all right?"

Katherine gave a self-conscious little laugh. "Of course. He just startled me. How do you think he is coming along?"

Consuela gave the question careful consideration, as she did everything, and answered slowly. "He will heal, but it might take much time. There is still a great deal of pain, on the inside as well as the outside of Senor Merrick." As she talked, her strong brown hands wrapped the soiled linen into a neat bundle.

Katherine hesitated on the landing and watched Consuela's wide back as the woman made her way down the stairs. How much time would he need? Thoughts whirling, she decided to check on her napping daughter before she went downstairs. The sleeping child lay curled on her side, her blanket clutched in one hand, and a rag doll in the other. Hannah embraced life with a gleeful energy that amused Katherine. Even in sleep, the child had her hands full. As she pulled the door closed quietly, her thoughts turned back to Merrick.

She was running out of time to have the deed for the ranch transferred to her name. By the time her attorney, Mr. Anderson, returned from Boston she hoped the outlaw would be healthy enough to leave. After convincing the attorney she had complied with the terms of Father's will, she could send Merrick out of the territory.

A commotion in the front room drew her to the head of the stairs. "Miss Kate!" Gibby shouted for her. "We got trouble." He barreled into view at the foot of the stairs. "Get your hat. We're riding to the south meadow." He disappeared, and she heard the front door slam.

Katherine had never seen her easy-going foreman so agitated. She called to Consuela that she was leaving and to take care of Hannah, and grabbed her hat on her way out the door.

Gibby and several of the hands waited on their horses for her out front. One of the men held her mount. When Hamlet saw Katherine, he leapt off the porch and ran huge circles around the horses, barking.

"Hamlet, be quiet." As she mounted her horse she questioned Gibby. "What happened?"

"Lost five head in the south meadow." As always, his reply was brief and to the point. He reeled his horse around and took off at a gallop before she could ask him anything else. The man sure hated to waste time talking.

She spurred her horse and followed with the men, Hamlet close behind her. The meadow lay at the opening to her valley, its far side fenced with barbed wire and bordered by the road to town. Generally Gibby didn't run the herd here in summer, but the season had been a dry one, and they needed the grazing.

They rode hard for about twenty minutes before Katherine spotted buzzards flying in lazy circles. The downed cattle lay east of the creek that bisected her property. They looked like big humps on the flat land. As she got closer, she could see insects swarming around the dead animals. The dog stopped short of the carcasses and stood with his head down, whimpering.

She dismounted and walked forward to get a better look. The smell of death hung thickly in the air. Dark blood stained the dry grass under the head of each animal. The gaping wounds in their throats crawled with flies. She stood transfixed, staring at the mutilated bodies. The steers had been butchered and left to rot. Her stomach roiled, and she turned away.

Rustling made sense, but not slaughter. After a moment she looked up at Gibby. "Why? Who would do such a senseless thing?"

The foreman's face set in a hard expression. "Can't say. Ain't never seen anything like it. Did you see the one closest to the fence?" He pointed to a steer about twenty feet away from the rest.

She shook her head. She had seen as much as she thought she could stand, but she followed him. The steer's throat had been cut like all the rest, but his huge side was mutilated too. Once more she had to look away.

Gibby stood quietly beside her for a moment before he spoke. "See what it said?"

She glanced up at him, startled, before she forced herself to look back at the dead animal. The cuts on his side weren't random slashes. The killer had spelled out a message. It said "wait" in big crude letters. Following the word were more slashes.

She took a deep breath to calm herself and choked on the rotting smell. "What does it say after 'wait'?"

Gibby leaned over and stared at the mangled steer. "I ain't rightly sure. I been looking at it, and I can't make it out."

Being unable to decipher the rest of the message made the warning all the more terrifying. Wait for what, she wondered?

Anger at the destruction of good stock overrode her fear. "Gibby, give me two of the hands. I'm going into Miles City to report this to Martin." Katherine had no intention of riding anywhere alone. The whole situation spooked her.

Gibby pulled a face and spat into the grass. "What do you suppose he can do?"

She knew Gibby had little use for Martin Denty, but he was the law. "Maybe some of the other ranchers have been hit."

Gibby waved at two of the hired hands who were still mounted. "You two go with Miss Holman into town. And stay out of the saloon. You're working."

Katherine moved closer to her foreman and laid a hand on his arm. "Check on Hannah for me, would you? Ask Consuela to keep her in the house. And take Hamlet back."

Gibby patted her hand and his expression softened. "Don't worry. She'll be fine. I'd never let anything happen to that child." He mounted, whistled to Hamlet, and rode off toward the house.

During the ride into town she scanned the dusty landscape. Nothing stirred in the afternoon heat. Whoever had done the cowardly deed was probably long gone.

Katherine tied her horse outside the sheriff's office and instructed the two hands to wait for her on a shady bench nearby on the boardwalk.

When she entered his office, Martin Denty came to his feet. She didn't have a chance to say a word. He scowled and shook his finger at her as if she were a naughty child. "I heard the news from over in Dennison. There's even a picture in the paper."

She'd known people in Miles City would find out sooner or later. She had just been hoping for later. "That's not why I'm here, Martin."

His face purpled at her reply. "Don't you think you owe me an explanation?"

His proprietary manner lit her short fuse. She owed him nothing. She faced him squarely, hands on her hips. "No. You have no right to ask!"

His flushed face contorted with anger. "People are talking, just like they done five years ago."

His retort stung her, more than she thought possible after all this time, but her pride would never let him see how his words had affected her. She raised her chin a notch. "I came here to ask for your services as sheriff, nothing more."

Denty trembled with anger. "That outlaw's giving you trouble already! If I have to arrest him and take him off your property, he'll hang. He gets into trouble, he gets his original sentence."

Close to losing her temper, she answered him in an

icy voice. "If you would stop ranting at me and listen, this has nothing to do with Merrick!"

He blinked at her words and she watched him visibly struggle to compose himself, his reply stiff and controlled. "Tell me why you're here." His clenched fists betrayed his lingering anger.

"We found five head of cattle slaughtered in the south meadow, by the road." She remembered the smell of dead flesh with such clarity she wondered if it had gotten into her clothes.

"You mean butchered?"

She shook her head. "Whoever did it didn't take any meat. And some words were carved into the side of one. It says 'wait.' We can't make out what else. Any reports like this from the other ranchers?"

Denty shook his head. "Could it be numbers after the word?"

She wasn't sure she understood him. "Numbers?"

"Twenty years ago the vigilantes left numbers. I'll get my deputy to stay in the office, and I'll ride out with you to take a look."

Katherine had no intention of waiting for him. She wanted to get back. "I'm going now. You'll see the steers from the road. I'll leave one of the hands there."

"Wait for me. I want to talk to you." Martin strapped on his gunbelt.

Halfway out the door she turned and faced him. "What you want to talk about is not open for discussion. I told you before, it's my personal business." What a pompous ass. He had no claim on her. Martin Denty had an incredibly thick skull. Furious, she wheeled around and left the office.

The two ranch hands jumped up from the bench outside. When neither made eye contact, she was sure they had overheard every word. She could just imagine the speculation this would cause in the bunkhouse tonight.

On the ride home she considered the sheriff's words as she scanned the range. If Merrick got into any trouble he would hang. That meant that if she couldn't handle him, and reported him to the law, she as good as signed his death warrant. It was a heavy responsibility she had taken on, more than she had ever realized when she made her impulsive decision to go to Dennison and claim a condemned man.

On the way back to the ranch they saw no one, but then she hadn't really expected to. She had told Sheriff Denty that what she had to tell him about her cattle had nothing to do with Merrick. Now a thought poked at her. *Could* the slaughter of her cattle have anything to do with the outlaw's presence? Or was it just a coincidence?

Katherine handed off her mount to one of the hands by the barn and headed for the house. As she climbed the broad front steps onto the porch, she heard wailing from inside the house. She recognized that furious cry.

Pushing open the front door, Katherine found her daughter and Consuela in a standoff in the front room. Hannah spotted her and flung herself into a frantic embrace of her mother's legs. She sputtered, babbling incoherently and pointed accusingly at the housekeeper.

Consuela nodded and greeted Katherine serenely. "*Hola,* senora."

Katherine leaned down and tipped her daughter's little tear-stained face up as she spoke to Consuela. "Let me guess. Hannah wants to go outside."

"Si. Senor Gibson told me of your wishes."

She wiped her daughter's face with her handkerchief and hid a smile as she addressed the angry child.

"Hannah, I left instructions that you were to stay inside until I returned. I want you to tell Consuela you're sorry for carrying on." She grasped the child's shoulders and turned the stiff little body toward the housekeeper.

Hannah's chin jutted out stubbornly for a moment, then she glanced at Katherine and appeared to consider the consequences of not doing what her mother asked. Finally she conceded. "I'm sorry."

Katherine smiled in approval, and then turned to Consuela. "How is our guest doing?"

"I think he is more awake."

Relieved to have some good news today, Katherine nodded at the housekeeper and then turned her attention back to her daughter. "Now, would you like to walk down to the barn and help feed the horses?"

The child brightened immediately, her anger forgotten in an instant. "Now? Now!"

"I will take her, senora. We can stop at the garden and pick vegetables for supper."

"If you see any strangers riding in, come back to the house immediately." Thoughts of the incident with the cattle were fresh in her mind.

The housekeeper nodded, and took the child by the hand. Katherine watched them go out the door. She sighed. Hannah had a temper like her mother when she did not get her own way.

Preoccupied with her thoughts, she headed into the kitchen for something cool to drink. As she walked through the dining room she heard a thud from upstairs. She hesitated midstep, and for an instant she felt as if her heart had stopped. Then she remembered she was not alone in the house. The bedroom Merrick occupied sat directly over the dining room.

Katherine forgot all about the cattle and took the

stairs two at a time. She didn't stop to knock, bursting into her father's bedroom.

Merrick sat on the edge of the bed, his freshly washed denims unbuttoned, but on. He must have had a struggle getting into his trousers with only one good arm, she thought. He was holding a shirt that had belonged to her father. One look at his broad chest and muscular bare arms above the bindings on his ribs told her he would never be able to wear it.

He looked up at her abrupt entrance into the room. She remembered those eyes, such a startling blue above his shaggy black beard.

"What do you think you're doing?" She blurted the words before she even thought about them.

He pushed himself to a standing position and swayed with the effort. "Ma'am?" His trousers slid down a bit over his narrow hips.

She watched with alarm as what little natural color he had in the unbruised areas of his face drained away, leaving his skin as white as the bandage around his head.

Katherine rushed across the room and caught him around the waist, her hand landing on his bare skin between the bandage and his pants. "Are you insane? You can't get out of bed." When she pushed her shoulder up under his good arm to steady him, he gasped with pain.

In an upright position he was even bigger than she had thought. With her arm around his waist, it took all her strength to awkwardly lower him to the mattress, then scoot out away from him and help him down onto the pillows.

Eyes closed, he spoke around shallow breaths, his soft drawl strained. "I thank you for your hospitality, ma'am, but I really need to be on my way. There's someone I have to find."

She imagined she could still feel the firm warmth of his skin under her hand, and smell the masculine scent of him. She also remembered in vivid detail how he had looked without those pants he now wore. She tried without much success to push her wanton thoughts away.

Her heart pounding, she backed across the room, needing to put distance between herself and the polite outlaw. Warily she watched him as his face contorted with pain and he gritted his teeth. Foolish man. Where did he think he could go in the shape he was in?

With that thought, Katherine had a realization. Wesley Austin Merrick had spoken just now as if he was a free man, able to leave her ranch if he chose to do so. At that moment she wondered just how much he remembered of what had taken place yesterday in Dennison.

4

Katherine stared at Merrick, dumbfounded. Bruised, battered, barely able to stand on his own two feet, he said he planned to leave. "Don't be ridiculous. You're not fit to go anywhere." Then another thought occurred to her. Perhaps he thought he still had to run from the law.

She decided to try to soothe him. "You're safe here, and you need to rest." He eyed her with a blatant look of suspicion.

How did you go about telling a dangerous man like Merrick that he was not free to leave the territory, or even the Rocking H? That he was married to you, a woman he didn't even know. She'd had some time to get used to the idea of being married to a complete stranger. She imagined the news was going to hit him right between the eyes like a stray bullet. It would be easier to explain her plan to him if he remembered what had happened in the sheriff's office during the hangings.

His voice broke into her thoughts. "Are you all right, ma'am?"

She realized that she clutched the door frame for support. "Yes, of course." Her face must have shown distress at what she had been thinking. She never had been any good at hiding her thoughts.

He shifted on the mattress and grimaced. She straightened and moved back toward the bed. Here he was, in pain, and he was asking her if she was all right.

He moved as if he was going to try to stand up again. "I need—"

She put her hand in the center of his bare chest and gently pushed him back against the pillows, interrupting his sentence. "You *need* to stay in bed and rest. I told you, you're safe. No one is going to hurt you." His thick chest hair felt warm and crinkly against her palm. Merrick resisted for a moment and leaned his body forward, against her hand, then slumped back on the pillows with a groan of pain. So ridiculously easy to subdue him, she thought, in spite of his size. He probably weighed twice what she did. Slowly she withdrew her hand from his chest.

She wondered what he remembered about what had happened in Dennison. The trial, the hangings, how much of it could he recall? Why didn't he ask about his friends? Even though they had been outlaws, she hated to be the one to have to tell him they were all dead.

"Where am I?" She saw the suspicion in his eyes as he searched her face.

Good, a question she could easily answer. "At the Rocking H ranch, near Miles City."

He seemed to consider her answer before he spoke again. "Who are you?"

"I'm Katherine Holman. Now be quiet, you need to rest." As she spoke, he closed his eyes and his breathing became less labored.

Like a coward, she decided she could wait until he felt better to explain to him about his situation. First she had to figure out what she would tell him. She toyed with the idea of not telling him at all about the marriage, and then immediately discarded the thought. People in Miles City already knew she had married him, and with the way news spread, he was bound to hear the fact from the hands before he left the ranch. She would stay with her original plan, and strike a deal with him. It just looked as if she might have to do it sooner rather than later. If he would stay until the deed was transferred to her name, she would help him leave the territory.

"Miz Holman?" His effort to speak ended in another grimace.

Ignoring him, she moved to the bedside table and carefully measured a dose of opiate from a small brown bottle the doctor had left for her father, adding a little water to the glass. Sliding a hand beneath his shoulders, she eased his head up. "Here, drink this."

He opened his eyes and looked at the glass, shaking his head. He made a face, and Katherine couldn't tell if his expression was for the bitter medicine, or because the sudden movement of his head caused him pain.

Her arm ached from the strain of lifting him, but she wanted him to take the medicine. Exasperated, she pressed the glass against his lips. "For heaven's sake, just drink it. I can't hold you up like this all day." She noticed the way his thick dark hair curled over her arm, and wondered if he usually wore it so long, or if he just hadn't taken the time to cut it recently.

For a moment, he pressed his lips together like a reluctant child, then he seemed to give up. Good thing. His show of temper had opened a deep split on his lower lip. Eyes closed, he sipped the bitter liquid. When she tipped the glass too fast, a bit of the medicine ran into his beard and down his neck onto his bare chest. He didn't seem to notice. He was asleep before she carefully placed his bandaged head back on the pillow. She propped his splinted arm up on a folded blanket, and gently pulled the quilt up over him.

Consuela appeared at the door. "Senora, do you need help?"

Katherine shook her head and explained to her housekeeper in a whisper. "He tried to get up. I just gave him some of father's medicine. I'll sit with him."

"Si."

"Where's Hannah?" She wanted Consuela to keep her child out of the room. She certainly didn't want Hannah exposed to an outlaw, and the last thing any sick man needed was a five-year-old whirlwind.

"She is in the barn with Mr. Hannibal. He will keep her until I go for her."

With Hannah safely accounted for, Katherine's thoughts turned back to Merrick. He couldn't go anywhere without clothes, could he? Katherine whispered to Consuela. "We're going to take all of father's clothes out of the wardrobe, and you can carry them out to the bunkhouse. The hands can get some use out of them."

The housekeeper responded with a simple nod. Together, Katherine and Consuela opened drawers and the wardrobe, stacking neat piles of her father's shirts, long johns, and nightshirts on the dresser. Katherine set one nightshirt aside. Consuela left the room with an armload of clothing, and Katherine closed the door behind her housekeeper. Going through her father's things had not been as difficult as she had expected.

Katherine settled into a chair by the bed and watched the quilt over Merrick's chest rise and fall with a steady rhythm. Earlier she had reached out and touched him to help him back into bed. Now, the sensations created by that touch came back to her. When she recalled his warmth, his scent, the texture of his hair, she felt a little warm and shaky. Reacting to an outlaw that way was something else she hadn't expected.

She leaned forward and poked his shoulder with her finger, checking to be sure that the drug had put him into a deep sleep. She undressed him again. The trousers, the only clothing he had managed to get into, were easier to pull over his hips than they had been the last time.

This time she didn't cover him, but instead looked her fill. His long, well-shaped body reached to the end of the mattress. Her eyes skipped to his big naked feet, and then traveled up his limbs. Bruises and swellings were an insult to the physical beauty of the man. Pale skin contrasted markedly with the thick dark hair that covered his legs and thighs. His manhood lay curved and nestled in a patch of curly black hair.

He shifted on the mattress, and her cheeks burned at the brazen way she had looked at him. Hurriedly she pulled the quilt up to his waist.

He's an outlaw, a rustler, she told herself, but the reminder didn't help much, with the image of his body burned into her brain. She scolded herself severely and got to work, trying to ignore her own agitation.

Carefully Katherine bunched up one of her father's nightshirts and eased the garment over Merrick's bandaged head, then wrestled his good arm through the sleeve. It was like trying to dress a sack of potatoes. She tugged at the hem of the garment, but his groans stopped her. Unwilling to risk the closeness and jostling needed to get the garment down past his hips, she left it bunched around his waist, and hastily covered him back up to his armpits with the quilts.

Relieved to have him decently covered, she stood back, her heart beating furiously. After a moment in which she tried to recover her nerves, she scooped up his denims and his boots, and carried them downstairs. She stuffed his belongings up on a shelf on the porch, and then she headed to the barn to fetch Hannah.

Wes awoke to darkness, naked under the sheets, except for a twisted nightshirt that was in danger of strangling him. What had happened to his trousers? Damn, it had taken a very painful half hour to get them on. Then he remembered the young woman, a neatly packaged little brunette with concern written all over her pretty face. She had said her name was Katherine Holman. Had she relieved him of his trousers? He wished he could remember. She had seemed awfully anxious that he stay in bed, and the memory of her jumpiness aroused his suspicions. What connection did she have with Watson and his gang?

Wes cursed the weakness followed by waves of pain that engulfed him every time he moved. He had been fooling himself earlier when he got up. No way could he have ridden his horse a mile today, even if he could have managed to get his boots on. Wes closed his eyes and rested against the pillows, shifting his splinted arm in an attempt to relieve the ache.

He'd been on the trail for months chasing Watson down. Now it seemed the only thing he could do was rest for a few days and get his strength back, before going after the rustlers again. He realized that facing Watson now would be foolish. He wouldn't stand a chance.

The woman had mentioned that he was at a ranch. But how had he gotten here? And why hadn't Watson killed him? He would feel better if he had his revolver on the nightstand beside him.

Damn it all anyway, he thought with frustration. He'd been so close to catching up with the rustlers who had killed Jim. The last thing Wes remembered was tying his horse, drawing his gun, and approaching the rustlers' camp on foot. After that everything was a blank. He thought he'd been nearer to a place named Dennison than Miles City.

He waited for the woman to come back so he could ask her what she knew. He remembered her small soft hands, the way she gently held his head and spoke to him like he was a child when he refused to drink that poison she called medicine. He hated the taste. The bitter dose took the pain away some, but it also robbed him of his ability to think clearly and made him so damn sleepy. He needed to stay alert if he was to get out of here alive.

If she had taken him in, she should know where the rustlers were headed, or she could find out. He'd ask her the next time she came in to see him. He closed his eyes and thought about her, her eyes, her soft skin, her scent. She smelled like springtime, like lavender. What connection could a woman like her have with a rustler like Watson?

Katherine pulled her lined denim jacket closed against the chill as she walked to the barn. In the distance she could see Gibby and some of her hands headed in from the south range. She had a few moments to check on her daughter before they arrived.

The afternoon had cooled and the feel of autumn had finally arrived. Time to unpack her heavy woolen clothing and air the garments. The thought made her a little sad. Winters in Montana were harsh and unforgiving, and this was the first winter she would be alone and solely responsible for the Rocking H.

The weather here in Montana was rarely consistent from year to year. Heavy snowfall or light, a rancher could always count on the temperatures dipping well below zero each winter. Freezing weather brought its own special problems to anyone who raised cattle. She hoped she could continue to outwit the elements, as her father had managed to do every year. She made a mental note to talk to Gibby about bringing the new breeding bulls into the pasture near the barn.

The warmth of the barn welcomed her as she stepped inside to watch Hannah. The smell of animals and hay filled the air. Her daughter wore a look of determination on her little face as she dragged a full bucket of grain across the dirt floor, leaving a trail in the hard-packed earth.

The old black wrangler, Hannibal Jones, saw Katherine and silently tipped his hat. Then he spoke to the child. "Little Miss, you be needin' any help?"

Her answer came unhesitatingly as she concentrated on her task, her face set in a serious expression. "No, I can do it." She stopped for a moment to rest and wipe her hands on her filthy pinafore.

Hannibal winked at Katherine, then spoke again to the child. "You let me know if you changes yo' mind."

Hannah answered with a grunt and didn't stop again until she had determinedly dragged the bucket to where Hannibal stood, leaning against a stall door.

He bent his twisted old body down to pat the child on the head, then picked up the bucket and poured its contents into a trough built into the door of Dynamite's stall. The gelding shook his mane and whinnied his approval.

Hannah spotted Katherine and squealed. "Mama, I'm helping."

"I can see that. You want to stay with Hannibal while I talk to Gibby?" Katherine smiled fondly at her daughter, pleased that the child enjoyed working. Some day the Rocking H would pass into her hands. Katherine would teach her child all there was to know about the ranching business, so she could run the Rocking H by herself, if need be.

Hannibal scooped up the empty bucket by the handle and took Hannah by the hand, heading for the room at the back of the barn where they kept all the spare bridles and saddles. The child had no problem keeping up with his peculiar rolling gait.

A bronc had thrown Hannibal into a fence fifteen years before, breaking his pelvis and back, ending his riding days. Her father had put him in charge of the barn. Hannibal's loyalty was born of unspoken gratefulness to her father. Most ranchers would have let the man go, but Julius Holman was a fair boss as well as an excellent rancher, and had always rewarded faithful employees. Katherine abided by the precedents he had set, firmly believing fair treatment bred loyalty to the ranch in the hired hands.

She heard horses approach and stepped out of the barn.

Gibby dismounted. He tipped his hat. "Afternoon, Miss Kate. Saw Sheriff Denty out at the south fence."

The image of the butchered cattle resurfaced to haunt her. "What did he say?"

"Nothing that mattered. He don't know what happened." Gibby's tone showed his dislike of the sheriff.

Something Denty had said today bothered her, and she wanted her foreman's reaction. She waited to speak until the hands filed past into the barn, leading their mounts. When it came to gossip, the men in the bunkhouse were as bad as little old ladies over the back fence.

"When I was in town today Martin mentioned vigilantes."

Gibby shook his head as he considered what she said. "That don't make no sense. What in the world would a bunch of vigilantes be gaining by cutting up your cattle?"

Katherine shrugged. She couldn't make any sense of what the sheriff had said either, unless it might be because of Merrick. She had to consider that there was an outside chance the vicious slaughter of the cattle had been done by some of her neighbors, who might object to her saving a rustler from hanging only to bring him into their area. She couldn't very well bring that idea up without explaining to Gibby who Merrick was and why she had brought him here. But she had to admit to herself she had had no trouble on the ranch like this before she saved the outlaw from hanging.

Katherine was skewered by Gibby's intense look and felt a twinge of guilt about hiding the truth from him.

"Might have something to do with that battered cowpuncher you dragged home from Dennison. A little bit of a coincidence there."

So Gibby knew after all. Martin must have said something to her foreman. "It's possible, I suppose." She would allow that the coincidence had to be considered. Katherine hesitated. She didn't need any more complications. The Rocking H had always had good relationships with its neighbors, and she hoped she could depend on them to continue to accept her now that she was the one running the ranch. They had stood by her even when the townspeople had shunned her after Hannah's birth.

"Why did you bring him here?" Gibby wasn't going to leave it alone. When her father died, her foreman had become her self-appointed protector.

Riled by his questions, she answered sharply. "He needed help." Now that was an understatement if she had ever made one.

Visibly annoyed, Gibby took off his hat and slapped it against his leather chaps. "Well fine, ain't you just the Angel of Mercy!"

Katherine took a step toward him and jabbed a finger in the middle of his bony chest. "I'm going to tell you the same thing I told Martin. The subject of Merrick is not open for discussion." She glared at him, daring him to challenge her.

Gibby, stiff-backed, muttered something to himself and then changed the subject. "You want riders out tonight?"

She welcomed the shift in conversation, but knew he would find an opportunity soon enough to open the subject again. She snapped her orders. "Five riders and make sure they carry rifles. If they don't have their own, they can come up to the house after supper, and I'll open the gun case."

"Yes ma'am. If you think of anything else you don't want to discuss, I'll be in the cookhouse." He wheeled around on the heel of his boot and stomped away.

His sarcasm stung. She knew Gibby had her best interests at heart, but taking on Merrick was something she had had to do on her own. Gibby had supported her as the boss after her father's death, but she knew he thought she should sell out or marry. He shared her father's belief that a woman lacked the strength needed to run a ranch. He didn't know about the conditions in her father's will, but he probably would have agreed with them.

She imagined what the old foreman's reaction would be if she told him that for a brief time after hearing the stipulations, she had toyed with the idea of asking him to marry her, just so she could retain the property. It might be worth telling him just to see the look on his face.

She called to Hannah and together they returned to the house. After feeding her daughter supper and putting her to bed, Katherine wandered out to the porch. The sun had just set and the purple glow of twilight bathed the rugged country that rolled gently away from her in a soft blend of deepening shadows. A drowsy quiet settled over the land. Animals who roamed in the daylight had settled down for the night, and the creatures who spent their waking hours in the dark had yet to stir. A single cricket chirped a plaintive sound.

In spite of all that had happened in the last few days, Katherine felt a certain peace steal over her as she looked out over her land. A cool wind blowing off the prairie lifted tendrils of hair away from her face and soothed her spirit.

Safety and contentment belonged to her on this piece of land her family had carved out of wilderness. Her mother, her father, and her brother, along with the babies that had perished shortly after their birth, were all buried on the rise in back of the house. She knew if she walked around the porch and looked to the west she would be able to see the markers on their graves silhouetted against the last of the fading light.

After her mother's death, Katherine had been sent away to Chicago to go to school. Her soul had longed to return to the prairie with its wide open sky. Every spring she had felt reborn when she traveled home for the summer. In her heart she knew she could never be happy living in a town, just as she knew her beautiful, innocent little daughter would never find acceptance there. She refused to have her child pay for a mistake that had been none of her doing.

Deep in her soul Katherine needed this land that she loved, the place to build a safe life for herself and Hannah. Nothing would stop her from protecting her child, whom she loved so fiercely, even if she had to marry an outlaw to do it.

5

Wes awakened to early morning light and lay tense and still, trying to identify the whooshing sound so close to his ear. He made a fist under the quilt, ready to strike. He turned his head slowly on the pillow, and not a foot from his face he saw a pair of unblinking brown eyes that studied him over the edge of the mattress. They were her eyes, Miz Holman's, but in a much smaller face. A riot of dark curls topped the little head. He let his hand relax.

The child, dressed in nightclothes, folded her hands on the bed and rested her chin on them. "Are you sick?"

Wes tried to speak and all he could manage was a croak. The little girl giggled. He cleared his throat and tried again. "I guess you could say that." That vile tasting medicine they poured down his throat made him feel vague and fuzzy, but the pain had lightened. He made a vow not to take any more. He ran his tongue over teeth that felt as if they were coated with cotton, and yearned for a good cup of coffee.

"I was sick once." She continued to watch him solemnly.

He wondered what kind of a response she expected. He didn't remember ever having a conversation with a child so young, even though he had plenty of nieces and nephews. The child continued to chatter, seemingly unconcerned that he failed to reply.

"My mama said, don't bother the man, he needs to rest."

Miz Holman. The woman with the soft brown eyes and thick hair was this child's mother. He didn't even know the lady, but he did remember how her hands felt against his skin when she so carefully cared for him. Wes wondered why the thought that she was married with a child perturbed him.

The little girl cocked her head to one side, a gesture he recognized. Miz Holman had studied him like that just before she had leapt off the bed yesterday. "Are you bothered?"

He had to smile at her turn of phrase, and the split in his lip pulled painfully. The loneliness of lying in bed had gotten to him, and he was glad for the child's company. "No, I'm not bothered. Where's your mama?"

She ignored his question and kept on talking. "Good. I can sing. You'll feel better. I feel better when Mama sings to me."

Wes closed his eyes and listened to the child's sweet rendition of a song he had heard cowpunchers on a cattle drive croon at night to restless steers. Where had a youngster like this learned that song? It seemed an unlikely lullaby for a little girl.

He listened to the words as she sung them in her clear, childish voice, and the lyrics had a poignancy that had never struck him before. Suddenly he missed his home and family very much.

> *Oh I am a Texas cowboy*
> *Far away from home*
> *If I ever get back to Texas*
> *I never more will roam.*

> *Come all you Texas cowboys*
> *And warning take from me,*
> *And do not go to Montana*
> *To spend your money free.*

The song as well as the visit ended abruptly when an annoyed voice called for someone named Hannah. The child turned and scampered out of the room, stopping briefly at the door to throw him a kiss. As soon as she disappeared, he realized he missed the little girl, and wished she would return and talk to him some more.

He lay in bed and listened to the comforting sounds of a house waking up in the morning. Someone was chopping wood, and he heard the twang of the metal door on a stove. It all seemed so normal, the noises, the child. The sense of danger that had pricked at him earlier faded a little.

Wes listened to make sure no one was coming before he worked himself into a sitting position, cradling his broken arm through the blasted nightshirt. Carefully he worked his splinted arm into the too-tight sleeve. The fabric gave with a loud ripping sound. He flexed his fingers, relieved to see they still moved at his command. Gingerly, he put his bare feet on the cold, bare wood floor. He felt a whole lot better than he had yesterday, his headache almost gone. He scratched absently at his chest, thinking a bath and a shave would go a long way toward helping him feel human again.

He looked around the room. Where the hell were his clothes? The nightshirt he wore barely came to his knees. Preferring to sleep nude, he hadn't worn clothes to bed in years.

Draping the quilt from the bed awkwardly over his shoulders like an Indian blanket, he tried standing. His stomach muscles balled up in a painful knot. He stretched his body upright slowly, then moved like an old man to the wardrobe. The door protested with a loud creak when he opened it. Empty. Someone had probably taken his things to wash them. He couldn't recall whether his pants had been dirty when he had struggled into them, but he did remember that the shelves of the wardrobe had been full of another man's clothes. Her husband's, perhaps? But where were they now? Probably moved into another room. And what about his saddlebags? All his shaving gear and fresh shirts were in them. He couldn't remember if he had seen them yesterday.

Wes shuffled back to the bed, easing himself down onto the mattress. His stomach grumbled with hunger. He ran his hand over the tender skin of his abdomen. The last meal he remembered had been cold beans out of a can.

That rustler Watson and his pals must have done this to him. He wondered why they hadn't killed him outright. His brother's murder hadn't been an isolated incident. Wes had trailed Watson from Texas, and along the way he had seen firsthand evidence of the man's cruelty.

The sound of horses from outside drew his attention. He got up again and made his way to the window.

A group of five riders pulled up outside the barn. He didn't recognize any of them. The men were armed with rifles, but he didn't see them carrying any game. Either they weren't very good hunters, or they hadn't been hunting food, because he had seen plenty of evidence of excellent possibilities as he rode through the territory. This was beautiful, rich country. He wondered if one of them might be Miz Holman's husband.

An old Negro man with a twisted back came out of the large barn to meet the group of riders as they approached. The riders dismounted and led their horses into the fine looking building. Everything Wes could see on the spread seemed to be in good repair. It looked like a prosperous, well-run place.

If there was no one else around, the black man would be easy to overpower. He shouldn't have too much difficulty getting a horse and a rifle if he couldn't locate his own. Staying in the saddle might be a little difficult, he allowed. He could only move at a snail's pace.

Again he wondered what connection a woman like Miz Holman could have to a rustler like Watson. Maybe her husband ran stolen cattle. He couldn't imagine that a sweet little thing like her would put up with buying stolen stock.

He shifted his gaze from the scene in front of the barn to the land beyond. It looked different here from where he had caught up with Watson. The prairie seemed flatter, and there were no bluffs or river that he could see. Where had they brought him? He could see a one-room log cabin, a stream out behind a bunkhouse, and open range beyond. In the far distance he spotted a herd of cattle.

This good land made him think of his family's ranch in Texas. Dad and his brothers would probably be getting ready for the fall roundup. Sam would be in town at his law practice, but Dave, John, and Bobby would be there to cover his absence. He missed them all. His thoughts had been so full of finding the rustlers who had killed Jim that he hadn't spared time to think of his family for a while. His last memory of his mother before he left Texas was on her knees, weeping over Jim's open grave. Wes had made his vow to bring Watson to justice the moment the first spadeful of earth had thudded hollowly on his brother's coffin.

He tensed up when he heard someone outside in the hallway. He braced his hips against the window sash for support and waited.

Katherine stood with her hand on the knob to her father's bedroom door. She had been avoiding Merrick long enough. The time had come to speak with him and let him know what his situation was. She wiped her palm against her green suede riding skirt, checked to make sure her white shirtwaist was properly tucked in, then knocked lightly before she pushed the door open. He wasn't in the bed. She caught her breath, and stepped into the room.

"Morning, ma'am."

Her glance swiveled to the window. Merrick stood there, outlined by the morning light, a quilt draped over his shoulders. His hairy, muscular legs stuck out of the ridiculously short nightshirt. He cradled his broken arm with his good hand and leaned his slim hips against the window frame.

Summoning her courage, she looked him in the eye. "Good morning, Mr. Merrick. You must be feeling better."

He nodded, then looked her up and down in a way that made her feel as if parts of her weren't properly covered. "Yes ma'am, I am at that." He said in a low throaty voice, smiling at her, his teeth very white against his black beard. She felt her apprehension grow. He smiled the way a wolf might while looking over his prey.

The swelling and bruises on his face were fading, making his features more clear. She guessed his age near thirty.

Katherine took a deep breath and straightened the cuffs on her shirtwaist. "I wanted, I mean, we need to talk." She chided herself for stumbling along. Hadn't she rehearsed this enough? His blatant maleness made her nerves quiver.

"Who are you?" His soft drawl interrupted her thoughts as he ignored her statement.

Flustered, she smoothed her skirt with her palms, feeling the reassuring lump in her right pocket. The small revolver gave her courage a boost. "Excuse me?"

"I know your name, but I don't know who you are." His blue eyes drilled her with an intent look.

She thought she had told him yesterday. Maybe he didn't remember. "My name is Katherine. Katherine Holman. And this is my ranch, the Rocking H."

His eyebrow cocked when she informed him the ranch was hers, as if he questioned what she said. He pushed away from the window frame and extended his good hand to her. "Pleased to meet you, Miz Holman."

She felt disturbed at his approach and took a step back. Pointing to the bed, she spoke more sharply than she had intended. "You had better get back in there." Her hand slid into her pocket and felt for the tiny pistol. She wondered if the gun would be at all effective in stopping a man his size, or more to the point, if she would have enough courage to even pull the trigger.

He lowered the hand he had extended, giving her a puzzled look. "All right." Gingerly he took a seat on the bed and leaned against the headrest. His nightshirt rode up his thighs. "This better?" Again he cocked one eyebrow up and watched her.

No, she thought, as she struggled to keep her eyes on his face and not on his legs. "You shouldn't be up yet." She knew she sounded rattled. She took a deep breath, trying to calm herself.

He pulled a pillow onto his lap and rested his splinted arm. "How did I get here?"

She had intended to do the talking, but Merrick seemed to have his own agenda. Fair enough. She would answer his questions, then tell him what she had come to say. "I brought you."

His eyes never left her face. "Why?"

She gave him the same reason she had given Gibby. "Because you needed help." His eyebrow shot up in that annoying way, as if he didn't believe her. "Now that you're better, we need to talk."

His eyes narrowed and he leaned forward. "Now that I'm better, I need my clothes, my horse, and my gun. I appreciate you taking me in, but I have business."

She flinched at his low, menacing voice and deliberate words. She knew all about his business. She refused to be intimidated. It was high time she told him where he stood. "You can't leave."

"I think I'll have to be the one to decide that, Miz Holman."

Alarmed, she realized he sounded like he planned to completely ignore what she had just said and leave today. Katherine took a step closer to the bed. "Really, you can't leave. The sheriff of Dennison said—"

He cut her off, cold. "Said he'd find Watson? That's up to me." His voice changed and now held a savage tone.

He didn't remember the trial or the hangings, but she did. "You mean to leave here to look for John Watson? The one they called Long Nose Jack?" She cursed the quaver in her voice. An outlaw like Merrick would take advantage of any weakness in her.

His intense gaze was still fixed on her. "Did he bring me here?"

She blurted out the answer to his question. "No. They hung him in Dennison." Watson was the rustler who had frightened the crowd at his trial by lunging and snarling at Judge Casey. Watson was said to be the leader of the gang.

The air left his lungs as if someone had punched him in the stomach. He closed his eyes. She studied his face, trying to read his expression.

He opened his eyes and drilled her with his blue eyes. "Are you sure? Did you see it?"

See it? In the middle of the night the vision still haunted her. She wished she had resisted the urge to look at the scaffold after the hangings when she had passed by on her way to the livery. She wondered from the intensity of his reaction if Watson had been kin of his. They looked nothing alike. "I was there." It had never occurred to her that someone might mourn a man like Watson.

He spoke again, so low she had to strain to hear it. "And the others? His gang?"

She swallowed hard and forced herself to look him in the eye. "They hung them, too." Carefully she watched him for his reaction. The second bit of news didn't seem to shock him as much as the first.

He ran his big hand over his face. "I guess it's over then."

Why didn't Merrick question why he hadn't been hung too? He stared past her at the floor.

Suddenly he looked drained and slumped against the headboard. "I guess I'll be heading home."

"I told you, you can't leave. The sheriff can arrest you if you leave." Then she added hurriedly, "Or if you give me any trouble."

His head jerked up and he stared at her. "What are you talking about?"

Explaining his situation to him was not going to be easy. Katherine chose her words carefully. "It's the law. The only reason they didn't hang you too is because I, uh, claimed you."

He couldn't have looked more surprised if she had lit the bed on fire. "They were going to hang me? Why?" He sat up straight and leaned toward her, bracing his good hand against the mattress. The quilt fell away from his broad shoulders and the buttons of his nightshirt strained at their buttonholes across his broad chest.

She studied the distressed look on his face. Why would the possibility of his own hanging shock him so much? Surely he had known the consequences when he did the crimes. Maybe he hadn't expected to be caught. "Because you were found guilty."

"Of what? When?" He looked tense, ready to leap from the bed.

She backed up another step and again her hand went to her pocket, the cold metal of the derringer reassuring against her trembling fingers. "Of rustling. At the trial with all the others."

He looked incredulous. "They tried me? With the rustlers?" He shook his head, as if trying to clear it, then shot her a suspicious look. "Where the hell was I? Here?"

She remembered what the men sitting in front of her the day of the hangings had said about the trial. She shook her head. "You were tied to a chair in the courtroom."

His brow furrowed. "I don't remember any of it." He rubbed his hand over his face again.

He looked so confused, she felt she needed to offer an explanation. "I heard you were unconscious." Hesitating, she decided to hazard a question that had bothered her since she had first laid eyes on him. "Why did the sheriff and his men beat you?"

He shook his head again, sending a shock of black hair over his forehead. Absently he pushed it away. "I don't think they did. I think it was Watson and his gang. The last thing I remember was sneaking up on their camp."

Her knees went weak as his statement sank in. His comment was so matter-of-fact, it sounded unrehearsed. When she spoke, there was a squeak in her voice. "You weren't part of his gang?"

"Hell, no. I'm from Texas." He sounded incensed that she would even consider the possibility that he was a cattle thief.

As if there weren't any rustlers in Texas, she thought with exasperation. She couldn't resist a sarcastic tone. "Excuse me."

She saw a small smile tug at the corner of his mouth as he explained. "I'd been trailing them for weeks. Watson killed my brother Jim when he stumbled on the gang while they were rustling some of our cattle."

"Oh dear." Her mind went blank, and she couldn't think of anything to say. Either he was a very good actor, or she had a much bigger problem here than she had imagined.

His voice brought her back to the here and now. "What did you mean when you said you claimed me?" He skewered her with an intense look.

Not meeting his eye, she gave him half an answer. "In the township of Dennison, there's a law that a woman can lay claim to a man who's about to hang."

Looking puzzled, he took a moment to digest her statement. The crease on his forehead between his eyes deepened. "And then what? You own me now? Do I have to work off time with you?"

She squirmed under his steady gaze. "Not exactly."

He stared at her, and his eyes narrowed. "Well, why don't you tell me exactly what it is I have to do?" His soft voice held a hint of menace. He swung his bare hairy legs over the edge of the bed.

What had happened to her resolve to be in charge of this situation? Unnerved, Katherine took another step backward. She decided on telling him another half-truth as she inched from the room. "Nothing. You don't have to do anything except stay here for a while. Then you can go home, back to Texas."

He shot her a skeptical look. His voice became very quiet as he stood, taking a step forward. "So I'm not indentured or sentenced to do time. What is my status here?"

"Ah, status? What do you mean?" Her mouth went dry. Every time she moved, he did, too. He wasn't getting any closer, but she wasn't getting any further away, either. Would he follow her out into the hall? Trying to remain calm, she assured herself that he was still weak.

If he got too close she could outrun him and yell for help. She took another backward step. Her bottom hit the edge of the open door.

He noticed she watched his mouth as he spoke and avoided looking him in the eye. She was hiding something, but this entire situation was so bizarre, he couldn't guess what that might be. He went over what she had just said, but it made no better sense the second time through.

She had an expression in her eyes that reminded him of a frightened rabbit facing a rattler. He had to admire her. She was terrified, but she didn't turn tail and run.

He wanted answers, and he wanted them now. "What would you call me, exactly? A guest?" He considered that for a moment and watched the slight shake of her head. "No, a guest can leave when he wishes. A hand? For how long? Do I get wages? What would *you* call me, Miz Holman?"

Her eyes got big and round as she blurted the word, "Husband." She sounded frantic. "I had to marry you."

He spoke over the sudden roaring in his ears. "What?" What did she say? Maybe he hadn't heard her right. He felt dizzy, and decided he'd better get back to the bed. He'd look like a fool if he passed out right in front of her. When he grasped the bedpost and lowered himself to the mattress, he turned back to her. She was gone. Damn.

Married. If Katherine Holman had reached out and slapped him in the face, it wouldn't have surprised Wes more. She had looked scared to death, backing out of the room with her hand in her pocket, which unless he'd missed his guess, held a weapon. Then she up and tells him he was sentenced to hang for a crime he didn't do in a trial he didn't remember. Why the heck had she married him to save him from hanging? She didn't know him from Adam, and she thought he was an outlaw.

His surprise gave way to anger. What had he ever done to deserve this? He supposed he should feel grateful to the little lady, but the entire situation was a mighty big puzzlement. He had assumed she already had a husband, but if she didn't, and needed one, why would she choose a condemned man? Her explanation didn't make any sense, and the confusion of the whole situation made him even more suspicious of her motives.

If he hadn't been standing up in the middle of the room when she hit him with that peculiar bit of information, he would have guessed he was dreaming. What a sorry set of circumstances. Married? Him? Damn.

The more he thought it over, the more he guessed the sheriff must have thought he was part of the gang. That was understandable, he supposed, if the lawmen had discovered him in the rustlers' camp. It bothered him that he couldn't remember anything of what had happened with the rustlers, but not nearly as much as the fact that Katherine Holman had married him. She acted like she was terrified of him, even after he told her he wasn't an outlaw. He could tell she didn't believe him about not being part of Watson's gang.

What fool politician would think up a law that allowed a woman to just up and marry a condemned man? What kind of a fool was Katherine Holman for taking that lawmaker up on his lunacy?

Something very strange was going on. If she needed a husband, she could have her pick. Available women in a remote place like the Montana territory were scarce. A good-looking woman like her, with a ranch, wouldn't have to resort to claiming a condemned man. Head pounding, he lay down and tried to make some sense of the puzzle, but too many pieces were missing. Married. Damn.

The first thing he needed to do was go back to Dennison, talk to the sheriff, and get cleared of the charge of rustling. Merrick had been a respected name for three generations of cattlemen in Texas. He wasn't about to leave this territory with the title of rustler attached to him. He'd go into town and telegraph his brother Sam. Sam was a lawyer and could tell him who to see about getting his name cleared.

Maybe his brother could also advise him about getting shed of a wife he didn't even remember acquiring. Funny thing was, the urge to get to know her better was stronger than the feeling that he had to get out of this crazy situation. That thought made him decide the blow to his head must have been harder than he realized.

In spite of his anger, Wes fell asleep thinking about big brown eyes, soft brown hair, and skin that smelled like lavender.

6

Shaken by her unsettling conversation with Merrick, Katherine continued to mull over what he had told her as she stepped onto the back porch and pulled on her warm sheepskin jacket. Why had she blurted out that she had married him? He had turned several shades of pale at that information. Mesmerized by his aggressive maleness, she had forgotten entirely that she had intended to be in charge of the conversation and inform Merrick what she expected of him. Disgusted with herself, she slapped her gloves against her riding skirt as she headed for the barn.

Winter was coming on and she had ignored her duties around the ranch long enough while nursing the outlaw—she frowned and corrected herself—the *possible* outlaw.

Unnerved anew by that thought, she needed to be away from the house to think. Somehow the whole situation seemed to have gotten out of her control. If he was telling the truth about being innocent, she didn't know what she was going to do. In either case he would have to stay until Anderson returned. In the eyes of the law he was still guilty. She wondered if that would matter to Merrick.

Hamlet sat outside the barn, waiting for her. The mutt always seemed to know when she was planning to ride out. She scratched him behind the ears and he wagged his long tail in greeting.

After saddling up, she rode hard toward the high north meadow. Gibby and his men were out that way to bring the herd closer to the house in case they got an early snow.

In spite of her best intentions, her thoughts turned back to her conversation with Merrick. As soon as she could, she would ride back to Dennison and talk to the sheriff, and try to find out more about Merrick, and the night he had been captured.

Not one cloud hung in the wide blue sky. The enormity of the land never failed to awe her. The natural beauty captured her thoughts, and the problem of Mr. Merrick faded.

The sounds of men yelling and the piteous bawling of a calf led her to a small draw near the stream. A cow, caught in a bog of mud, fought the efforts of the hands to drag her out. Two of the men had roped her and snubbed their lariats around their saddle horns. Their horses strained against the pull of the reluctant cow. She bellowed her displeasure, and that set her calf to bawling again. Several of the other hands sat watching, hollering advice along with derogatory comments at their companions. Gibby spotted Katherine and silenced the men. The hands treated her with respect, or they answered to Gibby.

She watched her men labor to save the cow. Every animal in her herd she considered to be an investment.

Katherine waved to Gibby and dismounted near the calf. He skittered away from her, but not before she had seen porcupine quills sticking from his snout.

"Wade, put that calf on a string for me." The wiry young cowpuncher waved his hat, and with a great show of style, threw his lariat around the calf, leapt from his horse, and wrestled the calf to the ground, lashing all his legs in one easy movement. She gathered some supplies from her saddlebag.

Katherine guessed the animal's age at about five months as she checked him over. Pleased at his general condition, she patted him on the flank. He rolled his eyes in fright until the whites showed, giving him a comical appearance. Using a pair of pliers, she pulled the quills from his tender snout, then rubbed the area with a foul smelling arnicated carbolic ointment. He howled at the treatment. "Silly critter. Next time, watch where you stick your nose."

"You almost done, Miss Kate?" Gibby rode over to where she knelt, working.

"Almost." Katherine checked the animal's ears for mites, gathered up her things, and got up off the ground.

"Good. The boys will have his mama out of there in a minute and she's hopping mad. They always act like getting stuck was our fault when we have to pull 'em out."

Katherine laughed, yanking Wade's rope off the hooves of the calf. The young animal struggled to his feet and bounded out of reach, shaking his head and snorting.

She wound the rope into a neat coil and handed it back to Wade before remounting her horse. She had no intention of being on the ground when the hands got the mother cow loose. No one in their right mind would face an angry mama on foot. Even Hamlet had enough sense to give the cow some space.

Gibby signaled to the men, who released their ropes. The cow plunged out of the gully and skittered away from the rescuers, bawling her displeasure. Smiling, Katherine took off her hat and used her bandanna to wipe the perspiration from her brow.

Katherine rode on with the hands and spotted the main body of the herd just after noon. Spread out across the range in clusters, the animals stopped grazing and raised their heads to watch the approaching riders. Gibby didn't even have to give any orders. Experienced hands spread out and loosely surrounded the animals, riding around them in tighter and tighter circles until the men on horseback had the steers bunched in a tight group. A choking cloud of dust rose and hung over the herd.

In the distance Katherine noted two animals that had not joined the herd. Immediately recognizable by their massive wide sets of horns, they were the only remaining stock from the herd her father had driven up the trail from Texas over twenty years before. Gibby spotted them at the same time. He started to signal to two of the hands.

Katherine interrupted him. "Get the herd moving. I'll get the longhorns." She pulled her bandanna up to cover her nose and mouth.

Gibby nodded, turning away to give the command to head out. The hands removed their hats and whacked them against their chaps, whistling and shouting to the milling animals.

The longhorns stood on a small hill about a hundred yards from the herd. To Katherine they looked as if they were disdainful of the white-faced cattle and held themselves apart.

She rode up to the animals, keeping a respectful distance. Those horns could be used very effectively as a weapon. She had heard stories of cowpunchers who had failed to keep a watchful eye and been gored.

She sat quietly atop her horse and spoke to the animals. "Yo Red, yo Bess. Time to move." Red turned his face to her and she could see his eyes, clouded with age. She doubted either one of them could withstand a winter storm out on the range, but there was no way she could shut them in. To her they were a symbol of the open range, and she would see to it they remained free until they died.

Red had led the original Rocking H herd up the trail all those years ago. Katherine had heard the stories from her father and Gibby a hundred times. She had only been two at the time, and had no memories of coming north on the drive, but that time lived for her in their tales.

She rode around behind the animals and removed her hat, slapping the brim against her thigh. Bringing them along would mean traveling in the dust of the herd, but she didn't care.

Her father had taken such a risk to bring his animals and his family to the Montana territory. Few people had had the courage to gamble their futures on the threat of hostile Indians, not to mention the bitter winter weather. One time she had asked him why he had decided to do it, and he had told her it was for the land. He'd never had to explain his feelings to her, even as a child she'd understood.

In 1856 Julius Holman had driven a herd north for a boss, and he'd fallen in love with the land. In those days it was free for the taking. Now things were different. Raising cattle had become big business.

Rustling was a business, too. Men like Watson made good money by stealing from legitimate ranchers. She remembered the clause in her father's will that stipulated she marry a man with experience in the cattle business. Rustler or rancher, Merrick fit the description.

Merrick. Katherine looked out over the bony backs and patchy hides of the two longhorns as they moved slowly in front of her. What was she going to do now? If he wasn't a rustler—and he had certainly sounded personally affronted that she might think that he was— did that change her plans for him? After pondering the question for a moment, she decided that his guilt or innocence really didn't matter, not where getting the deed to the ranch was concerned. All she needed was a marriage certificate, and some quick talking to convince the attorney. She turned her thoughts back to the business at hand, and away from the blue-eyed man in her father's bed.

In the last few years she had not had much of an opportunity to help move the herd. The men made the drive to the railroad in a few days now instead of taking weeks or months to get the animals to market.

The care of Hannah and the business of the ranch had kept Katherine at home. And, to be honest with herself, she was no longer comfortable being with the men in such close company. She had suffered so much gossip in town it had made her careful of her actions. She wanted to avoid any appearance of impropriety.

When the herd reached the wintering range, Katherine said a silent good-bye to the two old longhorns and kicked her horse into a gallop, riding around the herd until she caught up with Gibby.

"You want riders out?" Gibby asked. He took off his hat and used his sleeve to wipe his weathered face. His forehead stood out, stark white against the brown skin of the rest of his face and neck.

"For a couple of days, so they don't wander back. And make sure the men are armed." She hadn't forgotten the mutilated stock. She stood in the stirrups and quickly estimated the number of animals they had moved, pleased with the looks of the stock.

Gibby replaced his hat and motioned to the milling animals. "Half dozen calves in there we missed on the spring roundup."

"Get a fire going. We'll brand now. Then the riders can check the calves and make sure they're healing."

Gibby grunted his approval, and gave some quick orders. Within moments the seasoned hands had scraped a spot bare on the ground, and started a fire. Branding irons with the Rocking H symbol were produced from saddlebags and laid in the flames. Three men rode the perimeter, allowing the herd to spread out. Several others cut through the herd, roping the unmarked calves.

They worked as a team, rarely speaking. Each man knew what was expected of him and fulfilled his duty. Gibby allowed for no slackers in his outfit.

After the calves were roped and dragged to the fire to brand, Katherine checked their eyes and ears, doctoring any minor ailment she spotted before the bawling animals were set free to find their mamas. Hamlet lay by her side, unaffected by the distress of the animals. The air smelled thick with the odor of woodsmoke and singed hair.

Katherine's hands burned from the strong carbolic ointment she applied to the fresh brands. She paused sev-

eral times to pour water from her canteen over her hands
and wipe them on her bandanna, but it did little good.
The thick salve had been made to cling to skin no matter
what the weather and proved impervious to water.

Finally the riders had found all the unbranded
calves, and the men let the fire burn down and pulled
the irons out to cool.

She brushed at the dry grass clinging to her skirt.
"Gibby, I'm going to head back." Hamlet rose and
stretched, ready to follow.

"Want one of the men to go with you?" After she
refused his offer, Gibby tipped his hat and headed off.
Katherine caught her horse and mounted up, turning
toward the house. The ranch buildings were visible in
the distance. A thin curl of smoke from the kitchen
stovepipe hurried her along. Feeling satisfied with the
morning's work, she decided some of Consuela's chili
and tortillas sounded awfully good just now.

Wes watched her ride in, his eyes half closed as he
lazed in the shadows of the front porch. Katherine
Holman dismounted, leaving her horse at the barn.
Gingerly he shifted his weight in the old wooden rocking chair and rested his bandaged head carefully against
the back rail. He had been waiting for hours to talk to
her, to finish the conversation she had run out on this
morning. He had a few things to say to her about being
married.

He didn't like the idea of her, or any woman for that
matter, riding out on the range alone, with only a big
mutt for company. There were too many dangers out
there, too many things that could bring a rider down.
She would be safer if one of her men rode with her.

She pulled off her jacket as she walked up to the
house, the scruffy brown dog close at her side. He

appreciated the gentle sway of her rounded hips, and the way her neatly tucked-in shirtwaist accentuated her breasts. He had to admit, she made the looking easy.

Ever since she had left his room he had been planning how he would get back to Dennison and talk to the sheriff there to try to clear his name. He didn't know what he was going to do about Katherine Holman. Her marrying him like that put him in a mighty peculiar position, and for the life of him he couldn't figure out why she had done it.

Wes watched Katherine as, raising one arm, she took off her hat and slapped it against her thigh, sending a cloud of dust swirling into the warm afternoon air. He had time to see the sun pick up traces of red highlights in her hair before she put her hat back on. A layer of dirt coated her clothes. This was a woman who was not afraid to work like one of her men.

He would be able to ride tomorrow, but his curiosity was getting the better of him. Maybe he would let her think he was still too weak to go, and stick around until he figured out what she was up to.

She was halfway up the front steps when he cleared his throat and stopped her in her tracks. Her dog stiffened and growled, bristling hair rising on the back of his neck.

"Afternoon, ma'am." Merrick said from the shadows at the far end of the porch. She started at the sound of his voice, her hand flying up to cover her heart. He hadn't meant to startle her.

The porch, dim after the bright sun, had her squinting into the gloom. "What do you think you're doing?" she demanded, amazed to find him downstairs, awkward after their conversation this morning. She had planned to talk to him later.

He rose slowly from the old wooden rocker, uncoiling his length a little gingerly. She noticed that he held onto the chair for support even after he was up. The bandage on his head looked clean and new.

"Waiting for you to come back." He took a step away from the rocker into the sun. Moving with apparent difficulty, he grasped the railing around the porch, his eyes never leaving her face.

Katherine took a deep breath to steady herself and said curtly, "You should be in bed." His only answer was that annoying way he had of lifting one brow, his expression saying he didn't agree. Merrick had been sitting in her rocker, her favorite spot on the porch, where she liked to sit and survey her land in the evening as the sun disappeared behind the hill.

As far as she was concerned, no matter what he had said, his status as an outlaw was as yet undecided. He didn't belong on her porch, and she intended to tell him so. He had chosen her chair. It wasn't as if there weren't other places to sit, for heaven's sake, she thought, annoyed.

Seemingly unconcerned by Hamlet's growl, Merrick extended his hand to the dog. Ham left her side and approached Merrick. After a brief moment, the dog seemed satisfied that Merrick posed no threat, and curled up near him in a patch of sun.

Miserable judge of character, Katherine thought. The dog finds a stranger on the porch and after five seconds, lies down to take a nap.

Her gaze drifted back up from the dog to the man. Not only was he up, he had bathed and shaved off his beard, leaving only his mustache. He looked very different without the whiskers, and the handsomeness of his face stunned her for a moment. The beard had covered a strong, square chin and well-formed lips. She felt herself approving that he had left the mustache, it seemed to belong on his face.

She realized she was staring and cleared her throat. "Well, you seem to feel better." She realized she did not sound the least bit pleased, and certainly that was a good assessment of how she felt.

"You've been out branding." Not a question, but a statement. He had a deep mellow voice, with a little drawl.

Surprised, she took off her hat and used the back of her hand to brush her hair away from her sweaty forehead. "How did you know?"

"I'd recognize the smell of that salve anywhere."

Chagrined that the odor was so discernible, she couldn't think of anything to say. "Yes, well . . . "

"You know, that stuff will burn your skin. You ought to let your hands take care of the branding." His pretentious tone annoyed her.

Merrick had no business telling her what she should not be doing. Katherine snapped at him in reply. "I take care of my own stock. If the hands can do a job, so can I. Go back to bed." She stomped across the porch, ignoring his earlier plea that he wanted to speak to her, and went into the house. If he did follow her, she thought, it would take him the rest of the day to catch up, he was moving so slowly.

Just what she needed. A temporary husband who found out a few hours ago they were married, and already thinks he's the boss. It certainly hadn't take him very long to get around to making suggestions!

Katherine passed through the kitchen and grabbed the kettle on her way to the back porch. She hung her hat on a peg and poured hot water into a basin on the old dry sink by the kitchen door. She added some water from the pitcher and glanced into the cracked mirror hanging on the wall in front of her. Mercy, she looked like a hag!

Sweat plastered her disheveled hair to her forehead and dirt streaked her chin and cheeks. She scooped up the soap and lathered her hands and face. How she must have looked to him, coming in off the range like that. Immediately she chided herself. What did she care how she looked? He was temporary, very temporary! She didn't need to wear pretty dresses and be sweet-smelling from a bath just to impress the likes of him.

As soon as Anderson returned from Boston she would get Merrick out of her house, and out of her life. He had an unsettling effect on her, and she didn't like it one bit. Her cheeks flamed with color when she remembered how brazenly she had looked at his naked body. Perhaps if she hadn't undressed him that first night and seen what he looked like without his clothes, he wouldn't be having such an effect on her now. She splashed some cold water on her overheated face.

Briefly she considered moving him to the bunkhouse, then quickly discarded the idea. Anderson would be more likely to believe he was really her husband if Merrick resided in the house. Jerking a towel off the washstand, she dried her face and hands. Unable to resist one last peek in the mirror, Katherine smoothed her hair with her hands and decided she looked more presentable. She made a mental note to bring a brush downstairs and leave it on the dry sink, then she went to find Consuela and Hannah.

As she went to locate her daughter, she startled herself by realizing that in the last few minutes she had thought of Merrick as a stranger, and an annoyance, but not an outlaw. Was he innocent, or just a very convincing liar?

Katherine glanced out the front window on her way upstairs and saw him, sprawled, loose-limbed, in the rocker. His head lay against the high back of the chair and he appeared to be sleeping.

Merrick wasn't asleep, though he could be very easily, sitting here in the warm sunshine. He heard her stomping through the house. She sure managed to make a lot of noise for such a little thing, he thought. And was she ever touchy. What a temper. He still couldn't figure her out. In fact, there was a lot he couldn't figure out. He'd awakened to find himself in the middle of a giant puzzle. Now he understood how Alice must have felt when she tumbled down the rabbit-hole.

Well, he had a few of the pieces, and now that he didn't feel like he was in danger he supposed he could be patient for a while, and pick up a few more. He wouldn't chase after her, looking for answers, at least not yet. That spooked her too much.

The trip downstairs and a bath and shave had flat out exhausted him, and he hadn't even hauled the water. The Mexican woman named Consuela had done that. He doubted right now he could make it back upstairs without stopping part way to rest. He cursed his weakness and the vulnerable way it made him feel.

Cautiously he shifted his sore head into a new position against the hard wooden back of the chair. The wound itched like crazy, and he welcomed the sensation, a good sign of healing. If only his ribs weren't so bad. Every time he took a deep breath he felt as if his chest had been caved in. At least his teeth were all in place. They wouldn't grow back, ribs would.

As he drowsed in the late afternoon sun he admired the ranch. The operation appeared to be laid out in an orderly fashion. The big barn sat close enough to the house to be accessible, but not so close that the smell and flies would bother the occupants of the house. The corrals and fences were in a good state of repair. The low rambling bunkhouse looked like it had a new roof, and the attached cookhouse sported a covered walkway.

His thoughts drifted back to the way Katherine Holman had looked riding in. She had an easy way of sitting a horse that spoke to the fact she had probably ridden for a good part of her life. People who learned to ride as adults just didn't have the ease on a horse she possessed. Maybe she had grown up on a ranch before becoming a rancher's wife. He wondered if there was a polite way to ask her what had happened to her husband—he corrected himself—her first husband. According to her, he was her husband now. That thought made him jumpy. He wished he had more answers. Impatient, he had never been good at biding his time.

When she had walked out of the barn, before she knew he watched her, she had moved with an unconscious grace. She looked about eighteen, too young to be the mother of a child the age of her daughter. She must have married right out of the schoolroom. The thought bothered him, that she might have gone to some man so young. He smiled, remembering how tough and bossy she was under that feminine exterior. She might look young, but she would be a handful for any man.

Wes didn't have to see those big brown eyes to know how the sparks could fly from them when she got angry. He remembered that from this morning. No one would ever confuse her with a quiet, agreeable woman, but he figured to run a ranch she needed spirit.

He doubted the men who worked for her ever questioned her to her face. They must have respect for her, and follow her orders. He could tell by the way the place looked, the way it was run. It took a lot of strength to ride boss over a place like this.

Nothing he had seen so far gave him a clue as to why she had married him. He'd been considering that particular question all day. For the hundredth time he wondered why a pretty widow who owned a ranch would marry a man she thought was a rustler. He had meant to work up to asking just now when she had ordered him back to bed and stormed into the house. The whole situation intrigued him. Perhaps he would let her think he was weaker than he really was while he figured out what was really going on at the Rocking H.

The mutt lifted his head and propped his muzzle on Merrick's thigh. Wes scratched him behind the ears. He was a big dog, a good range dog. He looked part wolfhound. One of his neighbors in Texas had recently imported a breeding pair of pure-bred wolfhounds from Ireland to cut down on the coyote problem. The dogs made good pets. Maybe he'd ask for a pup when he got home.

Right now he decided to get back to his bed before he fell out of this chair. He contemplated the effort it would take to make it up the staircase, sure Katherine wouldn't have an ounce of sympathy in her if she found him sprawled on the floor in her parlor. He suppressed a groan as he hoisted his battered body from the rocker and headed for the front door.

7

Katherine threw two logs on the fire and returned to her desk. Merrick must have come in and gone upstairs when she went out to find Hannah. She hadn't seen him since she had stormed off the porch and into the house earlier in the afternoon. Now that the sun was down the temperature dipped, leaving a definite chill in the air. She pulled her shawl closer around her shoulders and settled into the huge wooden swivel chair.

Stock records covered the top of the desk. Meticulous entries of every date of purchase and breeding were made in bound volumes to keep track of her animals. Katherine was busy making entries on the calves the hands had branded today. The sound of a masculine clearing of the throat brought her head up with a jerk.

Merrick stood barefooted in the center of the room. He had cradled his broken arm in a makeshift sling. She carefully set her pen into the holder and dropped her hands into her lap, wishing he would stay in bed and out of her hair.

"Mr. Merrick." She waited for him to say something. He wouldn't have come all the way downstairs unless he had something to say, and she was pretty sure what subject he wanted to cover.

"I want some answers." He sounded tough, but he swayed a little while he spoke.

"For heaven's sake, sit down before you fall down!" Her voice sounded harsh and short, even to her own ears, as she pointed at the armchairs by the fireplace.

He stood beside his chair and waited until she was seated in the matching chair, never taking those blue eyes off her.

Who had taught a man like him manners? Katherine could see his drawn, tired face in the light from the lamp.

"Will you clear up some matters for me?" His mellow voice held that sound of Texas, so familiar in the speech of her late father and Gibby.

He made an effort at being polite, but she sensed his impatience simmering under the surface of his words. "I can try." She braced herself, not surprised he had questions. If he had truly lost all memory from the time the rustlers were captured until he woke up in her father's bed, Merrick probably felt pretty confused. She supposed he deserved some answers, even if he might be an outlaw.

"How did I come to be in jail?" He flexed his fingers and then made a fist, exercising the hand on his broken arm.

He was probably doing it unconsciously, she thought, but the movement of his big hand bothered her. Even with his broken arm those hands looked strong. She considered how safe two women and a child were sleeping in the same house with him. Maybe she would change her mind and move him into the bunkhouse after all.

"Ma'am?"

She jerked her attention away from his hand and back to his question. "The sheriff arrested you with the other rustlers. I don't know much about that. Just what I read in the newspaper." She glanced into the corner by the desk. "I still have the paper. Do you want to read the article?" Perhaps he couldn't read. She couldn't think of a polite way to ask him.

He shrugged. "Later. I have some more questions. When did the trial take place?"

"The morning after you were all captured. Judge Casey, the circuit judge, just happened to be in Miles City, and one of the deputies rode over to get him."

"Is that how you heard about it?" He grimaced as he sat up a little straighter.

She felt herself flush. "I took the wagon to Dennison the next day to pick up some supplies." Actually, she had known about the judge going to Dennison for the rustlers' trial. Martin Denty had invited her into town to have dinner with him and the judge as his guest. Then Martin sent word to cancel the invitation before she had had time to reply. In fact, she had been in the process of drafting a polite refusal when a deputy had shown up at the door. Katherine wondered if the citizens of Miles City realized they were paying Denty's deputies to deliver his personal messages.

"So this decision that you needed a husband was a spur of the moment thing?" The corners of his mouth twitched slightly under his black mustache.

The way he asked the question irritated her. He was making fun of her. "My decision and the reasons behind it are none of your business!"

Now he smiled outright, and the effect on her was immediate and intense, making her feel warm all over. "Well, not to be contrary, but I beg to differ. Since it was me you married, I think I have the right to ask."

She shrugged, and his smile disappeared. "You can ask all you want." She didn't think she had to tell him her personal thoughts on the matter. "Do you have any other questions?"

His expression hardened and she found she missed his smile. "Where exactly did the nuptials take place?"

Relieved he was not going to push the point of *why* she had married him, she still felt rattled. Katherine smoothed her skirt and took a deep breath, trying to calm herself. "In the sheriff's office."

He cocked an eyebrow at her. "Strange, I don't remember any of it. I was there, wasn't I?"

His skeptical tone infuriated her. "Of course you were there. And so were plenty of witnesses. And I have the certificate!"

"Did I sign it?"

He *had* needed a little help with that. His signature was barely a scribble, because a deputy had been holding the pen with Merrick's hand wrapped around it. "Of course." She hesitated for a moment, then gave in to her basic sense of honesty. "You did require a little assistance." Her answer sounded stiff.

"I see." He seemed to question the validity of what she said without saying so out loud.

She found trying to justify to him what she had done mortifying. Why, indeed, did she have to explain anything to him? He should be grateful. She answered him in a voice as sour as she felt. "I should think you might thank me."

"I think I'll wait until I know what really happened."

With that comment, Katherine lost her temper. He might as well have called her a liar. She jumped to her feet and came to an abrupt stop in front of him. He jerked back a little in surprise at her sudden movement. "Next time you're headed for the scaffold and a rope around your neck, I'll leave you be!"

She watched him flinch, the color draining from his face, leaving the yellowed bruises to stand out. He choked on his words. "Scaffold? You mean—"

She nodded, alarmed at his sudden change of color. Of course, if he really didn't remember anything, he wouldn't know how close he had come to dying. She felt contrite for giving him such a shock. "I'm sorry. For a moment I forgot you have no memory of that time."

He shook his head, suddenly looking too weary to speak. He raised his hand in a little gesture of defeat.

If she didn't get him upstairs, he might have to spend the night in that chair. "You really must go back to bed and stay there. You'll do yourself harm if you don't rest until you heal a bit more." She came around the side of the chair and placed a hand under his elbow, assisting him to his feet.

His first step wobbled a little. She pulled up against him to steady him. He put his arm around her shoulder, and allowed her to take on some of his weight. His arm lay warm and heavy across the back of her neck, and his hand applied a steady pressure where he gripped her upper arm.

As weak as he seemed, she sensed there was still a great strength in his body. She could feel the muscles in his torso and arm flex as he moved. His shirt smelled of soap and sunshine, and for just the slightest moment, she was tempted to turn her head and nuzzle her cheek against his chest. She jerked a little at that thought and must have hit against a sore spot on his ribs, because she heard him suck in a quick breath.

"Sorry," she murmured. His only response to her apology was a grunt of acknowledgment.

He didn't resist her help and allowed her to lead him to the bottom of the stairs before he pulled away from her, his hand lingering on her shoulder.

"Thank you. I can make it from here." He said the first two words in a low voice, and she truly didn't know if he was thanking her for helping him to the stairs, or for saving his life.

Katherine stood and watched him make his way slowly up the staircase. He certainly was stubborn about not staying in bed. The beating he had taken would keep a normal man down for a week, if it didn't kill him. She had thought that once he understood the gang of rustlers was gone and he wasn't being hunted by the sheriff, he might give in to the pain and stay in bed. She shook her head, not knowing what to think now. Her tidy little plan to inherit the ranch was starting to develop some cracks.

She turned and went back to her desk, thinking over what she had told him. Certainly he had had more questions than he had asked, but the information about the hanging had stopped him in his tracks.

Perhaps she would send some wires herself, to check on what he had told her about his background. If he was telling the truth, he would be anxious to clear his name. His innocence or guilt didn't make any difference to her, she reasoned, as long as she could keep the ranch. Later, if he wanted an annulment to officially end the marriage, she wouldn't try to stop him. With a jolt, she realized she had started to consider what he might want.

Weary from her day in the saddle and her exchanges with Merrick, she finished making her entries and closed the book. She turned the lamp down, until the room was lit only by the fire. The corners fell into shadow as she contemplated the last few days. This ranch would be hers in name. Maybe her plan was not working out the way she had envisioned, but at least it was still working.

She would talk to Merrick again in the morning. Perhaps she should tell him why she had married him. Being cordial to the man would only increase the chances of him cooperating with her later, when they had to face Anderson. The thought made her feel better, and she headed up the stairs to go to bed.

Katherine checked on Hannah, then paused at Merrick's closed door, opposite her own. No light showed on the threshold, and all was quiet. As she went into her room she heard his bed give off its familiar squeak. The noise had been there since her parents had transported the bed, in pieces, by wagon from Texas. When they put the frame together again in Montana, it had let off a distinctive squeak every time someone rolled over.

Katherine remembered how reassuring that noise had been in the middle of the night when she had awakened as a child, knowing her parents were close by. Now the noise reminded her of the big cowboy sleeping just across the hall. She lay awake for a long time, trying not to think about the way he had looked when he first got here, sprawled naked on that bed.

The next morning the sun peeked over the horizon, through the bare windows, and shone directly into

Wes's face. When he rolled over and buried his head in the pillow, it seemed that every muscle in his body protested. He had never stayed in bed. When you grew up on a ranch with five brothers, you learned to keep moving when you got hurt, or be labeled a sissy.

He could use the rest, get his strength back, and try to figure out what was going on here at Miz Holman's ranch. Watson and his gang of rustlers were hanged, so there was nothing more he could do about them. Wes had a hollow feeling, as if a place inside him, reserved for vengeance against his brother's murderer, was suddenly empty.

What he really needed to worry about was getting his name set right with the law. He wondered how long that might take. His gut tightened every time he thought of the fact that he was a convicted rustler.

When he did straighten things out with the sheriff, he could go home to Texas. He reasoned that if he was cleared of the rustling charges, his marriage to Katherine Holman could be declared null and void as well.

He could take the train. Traveling by rail would be much easier than the long ride home on horseback, feeling all used up the way he did. It would be hard to make camp and saddle his horse with his busted arm in a splint.

Hanged. He remembered the conversation with Miz Holman last night. She had saved his life. His surprise had been so great, he hadn't even thanked her properly when she told him. He'd have to find her today and tell her how grateful he felt to her. But none of what she said explained why she had married him.

If the story was true— He laughed out loud. It must be true. Who could make up something as crazy as that? Just then he heard a knock at his door. He hoped it was Consuela with breakfast. His belly was bumping up against his backbone. Her tortillas and a big plate of ham and eggs sounded mighty good.

"Come in." With his good arm he hoisted himself higher in the bed, up against the headboard.

The door opened, and there, instead of Consuela, stood Miz Holman with a tray. A shaft of sunlight brought out the deep rich color of her hair. She sure was a pretty little thing. He wanted to watch her take the pins out and see how far down her back that brunette mass would hang. According to her, she was his wife. That thought just wouldn't seem to stick.

"Good morning, Mr. Merrick. Are you up to eating breakfast?" Gracefully she crossed the room and set the tray down on his lap. Dressed much the same as she had been yesterday, he noticed the way her shirtwaist pulled against her breasts when she lowered the tray into his lap, and how her riding skirt clung smoothly to her rounded hips. He imagined his hands on her breasts.

Noting the flush on her cheeks and the fact that she didn't look at him, he thought she might have read his thoughts. Then he realized that his lack of a shirt must be embarrassing her. Well, if he got up to get one it would embarrass her more, because he was stark naked under the bedding.

He glanced down at the tray. "I could come downstairs and save you the trouble." His thoughts of eggs and tortillas evaporated. Porridge, dry toast, and a mug of tea. This was the kind of breakfast his mother ate. He never drank tea. Was this her idea of what a man needed to heal on? Maybe her husband had hurt himself and starved to death.

She focused on a spot to the left of his head. "No bother. I think you need to remain in bed. If you should tumble down the stairs, you will only do yourself more damage."

He certainly wasn't going to argue with her there. The weaker she thought he was, the more relaxed she would be around him. But if he was down in the kitchen he might be able to talk Consuela into some real food.

"I still hate to put you to the trouble." Besides, he was bored. Maybe she could join him in the bed.

She ignored his comment, and went on, talking to the headboard. "Mr. Merrick, I apologize for being so abrupt last night. Not remembering what happened to you must be difficult. Please ask me any questions you might have about the trial, and I'll try to answer them as best I can."

He found talking to someone who wouldn't make eye contact difficult. He wondered why she was so willing to talk today. He motioned to a lap robe folded neatly over the quilt rack. "I'm a little cold. Could you get that for me?" Perhaps if he covered up a little, she might relax.

She bolted for the robe, draping it across his shoulders when he leaned forward.

He was most curious about why she had married him, but after her response to that question last night, he hesitated to ask again. Maybe he could get her to talk about that later, when she got used to the idea that he wasn't an outlaw.

He spooned the bland porridge into his mouth, swallowed, and asked his first question. "How did I get here?"

She looked relieved, probably because he hadn't asked anything personal about the wedding. "In the back of my wagon."

She sure didn't seem inclined to elaborate for him. Well, they could stick to basics, if that's what she wanted. She sat down on a straight chair beside the bed, her spine so stiff it didn't touch the wood.

"My horse, and saddlebags?" He really wanted his own clothes.

She hesitated. "Sold."

"By you?" She had some nerve.

"Oh my, no. By the town of Dennison, to pay for the trial and the . . ." She looked uncomfortable and shifted her weight.

"The what?" Just what had the price of his horse bought, anyway?

"The scaffold." Her eyes met his this time when she spoke.

He whistled through his teeth. "That must have been one expensive bunch of lumber."

She looked relieved at his response, and even smiled a little. "I've never seen one like it. Five nooses. It must have been twenty feet long."

Damn, he'd liked that skewbald horse. He had trained Yakima himself. Not to mention his rifle and his saddlebags. "Think they'll refund me since I didn't use it?"

She laughed, and the sound went right to his heart. Those lips of hers looked very kissable. He must have been staring because she glanced at him and stopped abruptly, looking flushed and embarrassed.

Just as he opened his mouth to tell her how lovely she looked when she laughed, he was interrupted by a dog barking and a shout from outside.

At the sound, she shot off the chair. "Excuse me." She left the room and closed the door behind her. The room seemed very ordinary with her gone, and he wasn't sure he liked the sensations she'd left behind.

*   *   *

Her cheeks burned at the thoughts she had of Merrick when he looked at her the way he had. Katherine hurried down the stairs and opened the front door, almost colliding with the young hand.

"Wade, what's the matter?" She noticed his breathing came hard.

He started to talk, then, blushing, yanked off his hat. "Sorry to bother you, ma'am, but Mr. Gibson says he needs for you to ride down to the fence nearest the creek on the east range. And bring the medicine box."

"What's happened?" If one of the men was injured, she wanted to be prepared. She didn't want to waste time coming back for supplies.

He started to say something, then appeared to change his mind. "Some of the fence is down. I'll get your horse." He turned and left, vaulting the porch rail, before she could say anything else to him. He certainly was acting strangely, and that made her uneasy.

Why would she need her box for some fallen fence? Gibby wasn't a man to fuss unnecessarily, and if he told Wade to come and get her, she'd go.

She didn't mind making the ride out to the east pasture. It gave her a good excuse to get out of the house and away from Merrick. The more time she spent with him, the more she felt drawn to him. Just now, when he was asking her questions, she had actually imagined what it might be like to lie on the bed with him, to feel his arms around her. Those feelings made her very uncomfortable, because she knew they could only complicate her life, and leave her miserable when he went back to Texas. The big cowboy in her father's bed would walk out on her, just like all the other men in her life had left her alone.

Hamlet raced ahead of the riders. "I swear, that dog covers ten times as much territory as I do. I wish I had his staying power." She looked over at Wade and saw him nod, knowing that was the only response she was going to get. He had used up three days' worth of words delivering his message to her. Most of her hands were like him. She figured the bunkhouse must be a pretty quiet place, even in the evenings when everyone was in there.

Automatically Katherine checked the quality of the grass as they rode, pleased that the erosion near the creek bed seemed to have slowed a bit. They followed the banks of the creek until she could see Gibby and the other hands in the distance. Their horses grazed nearby under a stand of trees.

The wind changed slightly and brought her the smell of charred wood. The men stood in a cluster, their backs to Katherine. She waved and called her foreman's name. He turned and walked toward her.

As she dismounted, she could see that about fifteen feet of fence was not just down, but missing. She walked over to examine the area. The wire was gone, the posts had been burned, and all that stood were smoldering stumps. The odor of smoke hung heavy in the air. Why would someone burn fence posts? As dry as the grass was out here, they could have set the whole range on fire. She stopped suddenly, her thoughts making her queasy. Maybe that's what they'd meant to do, whoever had done this.

Katherine turned to speak to Gibby, and just then a couple of the hands stepped away from the group and she could see what they had been clustered around. She caught her breath in a gasp.

One of her men, a new hand this season named Tully, lay on the ground. Tully's eyes fluttered open and then closed again. She heaved a sigh. He was alive, but he must be in pain. Head down, Hamlet padded over to sit quietly by the injured man.

Gibby's voice broke into her horrified observations. "Found him about an hour ago. He was riding second shift last night.

Katherine winced as she saw the knot on his forehead. "Could he tell you what happened?"

Gibby took off his hat and scratched his head. "He don't know. He was lighting a smoke, heard a shot, and his horse went down."

He waved his hand in the direction of the trees by the creek. For the first time Katherine saw the shape of a horse on the ground in the shade.

"The fall must have knocked Tully out."

Katherine felt the same niggle of fear in the pit of her stomach that she had felt when she looked at the mutilated cattle. The well-being of her hands was as much her responsibility as that of the animals. "So he didn't see who did it?" Shading her eyes against the sun, she scanned the area around them.

Gibby replaced his hat on the back of his head. "Nope. Didn't see nothing."

Slowly anger replaced her fear. "Damn! Why would someone do this to Tully?"

"Maybe it wasn't aimed at Tully. Like the cattle, maybe it's some kind of warning. Except this time, some of the stock has gone missing, 'stead of being killed." Gibby slid his hands into his back pockets and balanced back on the heels of his boots.

"What kind of warning?" She demanded, having a fairly good idea what he meant.

Gibby lowered his voice so the other men couldn't hear their conversation. "Maybe some folks around here don't like you taking in a rustler. Or maybe he still has some friends left and they're trying to make a point."

"He isn't a rustler." How easily those words rolled off her tongue. When, she wondered, had she decided to believe that Merrick was innocent of cattle stealing? Or was it easier to accept his protestations of innocence because she had thought about lying with him in that bed?

Gibby's eyebrows shot up. "And just how do you know that?"

"Because he told me." The statement sounded lame as soon as she said it.

"Well, ain't that reassuring," Gibby replied with a snort, pulling the brim of his hat down.

Katherine wasn't going to defend Merrick to Gibby. If the cowboy in her father's bed was telling the truth, whoever was trying to scare her needed to be told Merrick had been mistakenly arrested with the gang. Or had she been so easily taken in by a man with a handsome face and a prime body? She didn't want to consider the possibility that that might be true.

She turned her attention to the mention of the missing stock. "How many head are gone?" She could see part of her herd grazing about a quarter mile east of where they stood.

Gibby jerked his head toward the herd. "Some of the breeding bulls seem to be missing."

If she lost her breeding bulls, then the number of calves in future years would be severely reduced. She had paid well for those bulls, and couldn't afford to lose them. "Send three riders out to see if they wandered off. Have them check the range beyond where the fence is down first. When they find the bulls, bring them down to the corral by the barn."

Katherine left Gibby to follow out her orders and went to get her medical supplies. When she approached Tully, the other hands standing around nodded politely to her and stepped back. She knelt down on the ground in front of him and put her hand on his arm.

He opened his eyes and swallowed hard when he saw who it was. "Sorry, ma'am."

His greeting surprised her. "Sorry for what, Tully?" She pulled the cork out of a bottle and poured some of the brown liquid onto a clean square of linen and dabbed the split skin on his forehead.

"Being took by surprise. The horse. The fence." He winced as she cleaned his wound.

"For heaven's sake, that wasn't your fault." She held a canteen to his lips and tipped it so he could drink. She knew Tully liked spending his Saturday nights in the saloons in town. On several occasions she had heard him come home in the early hours Sunday morning, singing at the top of his lungs. "I'm sorry this isn't whisky."

Tully managed a smile. "You ain't the only one."

She smiled back. "You just hold on tight. Anything feel broken?"

"Nope." He said nothing else, just closed his eyes.

How was she going to find out who had done this to Tully? And why? That little voice in her head she didn't want to hear but couldn't afford to ignore whispered to her. What if all this hurt was connected somehow to Merrick?

8

Accompanied by four of her men, Katherine rode home beside Tully, amazed that the man could stay in the saddle. Even Hamlet acted subdued, as if he sensed her feeling of disquiet. The group of riders stopped outside the bunkhouse. Two of the hands dismounted and slid Tully off his mount and helped him inside.

Katherine called to the man who had come to fetch her earlier. "Wade, come up to the house and get some salve for Tully."

Wade tipped his hat to her. "Thank you, ma'am, but we got some inside."

"And whisky, Wade." She would never dare invade the sanctity of the bunkhouse by bringing a bottle down, but someone could come up to the house to get some whisky.

He grinned. "We could probably scare some up."

"You see that Tully gets salve on his head, and put him in his bunk with a good dose of whisky." Then she thought of one more thing. She called after the departing man. "And Wade, make sure he's in a bottom bunk."

Wade nodded and disappeared into the building where the cowboys all slept. She made a mental note to check with Gibby later and see how Tully was getting along. She felt responsible for the man's pain, just as she felt responsible for everything that happened on the Rocking H.

Katherine left her mount at the barn with Hannibal, and walked toward the house, wondering if Merrick could have any connection to the incidents at the ranch, or if it was just coincidence that they had started when she brought him here. The link seemed unlikely, but she couldn't ignore the possibility. Someone out there threatened the safety of her ranch and her family.

For the second day in a row the man who filled her thoughts sat in her rocker on the porch. He had moved the big chair out of the shady corner. Sound asleep, his large frame sprawled on the chair. A copy of Mark Twain's *Adventures of Tom Sawyer* lay open across his stomach. She had read that same book to her father as he lay dying upstairs. Well, that answered one of her questions. The man could read. What about all the other questions? The incident with Tully this morning made her unsure whether her instincts about Merrick's innocence might be wrong. Was Merrick what he claimed to be? Before all this had happened, she would have described herself as a good judge of character. How could she be sure she was not making a very costly mistake if she trusted him?

She stood on the porch for a moment and studied him. A shaft of sunlight fell across his broad chest. His shirt, top two buttons undone, revealed a growth of dark hair, blacker than the hair on his head. Katherine's eye traveled upward. He hadn't shaved yet today, and his beard showed heavy on his cheeks, obscuring some of the fading bruises, but not the strong angle of his jaw. His eyes were closed, but she didn't have to see them to remember their shade of blue. His wavy dark hair was longer than fashion indicated, but its length was understandable if he had been on the trail. The bandage that had been around his head earlier this morning was gone.

Her gaze traveled down, past the strong chin and the tuft of hair at the collar of his shirt, down his broad chest, and over his middle. She wondered if he had taken off the bandage around his ribs, too. He must have when he bathed. Perhaps Consuela had helped bandage him up again. She made a mental note to ask the Mexican woman. She lingered at his waist. The belt he wore gathered in his trousers a little. He must have lost weight since his capture. Down her gaze went, lingering for a moment on the buttons on his pants, remembering what he had looked like with them off. She felt a blush creep up her cheeks.

"Like what you see?" His low, teasing voice startled her and she jumped, her gaze swinging back up to his face.

"I, ah, thought you were asleep." She sounded lame. Why did he have to wake up just when she reached *that* part of him? She felt warm, and resisted the urge to fan her face with her wide-brimmed hat.

"You didn't answer my question." His lips curved under his mustache in a lazy, teasing grin.

For a moment she drew a blank and couldn't remember his question. Then she did and felt annoyed. How rude of him to draw attention to a situation he knew was bound to embarrass her.

"And I don't plan to." She kept her voice tart. He certainly could annoy her with very little effort. She lowered her eyes once more and focused on the book. She very much wanted to change the subject. "Where did you get that book?"

He picked up the volume in one of his big square hands and looked at the spine of the book. "In the drawer of the bed table in my room. Why?"

His room. But what did it matter how he referred to the place where he slept? The situation was very temporary, she told herself. "No reason. I just wondered."

His next question made her wary. "Do you have a minute? There's still a lot I didn't get to ask this morning."

She nodded. Now was as good as later. For every question he asked her, she could question him. She could sent a few telegrams and confirm what he had told her about his family in Texas. She shuddered, remembering how helpless Tully had looked lying on the ground.

"What's wrong?" He threw her a look of concern.

"Nothing." She put Tully from her mind and pulled off her hat. Then she took a seat on the porch swing, across from where he sat.

Merrick pulled himself up on the rocker and closed the book he had been reading, placing it carefully on the wooden floor beside him. He enjoyed the flush he could bring to her cheeks just by teasing her. After the look she just gave him, and the way she blushed, he had no doubts now about who had removed his trousers when he had first arrived at her house. Now he wanted her soft white hands pulling his denims off while he was wide awake.

"What happened this morning? I heard one of the hands come and get you. He sounded all riled up." He watched her carefully, still curious to find out what this whole situation at her ranch was really about. He had heard riders coming and going in the middle of the night last night. There was a lot more going on here and she seemed unwilling to tell him.

She had been friendlier this morning, before she was called away. Now he felt her pull back again, snipping at him the way she had when he had first awakened. What had happened to change her attitude toward him? He guessed it had something to do with the reason she had ridden out in such a hurry this morning.

"Some fence was down." Her answer sounded guarded. Nervously she pulled off her gloves and twisted them in her hands. He doubted that she realized her gestures made her look uneasy.

"Your man sounded pretty agitated if it was just some fence." He watched her taut expression as he spoke.

Her chin came up. She looked him in the eye, hesitating for a brief moment. "One of the hands was injured."

"Bad?"

"No." She continued to stare at him.

So she was having trouble on her ranch. Could that be the reason she had married him? It still didn't make any sense.

He continued to hold her gaze. "I need the loan of a horse tomorrow. I want to get word to my family and clear my name." And once his name was cleared, the marriage could be annulled.

She looked startled by his request. "Tomorrow? You can't make that kind of ride tomorrow. You're not well enough!"

At this point, he didn't care what her opinion of the state of his health might be. He needed to contact his family and get cleared of the charges against him. "Thank you for your concern, ma'am, but I'm feeling much better." Perhaps he was playing up his weakness a little too much.

"You don't have to make that long ride. I'll take you in a wagon later in the week." She sounded as if the subject was settled.

Bossy woman, he wasn't going anywhere in her wagon. Perhaps he hadn't made himself clear. "Ma'am, I can go by myself."

Abruptly she stood. Her hat and gloves fell unnoticed to the board floor of the porch as she addressed him in a firm voice. "You can't leave the ranch without me. The sheriff will find you and hang you!" She turned abruptly and walked into the house.

Well, damnation! He thought he had convinced her he wasn't one of the rustlers, and now she was treating him like a coiled rattlesnake. Why the hell had she married him and brought him here, anyway? And if she didn't trust him, why did she want him to stay?

Wes levered himself out of the big rocker, and stood stretching for a moment, trying to get the kinks out of his body, before he followed her into her house. The mutt started barking and ran toward the road. Wes looked over his shoulder and saw a carriage approaching the house in a cloud of dust.

He stuck his head in the front door. She was standing in the middle of the parlor, her arms crossed over her chest. "Miz Holman? You've got company."

As she brushed past him to look out the door, he caught a whiff of perfume. Lavender. She smelled mighty pretty.

She stared at the approaching carriage for a moment, then muttered something he didn't catch.

With a determined look, she turned and pushed him into the house and said in the best schoolmarm voice he had ever heard, "Go upstairs and lie down. You need to rest." She closed the front door firmly behind them.

The bossier she got, the more stubborn he felt. "No. We need to talk." He wondered who the women in the carriage were that they had her so spooked.

"Later." She looked nervously over her shoulder out the front window.

She apparently had no intention of letting them meet him. She looked all undone, and a little frantic.

"No." He decided not to cooperate with her unless she promised him something in return.

She surprised him when she moved in close and laid a hand on his arm, gazing up into his face and softly pleading with him. "Please?"

Her plea, combined with her warm closeness, almost made him lose his resolve. He wanted to drag her into his arms and kiss her silly. He cleared his throat and bent down to whisper in her ear. "I'll make you a deal. I go upstairs now, and you answer my questions when your company leaves."

She hesitated for a moment, her hand trembling on his arm, then she nodded in agreement. He walked slowly across the parlor to the stairs and glanced back over his shoulder to see her gnawing on one of her pretty little knuckles. Deliberately, just to see what she might do, he took the stairs slowly, gripping the banister as if he needed the support. When he reached the middle of the staircase, he turned a second time as a knock sounded at the front door, and watched with amusement as she flapped her skirt at him, shooing him as she would a chicken. The action gave him a glance of her trim ankles.

She was one interesting woman, he thought, as he entered his room and lowered himself to the bed. He dozed, wondering who Katherine's visitors might be, and why she was so anxious to have him out of the way.

Katherine waited until Merrick reached the top of the stairs and stepped out of sight before she opened the door to her visitors.

"Mrs. Moody, what a pleasant surprise!" Katherine forced herself to smile at the large woman in the horrible light green dress. She turned to Mrs. Moody's companion. "And Virna. I'm so glad you could come, too." If there was one person on this earth she didn't care to see at this or any other time it would be Sapphira Moody, town gossip. She always thought of Mrs. Moody and her daughter-in-law Virna as one person. They lived together, traveled about together, and everything Sapphira said, Virna would validate with a nod.

Mrs. Moody glanced past Katherine into the front room. "I've made elderberry wine, dear, and I wanted to bring you a bottle to celebrate your wedding." Mrs. Moody held out her offering and Katherine accepted the gift. "And your mail." She elbowed Virna, who silently handed over two newspapers and a bundle from the post office.

"Thank you." Katherine knew the real reason they were here. They had heard about Merrick and wanted to lay claim to being the first women in Miles City to lay eyes on him. Not if she could help it!

Katherine ushered them into the parlor, and saw that they seated themselves on comfortable chairs before she spoke. "Let me arrange for tea."

Mrs. Moody shifted her large bulk on the chair. She reminded Katherine of a fat hen settling on her nest. "That would be lovely, dear."

Katherine looked at Virna and waited for her to nod. She was not disappointed. She forced a smile for her guests and then turned and made a sour face as she headed for the kitchen, the bottle of wine tucked under her arm. She left the bundle of mail and newspapers on the hutch in the dining room, and carried the wine into the kitchen.

She found Consuela and Hannah out back, working in the garden. Her daughter squatted on a patch of bare earth, digging furiously with a small hand shovel. Hamlet lay snoozing close by in the shade of an alder tree.

"Consuela, can you come here for a moment?"

Consuela dusted off her hands and approached Katherine. "Senora?"

"Consuela, we have guests. Will you please make tea? Leave the door open and you'll be able to see Hannah." Katherine didn't need to tell the old woman to keep the child out of the parlor. Consuela knew how much Katherine tried to protect her child from the scorn of the townspeople.

"Si." She plodded up the back steps, stopping long enough to stamp the dirt off her shoes. She took the bottle of wine from Katherine's hands.

Hannah ignored the adults and continued to concentrate on her digging. Katherine returned to the parlor, her mouth fixed with a smile that she hoped looked less false than it felt.

Unwilling to wait for questions she had no intention of answering, Katherine jumped in and joined them at their game. "Well, ladies, what's new in Miles City?"

Mrs. Moody immediately took the bait and launched into a description of the extravagant new set of carved bedroom furniture the dry goods merchant's wife, Mrs. Rivens, had ordered from St. Louis. Sapphira warmed to her subject, leaned forward, her voice lowered in a conspiratorial tone. "Someone in her family must have died and left her money, because I know for a fact that their finances could not support such a purchase." She smoothed the pea-green folds of her silk skirt, obviously pleased to have imparted that little tidbit of information.

Katherine wondered if Mr. Moody realized his wife was privy to the personal finances of his customers at the bank, and that she was speculating about them in other people's parlors. She suspected the knowledge might just cause him a case of apoplexy, but she doubted he would confront his wife and demand she stop her gossiping. As far as Katherine knew, no one yet had had the nerve to stand up to Mrs. Sapphira Moody.

Consuela set the tea tray on the small table beside Katherine.

Mrs. Moody accepted a cup and looked toward the stairs. "Will your husband be joining us?" There was a little dramatic pause in her question, just before the word "husband."

Katherine tried to picture one of the delicate tea cups in Merrick's large hands as she offered an excuse. "No, I'm afraid he isn't very well."

Mrs. Moody looked disappointed and made a charitable comment about his health and recovery, then launched into gossip about the new robes for the church choir, the rebuilt stove in the sitting room at the hotel, the possibility of enlarging the lending library, and Mr. Norton, the owner of the town's only shoe store, who had closed up shop to move back to Chicago to take care of his ailing mother.

Every time Mrs. Moody switched subjects, she paused and looked pointedly at Katherine, dropping little comments, openings for her to tell them what they were dying to hear. Katherine had no intention of giving them the satisfaction of returning to Miles City armed with more gossip, and the laws of polite society forbade Mrs. Moody from asking more personal questions about Katherine's husband and marriage. As obnoxious as the woman might be, no one would ever be able to label her impolite.

After Mrs. Moody drank two cups of tea, and ran out of gossip, she declared it was time for them to leave. Katherine could tell by the thin line of her lips and the abrupt thank you that the woman was annoyed, and it gave Katherine a perverse sense of satisfaction. Mrs. Moody never came to visit unless she wanted something, and Katherine was darned if she would give it to her. Virna hadn't said ten words the entire time.

Katherine smiled and said good-bye at her front door. "It was so kind of you to call. Thank you for the wine, and for delivering my mail."

Mrs. Moody gave her a curt nod and lumbered down the porch steps, dragging Virna with her. Katherine closed the door and leaned against the smooth wood, letting out a loud sigh. She anticipated that Mrs. Moody's visit today was probably the first of many, if she knew the woman. Sapphira Moody was as tenacious as a hound at a squirrel hole.

She heard the carriage drive away and waited for a moment, then opened the front windows. The fresh air smelled wonderful after being trapped in the parlor with Mrs. Moody's cloying perfume.

She sorted through the mail, then opened the newspapers to the front page. One glance told her why Mrs. Moody had appeared for tea. There, in the middle of the front page, was a photograph of Katherine standing near the scaffold in Dennison. The headline read: Miles City Woman Claims And Marries Condemned Man. She sighed and refolded the paper, not wanting to read the article. Now she knew why there had been a photographer at the hangings. How quaint, she thought, a picture of her wedding day.

Katherine needed some fresh air, and headed for the bunkhouse to check on Tully. By the time she reached the barn she could hear him from inside the bunkhouse, singing a bawdy song, well on his way to a high lonesome. So much for Mr. Tully. It would do no good to inquire about how he felt. He wouldn't feel much of anything until tomorrow at the earliest. What a day. She was tempted to go get a bottle of whisky from the house and join him.

9

Katherine sat on the porch in her favorite chair, the same chair Merrick had been sprawled in earlier. She wanted to believe him, she really did. Heaven knows her life would be easier if Merrick was innocent. But how could she accept what he said? The problems she was having now had all started when she brought him to the Rocking H.

A cloud of dust in the distance alerted her to a rider coming up the road. What now? Mrs. Moody and her shadow Virna were all the visitors she needed for one day. She watched the figure approach. After a few moments she recognized the sheriff, Martin Denty. Well, great! She glanced at the position of the sun. Whenever he did come, he made sure it was near time for a meal. Consuela was in the kitchen preparing supper.

Katherine knew Martin. He had come for the same reason Mrs. Moody had visited. Unlike Sapphira Moody, he would stick around and talk her ear off until she invited him for a meal. She didn't have the energy this evening to try to wait him out, and her mother had drilled the rules of hospitality into her so often she wouldn't tell him to leave. Might as well go ahead and invite him in, get him fed and out quickly.

His visit would cut into her time to play with Hannah and her work time on the books after her daughter went to bed. She got up and walked through the parlor, past the front stairs, and on into the kitchen.

Consuela and Hannah were standing together at the table, Hannah on a chair, making biscuits. "Sheriff Denty is coming up the road. I'm going to invite him for supper."

Consuela nodded. "Si, senora."

"Please feed Hannah here in the kitchen, but first take a tray up to Mr. Merrick. Ask him to stay in his room." Consuela nodded again, and helped Hannah press down on the cutter to make a biscuit. The little girl concentrated on what she was doing, her bottom lip captured by her small white teeth.

Hurriedly Katherine went through to the dining room and mechanically went through the motions of setting the table while she listened for Martin's knock. She opened a drawer in the hutch and removed a cloth, then centered it on the dining room table, smoothing the white linen. She placed the silver candle holders in the middle of the table. There was enough length on the candles to last through dinner.

She much preferred to eat in the kitchen, a much cozier room, but she would treat Denty like a guest. He would never be invited to share the familiarity of her kitchen table, as a friend would.

Finding matches in a porcelain box, she lit the candles. Then she carefully took down two of her mother's

china plates. Their delicate eggshell color looked
creamy in the dim light. Next came two of the fragile
stemmed wine glasses that had been a wedding present
to her parents. A friend of Julius's from the east had
shipped them all the way from Venice, Italy. She held
them up to the candle and they shimmered with all the
colors of the rainbow. Someday she wanted to sail
across the ocean and see the city where this fantastic
glass had been made. As a child she had thought it must
be a magical place.

When the table setting was complete, Katherine
returned to the porch, wondering what was keeping
Denty. She spotted him tying up his horse near the
trough, just outside the barn. The sun hung low on the
horizon.

He lumbered toward the house. "Evening, Katherine."
He removed his hat, and tracked mud up the steps of her
porch.

"Martin, isn't it a little late for you to be riding all
the way from town?" She would not let him into her
house without a comment on his timing. He knew when
they had supper.

"I came to tell you my news. I didn't come from
town. I came from my place." He stopped in front of
her, his hat held between his two hands over his ample
belly.

As far as Katherine knew, he rented a room at Mrs.
Porter's boarding house in town. "Your place?"

"That's my news. I bought the old Chapman place.
Signed the papers yesterday." The land he mentioned
lay to the south of the Rocking H.

Katherine had never considered that Denty might
have enough money to purchase land. She'd heard the
bank was reluctant to lend money to a rancher right

now, when land values were down, especially on a place that had already failed. And Sapphira had not mentioned any transactions involving Denty this afternoon. She wondered how the sheriff had managed the finances.

The land at the Chapman place was not as good as hers for grazing, and Mr. Chapman ran a much smaller herd. He had lost some outbuildings in a fire this past autumn, and unable to afford repairs, he had finally given up and moved back to his family's home in Virginia. Using all her available cash, Katherine had purchased his stock.

"Well, how about that?" She didn't much like him as sheriff, and guessed she probably wouldn't feel any differently about him as a rancher.

"Guess that sort of makes us neighbors, don't it?" He smiled at her, revealing crooked, tobacco-stained teeth.

"Only if you jump right over the Eckhart place." She didn't want to encourage this neighbor business, or he'd be here all the time, looking for a meal. She'd known for a long time how much Martin liked his meals.

"I wanted to check on that rustler. He giving you any trouble?"

She had been expecting that question since he rode up. "No." Not unless you count the way he makes me blush when I think about how he looked with his pants off. Immediately the thought alone brought heat to her cheeks and she knew she was blushing. Again.

"You keeping him in the bunkhouse?" Martin made Merrick sound like a piece of furniture.

Katherine decided that was none of Denty's business, so she didn't answer him directly. "He still doesn't get around. They beat him badly."

"Are you sure you're telling me the truth?" He squinted up his little eyes and studied her face. "I know you've been having troubles."

Did he know about Tully already? She hadn't sent anyone to town with that news. She drew herself up and looked Denty square in the face. This man had an uncanny ability to say just the thing that could make her mad. "Are you questioning my honesty?" she snapped.

He backed off a step, holding his hat out between them like a shield against her anger. "No, no Katherine. I would never do that. I'd just feel better if I could see him." He looked distinctly annoyed at her irritation, a fact that made Katherine happy in a perverse kind of way.

"Well, you can't. He needs his rest and I don't want him disturbed. I told you in town that I wasn't going to discuss him, and nothing has changed." What she did with Merrick was none of Denty's business. Or Mrs. Moody's or Virna's, or anyone else in Miles City.

Denty's mouth thinned to a hard line. "But he is my business if he makes any trouble. You know that. And he will Katherine. He's an outlaw."

"If that happens, and I doubt that it will, I'll let you know." She took his hat and hung it on a peg just inside the front door. "Supper's ready. You go ahead to the dining room and I'll be along directly."

Katherine headed to the kitchen and kissed the top of Hannah's head as she sat at the kitchen table eating her supper.

"That man here, Mama?" Hannah didn't like Martin Denty.

"Just for supper. He'll be gone soon, and you and I will read stories." Her father had always told her that children and animals were good judges of character.

Hannah made a face. "Tell him not to dawdle."

Katherine wondered how many times she had said just these words to her little girl while they ate. "I will. You mind Consuela." Her daughter nodded, and Katherine and Consuela scooped up the serving dishes and carried them through into the dining room.

Martin had placed himself at the head of the table and sat waiting, fork in hand. Since her father's death, that had been Katherine's chair. It annoyed her that he felt free to take it. She took a dish of pot roast and set it down in front of him a little harder than she should have. The gravy splattered the table cloth.

"Katherine, be more careful!" He spoke to her as if she were a child. He never bothered to greet Consuela, noisily digging into the meal before Katherine could take her place at the table.

Wes Merrick might be a convicted outlaw, but his manners far surpassed those of the sheriff.

Katherine poured some of the elderberry wine Mrs. Moody had brought today when she visited, enjoying the flavor. The overbearing woman did know how to make good wine, Katherine thought sourly.

The meal progressed in silence, except for the rude sounds Martin made while eating. It seemed as if they had been in the dining room for hours, but judging from the length of the candles, Katherine realized that it only felt that way. The clock on the mantle in the living room struck six. He had only been there for half an hour. Denty made an attempt to cover a belch and then wiped his greasy hands and face on the white napkin. Consuela would have to boil the linen to get it clean, Katherine thought with disgust.

Katherine could stand no more of his company. Without saying a word she jumped up from the table, grabbed two dishes, and carried them into the kitchen. When she came back for another armful, Denty was gone. She found him in the living room, about to light a cigar.

"Martin, save that for your ride home." She had no intention of letting him light that cigar inside and then have her front room smell like stale smoke.

"I like it right after dinner," Martin protested, too obtuse to understand her not too subtle suggestion that he be on his way.

Katherine took his hat off the peg and handed it to him, then she opened the front door and gestured to his horse. "Fine. I have a lot to do, so I'll say good night." Being subtle with Martin Denty didn't work.

"But Katherine—" he sputtered, annoyed.

"Good night, Martin." She waited until he stepped through the door, then she closed it behind him. If he was annoyed with her, perhaps he wouldn't come back so soon.

Katherine pulled aside the lace curtain and watched impatiently until Denty was headed out to the road. Gibby was due up to the house to discuss ranch business, and she needed to get on with her evening. She walked back into the kitchen, where Consuela had filled the washtub and was peeling the pinafore off a very dirty, protesting little girl.

"Thank you Consuela, I'll do this while you do the dishes." She unbuttoned Hannah's dress and pulled the sleeves down the little girl's arms. Katherine lifted her onto a chair and unbuttoned her hightop shoes. The child's socks were stiff with dirt.

"Hannah, it is beyond me how you can get your socks so dirty with your shoes on." Hannah shrugged and looked unconcerned. Katherine sometimes felt her daughter knew there were things her mother needed to say to her, and the child just patiently waited until Katherine finished with them, then went on to things she wanted to talk about.

"How did the man get hurt?" Hannah held up her arms so Katherine could lift her into the tub.

The question puzzled Katherine. Did Hannah know what had happened to Tully? "What man?"

"The man in Pop Pop's bed." Hannah dropped the soap in the water with a plop, then chased it around the tub.

Katherine caught the lump of soap as Hannah's words sunk in. "Did you go in Pop Pop's room?"

The little girl looked as guilty as a child caught with her hand in the candy jar. "A little."

A little knot of dread formed in her stomach. It was one thing for Katherine to take a chance on the rustler, but she didn't want her daughter anywhere near him. She put her hands on Hannah's cheeks and turned the little face up so she could look her daughter square in the eyes. "You are not to go in Pop Pop's room. Understand?" Hannah nodded. "If you do, I'll spank you."

Hannah's eyes got big and round. "Yes, Mama."

Katherine had never laid a hand on her daughter, but she wouldn't hesitate to carry out this particular threat. She would do anything to insure her daughter's safety.

Katherine finished washing Hannah's hair, and rinsed the complaining child with a bucket of warm water. "I swear, you would look like a grimy little piggy if you had your way. Doesn't it feel nice to be all clean?"

Hannah shook her head stubbornly, her teeth starting to chatter. Katherine wrapped her in a towel and sat down with the child on her lap. She rubbed her child's curly hair, getting the moisture out, and realized that the way Hannah was growing she wouldn't be able to hold her like this for much longer. She dropped a kiss on the back of Hannah's neck and the child giggled.

"What story do you want tonight?" Katherine asked as she pulled a flannel nightgown over Hannah's head.

"Dragons and princesses." Hannah sounded sure of her choice.

"King Arthur?" The child nodded vigorously, and Katherine took her by the hand and led her upstairs to her room.

Katherine lit the lamp, and settled down in a chair beside Hannah's bed. As she read she tried some short-cuts in the rather long story, but Hannah would have none of it. Her favorite, she knew the book by heart, and caught Katherine every time she tried to condense the plot. The child also insisted on inspecting every picture and discussing its contents. Finally they were finished. Hannah let out a dramatic sigh, and intoned, "Happy ever after."

If only it was so easy, Katherine thought, as she listened to Hannah's prayers with half an ear.

"Good night, sweet girl." She brushed the hair aside and kissed Hannah's forehead, savoring the sweet smell of a clean child.

"Night night, Mama." Hannah threw her arms around Katherine's neck and gave her a noisy smack on the cheek. Then she rolled over and burrowed into her pillow.

Katherine took the lamp with her when she left her daughter's room. Consuela had built up the fire in the office, making the room warm and inviting. Gibby arrived, hollering to her from the front door before coming through the front room into her office.

She greeted him and asked him about Tully.

"He'll do all right, I reckon. If I had to guess, I'd say he'll be more bothered by a hangover tomorrow than he will by getting throwed." Gibby scratched at his thinning hair.

"Did you find any of the missing stock?" Katherine opened her breeding book to the page that held the current records of the ranch's bulls.

"Found one bull. Three are still missing." He gave Katherine the details and waited while she entered some notes in her book. "Got any notion over who could have done it?"

"Not a clue. But I can understand the theft of the stock better than the mutilations. Those animals are valuable." The ranch would suffer future losses if the bulls were not located by breeding time. Losses she couldn't afford. Would she gain possession of her property only to have to sell it down the road?

"Some of the boys checked at Eckhart's place, and down to Chapman's. Did you know Denty bought the old Chapman place?"

Katherine looked up from her writing and nodded. "He stopped here at suppertime."

"Where'd he get the money to buy it?" Gibby apparently had had the same thoughts she had.

"I have no idea. I couldn't think of a polite way to ask."

"Since when did you start being polite to Denty?" Gibby asked her the question with a grin.

Katherine smiled at her foreman. "Shame on you, Gibson Sawyer, I'm always polite."

Gibby replied with a snort, indicating how dubious he felt her answer was. "The hands over to Denty's made our boys feel a mite unwelcome. They were all new to these parts, according to Jake and Danny."

"Perhaps they just don't realize how neighborly folks around Miles City tend to be. I'll mention the lack of hospitality to Sheriff Denty the next time I see him." It was odd that all his men would be new. "With winter coming on I'd think he could pick up hands from the other outfits around here."

Gibby nodded in assent, and got up and added a log to the fire. The chill announcing the coming winter had crept into the evenings. He returned to his chair, sat, and propped one boot over his opposite knee.

Movement at the door caught her attention, and she looked up, expecting to see Consuela bringing them coffee. Instead it was Merrick. He stopped in the doorway, his wide shoulders filling the opening. Her heart responded to his presence with an increased beat.

He held her father's copy of *Tom Sawyer* in his good hand. His other arm was still in a sling. "Sorry, Miz Holman. I didn't mean to interrupt. I finished reading this and came to get another book." The warm tones of his voice washed over her, and for a moment she lost her train of thought.

Gibby swiveled and stared at Merrick. There was nothing she could do but introduce them. "Mr. Merrick, this is my foreman, Gibson Sawyer. Gibby, this is Wes Merrick."

Merrick immediately tucked the book under his bandaged arm and extended his hand. Gibby rose out of the chair and shook Merrick's hand, looking the younger man over as if he were stock the foreman was thinking about buying.

Merrick spoke first. "The ranch is a fine-looking operation, Mr. Sawyer."

Katherine watched Gibby visibly relax as he listened to Merrick. It was her turn to stiffen. Why did Merrick automatically give the credit for the well-run ranch to Gibby?

Gibby resumed his seat. "You done some work on a ranch?"

"I grew up on a ranch. My father has a spread down northern Texas, in Moore county. The Shamrock."

Annoyed at Merrick for giving Gibby credit for the Rocking H, Katherine interrupted the conversation. "Excuse me, but we have some work to do, Gibby." Both men turned to look at her.

Merrick's eyebrow rose a little. "Sorry. I'll get out of your way. Come and tell me when you're finished." He looked amused as he walked to the bookcases lining the walls and placed the copy of *Tom Sawyer* back on the shelf. Then he selected a new book and left the room.

She watched him disappear through the doorway.

Gibby waited to speak until Merrick was gone. "How come if you two are married he calls you Miz Holman?"

Katherine really didn't want to discuss her arrangement with Merrick, but she knew Gibby. Unless she gagged him, he wouldn't quit pestering her about it until she gave him an explanation.

She propped her elbows on the desk and rubbed at her temples with her fingertips, trying to relieve the headache that had begun this afternoon when Mrs. Moody arrived. "I needed a marriage, a valid certificate, to inherit the ranch." There, she had said it. Actually, she felt relieved that Gibby knew.

"Why? Didn't your daddy leave you this place?" Gibby looked confused.

"Not outright. His will stated I had to be married within six months or the place would be sold." Katherine rubbed her hands wearily over her face. "He didn't trust me to run the Rocking H by myself, even though I took care of everything for almost a year before he died. I only had eight weeks left."

"You could have come to me. Your Pa would've had a fit if he knowed what you done."

"My father's the one who left me in this mess."

"Why didn't you just marry up with one of the fellows around these parts? Why did you go and get yourself a condemned man?" Gibby leaned across the desk as he spoke and patted her hand, his voice kind. "Didn't you know what a risk you were taking?"

Katherine noticed he didn't disagree with the clause her father had placed in the will. "Of course I knew. I needed to be married, but I didn't want a husband."

Gibby blinked. His mouth fell open. "Huh?"

"As soon as Anderson gets back and I get the deed transferred into my name, Merrick can leave." Katherine didn't understand why Gibby was having trouble understanding what she was telling him. It made perfect sense to her.

He took a moment to respond. "What happens when you want to marry someone, I mean when you want a husband, and you already got one?"

Katherine stood up, turned her back to him, and looked out the window into the dark night. She could close her eyes and see the view, she didn't need daylight. "I'm not going to want a husband—ever."

"Why not?"

"If Gerald hadn't died, I would have married him. You know how the men in town think of me now, because of Hannah."

Gibby snorted in disgust. "Gerald was a weakling. There are plenty of men who would be proud to marry you." She could have predicted his response, knowing he felt the same way about Gerald as her father had. Defending her dead fiancé would be a waste of breath.

"And accept Hannah as their own child?" She waited for an answer, and his silence spoke volumes. She softened her tone as she turned back to look at her foreman. "Trust that what I say is true, not just my imagination, Gibby. They all treat me differently than they did before. No one is outright rude, but I notice it just the same."

"Here, on the ranch?" His hands balled into fists. She watched her bantam rooster protector with fondness.

"No. The only one who ever said anything was a new man. Papa fired him on the spot."

"Sorry, Missy. I didn't realize. If you ever have any trouble with any fella, you come to me." Katherine appreciated his fierce words. She felt better, knowing he was there. She smiled, acknowledging his statement of protection. She was glad she had finally told him about her situation.

Katherine knew she need not admonish Gibby to keep silent. He had always been completely loyal to the Holman family and the Rocking H. She decided they had spent enough time talking over her marital state. "We need to talk about getting ready for winter."

"You going to let some of the hands go?" He asked the same question every year.

Katherine knew Gibby felt responsible for his hired hands, but the ranch could not afford to keep a full crew on through the winter. "We'll have to, there just won't be enough work to justify keeping them. I want to make a list of repairs we need to do."

"First thing, we need to stock up the line shacks. The cookshack needs a new roof, or at least a good patch job. And we need to keep a few of the fellows to hunt wolves. We lost a lot of stock to those varmints last winter. If you want to make a little extra money and cull the herd, we could get rid of a few of the cows who've been dry for two seasons and butcher them down for hides and tallow."

Katherine wrote as Gibby spoke. The idea of thinning a few head out of the herd appealed to her. The hides and tallow would bring in much needed cash. If the winter proved to be a harsh one, some of those older cows were bound not to survive anyway.

"That all sounds fine, Gibby. How do you want to decide which hands stay?" This was the hard part, deciding who drew pay, and who would leave and find other work for the winter months. Usually the more senior hands stayed year round, but there were no guarantees when you hired on, and the men knew it.

"Bo and Randy have a job at the blacksmith's in Miles City. Some fella from New Orleans settled in town and ordered an iron-worked front for his store that'll take months to build. So we don't have to worry about them two." Gibby leaned back in his chair, tipping the two front legs off the floor.

Katherine started two columns on a fresh page in her daily ledger. "How about Tully? I feel badly about what happened to him. He should stay at least until he can get himself a new horse."

Gibby nodded. "He's a good worker."

"If we keep him, along with Wade, Jake, and Danny, do you have enough work to keep them busy?"

"Sure thing. That number sounds just about right." Gibby pushed off the chair and came to his feet.

Katherine stood, too. She knew he had done about as much talking as she could expect out of him for one night, but she had one more question. She walked with him out of the office and into the parlor. "Any word in town about the cost of feed? Prices going up?"

"I put in our order with Mr. Jenkins over to the feed and grain. He seems to think things will stay the same, unless the winter gets real bad." He took his battered hat off the peg and put it on.

And they wouldn't need extra feed unless the winter did get bad. It seemed to Katherine for every two steps she took forward, she fell one behind. "Thanks, Gibby. Let the boys who will be leaving know right away so they can make plans. I'll pay them when they're ready to go."

In answer, Gibby nodded and opened the front door. A blast of cold air ruffled Katherine's skirt and caused her to shiver after the door had closed behind her foreman.

She tried to think of the long bleak months ahead as a season you had to endure to get to spring. Katherine went back to the warm office and her ledgers. She had enough in her account at the bank to pay off the hands and buy feed. Any other expenses would have to ride until they had some cash coming in. Unless they found those bulls, a year from now things would be looking mighty bleak.

Katherine worked in the lamplight until her eyes burned and the fire died down, no longer giving off heat. She closed her books and banked the coals in the fireplace. Her plans for wintering had been made as well as they could be. Something unforeseen always happened, but she wouldn't waste time worrying.

She took the lamp and went on up to her room. No light showed under Merrick's door as she passed it on the way to her own. Confused at her own feelings about the man, she didn't mind putting him off until tomorrow. She stopped in and checked on Hannah. The child had burrowed under the quilts so that only the very top of her head showed. Before too long Consuela would have to light the fireplaces in the bedrooms each evening.

As she undressed and readied herself for bed, she remembered Merrick, standing in the doorway to the office, looking as if he belonged there. He had told Gibby he had been raised on his father's ranch. He had the tough, suntanned look of a man who spent his hours working outside, in the saddle. Like a rancher. Or a rustler.

Katherine crawled between the cold sheets and fell asleep, trying to picture him working a herd. The image came all too easily to her mind.

When she woke in the morning, she vowed not to think about the rustler sleeping in her spare room anymore before she went to bed. It seemed as if she had dreamed of him all night, and most of her dreams had nothing to do with cattle.

Up at dawn, Katherine dressed in a calico blouse and riding skirt. Today she planned to ride more of the range to decide where the herd would be moved this week. She glanced out the window, looking for signs of weather, gratified to find only a clear blue sky.

She whistled on the stairs, and then laughed aloud when she remembered how superstitious her mother had been about whistling in the house. She had been scolded about it more than once as she was growing up. She could almost hear her mother's voice saying, "Whistling girls and crowing hens always come to no good end."

Her good mood ended abruptly when she entered the kitchen and found Merrick sitting at the table, having breakfast alone with her daughter. Katherine paused in the doorway. She had admonished Hannah not to go into his room, but she had failed to think about what to do when the man was up and around.

"Where's Consuela?"

Merrick pushed back his chair and stood politely at the sound of her voice.

Hannah turned and grinned at her mother. She had a big smear of berry jam on her face. "Mama, are you hungry?" Katherine noticed the child had gotten dressed, a requirement at Katherine's table, even for breakfast, but that her feet were bare.

She ignored Hannah's question, speaking sharply to the child, "Go upstairs. Get your shoes and stockings."

Hannah stared at her for a moment with a wounded expression on her face, then scrambled out the door past her mother.

Katherine waited until she was sure her child was out of earshot before she spoke. Merrick had remained standing, facing her. "Mr. Merrick, I would appreciate it if you did not spend any time alone with my daughter."

He flinched as if she had slapped him, then a stiff expression crossed his face. He threw his wadded up napkin onto the table beside his plate, and brushed past her into the dining room without saying a word.

She hadn't meant to sound so abrupt. She heard Hannah's bare feet slapping on the staircase, and the sound of the child's voice as she said something to Merrick. When Katherine followed him to apologize for her rash comment, she saw Merrick at the top of the stairs, headed towards his room.

Hannah stood on the bottom step, staring after him, her bottom lip quivering. She turned to look at her mother, a questioning expression on her little face.

Katherine took her daughter by the hand and led her

into the kitchen. "Hannah, Mr. Merrick has been sick, and I don't want you to pester him. Do you understand?" She lifted Hannah onto a chair and helped her pull on her stockings.

The child nodded, her eyes wet with unshed tears. Uncharacteristically, she didn't question her mother. Just as Katherine finished fastening Hannah's shoes, Consuela came through the back door with a bucket of milk.

"Good morning, senora." She set the bucket on the dry sink.

"Consuela, don't leave Hannah alone with Mr. Merrick." Katherine watched as a flash of fear crossed the old woman's face.

"Everything is all right. I just don't feel right about her being alone with him." Katherine could tell by the woman's face that she wanted to ask questions, but held them because that was her way. Not sure how much Consuela knew about Merrick, she felt the woman did deserve an explanation. They could talk this afternoon when Hannah napped.

Katherine leaned over and kissed the top of Hannah's head, then carried Merrick's half-finished plate of breakfast over to the sink. She knew she had upset him, but her daughter's safety was more important than any wounded feelings he might have. She poured herself a cup of coffee and joined her daughter at the table as the child struggled with her stockings.

Katherine buttoned the child's shoes. "Consuela, I'm going to ride out today. Keep Hannah with you." She finished her coffee, anxious to get out and ride in the clear early morning air. She turned to the child. "You mind Consuela."

"Mama? When I'm bigger can I go, too?" Hannah appeared to have gotten over her hurt.

Katherine wiped the jam off her daughter's face. "Of course. You have to learn to run this place, because some day it will be yours."

Hannah's eyes got big and round. "All mine, by myself?"

Oh, my darling daughter, Katherine thought, hopefully you won't be by yourself. You will find someone who will love you and not leave, whatever the reason. Katherine tore herself away from her thoughts to answer her daughter's question, fighting the lump in her throat. "That's right, all yours."

Hannah looked awestruck, and Katherine wondered if the child was old enough to understand the gravity of this conversation. This ranch was Hannah's future, and Katherine would teach her daughter everything she needed to know to make a success of the place by herself. Then, if she did marry, she could be a partner, rather than become a subservient wife.

"I have to go. You be a good girl and mind Consuela."

"You already said that."

Katherine tugged on a curl of Hannah's hair. "Sometimes, young lady, it needs to be said more than once. Give me a kiss."

Obediently the child turned her clean face up for a kiss. Katherine decided to take two. She never knew what condition that face would be in by the time she returned.

Merrick paced across his room, furious. That scene in the kitchen had left a bad taste in his mouth. He had been sitting at the kitchen table, enjoying a big breakfast prepared by Consuela, and having a conversation with little Hannah, when Miz Holman burst in and informed him in no uncertain terms that she didn't want him anywhere near her daughter.

The woman marries him off the gallows, brings him home, nurses him, then yells at him for having breakfast at her table. What did she think he was, anyway? Some kind of pervert who would hurt a little girl? Obviously she didn't believe that he was not a part of the rustlers' gang. Well, he'd prove it to her. He'd ride into Dennison, telegraph his brother, and get his name cleared. Then he would head home to Texas.

The truth of the matter was that he didn't feel the pull of home the way he had at first. It hadn't taken him long to fall in love with Montana, with its rolling prairie and big open sky. He had heard there were beautiful mountains to the west, and he wanted to see them.

He also had to admit, if he was going to be completely honest with himself, that, as crazy as she acted, he had a yen for Katherine Holman that surprised him. As much as she annoyed him with her suspicions and her bossiness, she got to him. She claimed they were legally married. He wondered what it would be like to spend the rest of his life with her. Would she be as feisty in bed at night as she was running the ranch during the day? Just the thought of her made him hard. He paced the room and decided he needed to get out of the house. All the time he was spending inside was making him think loco thoughts.

Wes hesitated at his door when he heard her footsteps hurry down the front stairs. He walked across his room, leaned against the sill, counted to five, then looked out his window. Sure enough, Katherine Holman rushed out of the house and across to the barn. He liked to watch the way her hair fluttered in the breeze when she hurried along.

She probably planned to ride out. Alone. The fact that she went alone was just one more thing that annoyed him about the woman. She should take someone with her.

Intent on catching her before she left, he headed out the front door. There were a few things he needed to say to her after her stinging insinuations this morning at the breakfast table.

The sun felt good on his face as he walked to the barn. Before she had ambushed him at breakfast, he had planned to tell her he would start to work today, to pay her back for her strange hospitality. With his arm still in splints, there were limitations on what he could manage, but if this outfit was anything like the spread at home, there was always mending.

Heaven knew he needed the distraction work would provide. If he sat around inside much longer, he'd go crazy with thoughts of Katherine Holman. He honestly couldn't say if he had her all alone whether he would shake her or kiss her until he got her out of his system.

Katherine adjusted Dynamite's cinch in the warm, dim barn. Her horse was famous for puffing up his belly while he was being saddled. She heard footsteps behind her and turned. Merrick came to a stop beside her, his hat in his hand, his expression grim. "I think you owe me an explanation about what you said this morning." His jaw clenched and she could see his pulse beating in a small vein at his temple.

She glanced across the barn, and kept her voice low so Hannibal could not hear what she said. "I didn't mean to hurt your feelings, but I don't know you, Mr. Merrick. I protect my daughter from strangers." Her heart told her he was what he said he was, but when it came to her daughter's safety, she dared not trust just her heart.

He shifted his weight and leaned his taut body closer. He spoke, his voice low and furious, his breath warm on her cheek. "I don't know why the hell you brought me here, lady, but know this: I am an honorable man." He spun on his boot heel and left the barn.

You probably are, she thought as she watched him walk toward the cookshack, but I can't take a risk, not with my child.

Katherine mounted up and rode out. She stopped on the hill behind the house and knelt for a few moments at her family's graves. Some day she would rest beside them. It was comforting in a strange kind of way to know that she would stay on this land, even after she died.

The last of her family was right here, in front of her. What would become of Hannah if something happened to Katherine before the child was grown? There were some distant cousins left behind in Texas when her parents relocated in the Montana territory, but she didn't consider them, for her folks had not had a kind word for them that she could recall. Katherine knew Gerald had some relations living in Chicago, but she wouldn't think they would welcome a child born out of wedlock to a deceased relation, and she would never place Hannah somewhere where she would not feel welcome.

She wanted her daughter right here, on the ranch. She would have to make some provision for Hannah so the child would have clear title to the ranch. Perhaps Gibby would consent to be Hannah's guardian. She knew how much he loved the child.

Katherine climbed back on her horse and proceeded to ride a wide arc to the north. Clouds gathered low and gray on the horizon, and she guessed they might be getting some snow in the near future.

She rode for two hours, stopping now and again to pull up grass and check the moisture in the soil. Pleased with the way the range looked, she headed back to the house. A hot cup of coffee sounded mighty good, and she looked forward to the warmth of the kitchen.

Her house had not been the refuge it generally was these last few days, with Merrick up and about. His presence unsettled her, but she could hardly confine the man to his room, and she never knew where she would come across him. He might be in the kitchen speaking Spanish to Consuela, or looking for a book to read in her office, or sprawled in her chair in the sun on her front porch. He seemed to take up so much space. She had become acutely aware of him just *being* there.

She assured herself his departure would be a relief, but a part of her would miss the thrill of having a man in her house. Merrick's presence brought a tension to her insides and made her feel more alive. She pushed the thought away, telling herself her only concern should be getting the deed to the ranch and settling Hannah's future. Merrick was only a tool to insure these things would happen.

With a start, she realized she was almost back at the barn. She had been so lost in thought that she hadn't realized how far she had ridden. She rode through the big doors, and saw him.

Merrick glanced at her as he heaved a saddle onto a horse's back with his good arm, then reached under the animal to catch the cinch. His shirt tightened across his wide back.

"Where are you going?" she said as she swung her leg over her horse to dismount. She thought she had made it clear he couldn't just leave.

He gave her a sour look. "Just for a ride." He put his boot in the stirrup and grimaced as he swung his weight up onto the animal. "You better make up your mind what you want, lady. You don't want me around, but you won't let me leave." He rode past her, looking like he was made to be on a horse.

Katherine watched him as he rode away. She decided she would have to tell Merrick why she needed him here until Mr. Anderson returned. After all, her plan would require his cooperation. She had better make friends with him soon.

She left her mount with Hannibal and headed past the garden to the kitchen, via the back porch to take off her muddy boots. What was left of the vegetable plants had withered in the last few cold days, making the garden look bleak and uncared for. Consuela had finished canning a month ago.

Katherine's fingers and the tip of her nose tingled with cold. She looked forward to sitting near the stove with her coffee, hearing what Hannah and Consuela had done that morning.

When she opened the back door, the aroma of cinnamon and coffee greeted her. She stood inside the door for a moment and enjoyed the quiet warmth of the empty kitchen. Consuela and Hannah must be upstairs.

Katherine helped herself to a cinnamon roll and poured a cup of coffee from the pot that always sat on the back of the stove. She finished the roll, and with the coffee in hand went to find the other female residents of the house.

"Consuela, Hannah, where are you?" Katherine called as she headed slowly up the stairs, balancing her cup of coffee so it did not spill.

"Here, Mama. In the man's room." Hannah's voice drifted down the hallway, from the room where Merrick slept. She ignored her coffee now as it splashed in the cup, and hurried to the door. Hannah was there, all right, but so was Consuela. The housekeeper had stripped the linens and the oilcloth from the bed, and opened all the windows to air the room.

"Senora, Senor Merrick has gone to the barn. He said he wanted to help."

Katherine nodded. "I saw him."

"I'm helping Consuela, Mama." Hannah sat on the floor, wrestling a pillowcase off one of the feather pillows.

Katherine, relieved that Hannah had not disobeyed her by going into Merrick's room to visit him, relaxed her white-knuckled grip on her coffee cup. "Of course you are, sweeting, and you're doing a very good job, too.

Katherine was curious as to what Merrick might have done to help out in the barn. Weak as he still must be, she didn't want him overdoing it or getting in Hannibal's way.

". . . and left a message for you on the desk." Consuela snapped a clean sheet by two corners and the snowy linen drifted down over the mattress.

"Excuse me?" Katherine forced herself to stop thinking about Merrick.

"A boy from town. I put it on your desk." Deftly Consuela tucked the linen in at the corners of the feather mattress.

A message from town. Could Anderson be back so soon? Butterflies quivered in Katherine's stomach. She turned, set her coffee cup on the dresser, and hurried down the steps.

The message was from Mr. Moody, the banker. True to his word, he had sent word to inform her Mr. Anderson had returned from Boston on the evening train yesterday.

Katherine stuffed the note in the pocket of her skirt and ran back up the stairs to change into her gray dress. She would not waste one moment of time before she spoke to George Anderson. He must have already heard gossip about her marriage, but she figured the sooner she got to him, the better.

While she changed, she hollered to Consuela to have Hannibal get the buggy ready. She took the pins from her hair, brushed it, and twisted it back into a knot, perching the hat that matched her tailored gray outfit on top of her head. She looked out the window and saw Hannibal driving the buggy to the porch steps.

Katherine returned to Merrick's room and said good-bye to Consuela and her daughter. As she went down the stairs, she wondered when she had stopped thinking of the room as her father's and started thinking of it as Merrick's.

She stopped long enough in the study to get the certificate of marriage and slide the document into a leather envelope. The document would look more official presented that way, she reasoned, than pulling it from the pocket of her skirt.

She felt much more composed than she had the first time she had set out to see Mr. Anderson. Now she could put forth the argument that Merrick had been unjustly accused of rustling. She wouldn't hesitate to point out his innocence, even though she had no proof.

Katherine pulled up in front of the bank and, clutching the leather envelope, hopped down to the ground. She would try the bank first. If Anderson wasn't in his

office, she'd call at his home. She tucked the envelope
under her arm, tied her horses to the railing out front,
and shook out her skirt, brushing the dust off before
she entered the bank. Mr. Moody sat at his desk behind
the railing that separated the room into two halves.

Mr. Moody looked up as she pushed through the
swinging portion of the barrier. "Thank you for sending
the message out to the ranch, Mr. Moody. I appreciate
it. Is Mr. Anderson in?"

The banker heaved his round body out of his chair.
"Your timing is perfect. He arrived in his office a few
moments ago. I believe he is expecting you." He gestured toward the attorney's office door.

I'll bet he is, thought Katherine, sure he had gotten
an earful on her activities since he returned home to
Dennison. With a polite nod at Moody, she crossed
over to Anderson's door, knocked once, and heard the
lawyer's voice call for her to come in.

Nothing had changed in the office since she had been
there just after her father's death to hear his will read.
The same cracked leather covered the chairs, and the
stale smell of pipe smoke hung heavy in the stuffy, overheated air. All of her embarrassment and anger that day
came back to her as she walked through the door.

George Anderson unfolded his tall, narrow frame
from behind his desk and formally greeted her with a
jerky little bow. His rumpled suit hung loose, and comb
marks showed plainly where he had plastered his thinning hair over the large bald spot on the top of his head.

"Good day, Katherine." He extended his hand across
the desk.

Katherine appreciated the unexpected business-like
gesture. She grasped his limp hand in a firm handshake,
and then let go quickly. "Good day, Mr. Anderson. I'm

glad you're back. I hope your wife is well. We didn't expect to see you so soon." It occurred to her that she should ask about Anderson's father's health, but she wasn't sure how to phrase the awkward question. She didn't know if the elderly gentleman was alive or dead.

He indicated that she should sit in one of the seats opposite his desk, then he folded his tall, thin frame back into his desk chair.

"I hadn't expected to return so quickly, but by the time I reached Boston, my father had already passed."

That statement made the situation easier for her. As Katherine murmured some words of condolence, and Anderson thanked her, she became impatient, wanting to get down to the business of the deed to the ranch.

"The funeral was scheduled for the day after I arrived, and I stayed just long enough to see my mother settled back into her routine. I couldn't leave my practice for any longer than necessary." He spoke matter-of-factly as he made fussy little gestures, lining up the papers on his desk in neat rows.

She shifted in her seat. He made it sound like he had clients lined up outside his door. Well, she might be the only one, but she had been anxiously waiting for his return. She needed to convince the attorney of the fact that she had acquired a husband, before said person left the territory.

Clutching the leather envelope in her damp hands, she decided to proceed with her business as if he knew nothing about her marriage. "Mr. Anderson, I came to let you know that my marital status has changed. I am now a married woman, and I would like the deed to the Rocking H transferred officially to me." She pulled the certificate of marriage, complete with Judge Casey's signature, from the leather envelope, and handed it across the desk.

George Anderson accepted the document, then he placed a pair of spectacles on the end of his nose without saying a word. He looked at the certificate for what seemed like a very long time to Katherine, then he peered at her across the top of his glasses. Nerves made her want to fidget, and she made herself sit very still.

He cleared his throat twice before he spoke. "I have already heard about this unorthodox situation. Where is this Mr. Merrick now?"

Katherine sat up a little straighter. She could feel perspiration forming under her arms and between her breasts. Anxious as she was, she hoped her voice wouldn't quaver. "Just now he is at the Rocking H." She almost had to bite her tongue to keep from babbling on because of her tightly wound nerves.

"The will stipulates he must have knowledge of the cattle business."

"His father has a ranch in northern Texas. He grew up there."

George Anderson's demeanor cracked, and his voice rose as he slapped the flat of his hand on his desk. "Katherine, he's a rustler, a condemned man!"

Katherine jumped, then swallowed hard and plunged ahead with her argument. "He was convicted unjustly. He is innocent of rustling." She spoke with a certainty that she didn't have to force. The words sounded true to her own ears.

Anderson stood up and leaned across the desk. "Not according to Sheriff Denty."

Katherine swelled with anger. Denty had certainly wasted no time coming to Anderson. How dare Martin interfere? She had made it clear to the sheriff several times that he had no claim on her. "I certainly hope you did not discuss anything that had to do with me or my father's will with Martin Denty!" She wondered if Martin's recent proposals of marriage were due to the fact that he knew about the clause in her father's will.

Anderson had the good grace to blush at her veiled accusation of a breach of ethics on the attorney's part. "Of course not. We spoke only in general terms. He's as concerned with your well-being as I am."

She was sure Martin Denty was more concerned with her property than her personal state of being. "Well, you can believe the rumors, or you can believe me." Agitated, she rose to her feet as she spoke, unable to sit still. And what was she going to do if Anderson refused her claim?

The attorney regained his outward composure, turned, and took some papers out of the file case behind him, then resumed his seat before he addressed her. "Please, Katherine, sit down."

Katherine tugged on the hem of her jacket and smoothed her skirt, straightening the evidence of her agitation. She sat down, waiting for him to speak. She was so wrought up now that if she said anything she would probably put her foot in it.

Anderson held a copy of her father's will in one hand. In his other hand he held her marriage certificate. He looked back and forth between the two documents until she thought she might scream.

Carefully he laid the two documents down on the desk blotter, side by side. He cleared his throat. "If you truly have a marriage with this man you have fulfilled the requirements of the will in letter, if not in spirit."

Katherine opened her mouth to protest, and Anderson held up a bony hand to stop her. "Let me finish. I could tell the day I read that clause in your father's will to you what a blow it must have been."

Katherine leaned forward and laid both her hands on his desk, palms down. "You have the certificate in your hand that proves I'm married." She wanted to reach across the desk, grab him by the front of his dingy white shirt, and shake him.

"That proves only that you acted foolishly and went through a ceremony. Being married is another matter. I have a duty to your late father as his attorney and his friend. I will have to meet Mr. Merrick. Perhaps you could bring him to my office."

Katherine thought quickly. She didn't have any intention of parading Merrick through town for everyone to gawk at. "I'm afraid his health is not good. He couldn't manage a trip to town." She paused and thought for a moment. "Why don't you and your wife come to the ranch and have dinner with us? Does Saturday suit?" She held her breath as she waited for his answer.

Once more George Anderson uncurled his skinny length from his desk chair. "That would be fine."

Now that Anderson was coming to inspect her husband, Katherine had left herself no choice. She would have to explain the whole situation to Merrick. After her run-in with him this morning, she hoped he would agree to cooperate with her and act like a husband at dinner this Saturday with Anderson, so the lawyer would accept her marriage. Then she could get the deed transferred to her name before Merrick left Montana. That thought should make her feel good, but oddly, it didn't. Katherine relaxed the fists she had made in her lap and stood to face the attorney.

Anderson continued speaking. "I don't approve of what you've done, and neither would your father. I just hope you won't come to regret this rash act."

Admittedly, marrying Merrick practically off the scaffold had been rash, but she didn't regret doing it. Lately, she had begun to fear her regrets would come later, when the big cowboy left the Rocking H. At least the ranch would be hers, legally. She turned her attention back to what Mr. Anderson was saying.

". . . name transferred and legally registered." His hand held a pen poised above a tablet of paper. He stopped talking for a moment and peered down at the marriage certificate. "I want this to be correct on the deed if and when it is to be transferred into your name. Merrick is spelled with two Rs and a K on the end, correct?"

Katherine nodded, speechless. Of course, she thought, how stupid of her. The name on the deed to the Rocking H would be Merrick. Katherine Adora Holman Merrick. She was stuck with it. And to add insult to injury, on the deed, his name would probably be listed first.

10

Wes gingerly settled his large frame back down on the sturdy bench in the small room at the back of the barn. The short ride had done him good, working off some of the anger he had wanted to direct at Katherine Holman. He tried to see things from her point of view, but his honor had been questioned too many times lately for him to be willing to ignore a slur like the one she had directed his way this morning.

He sorted through a box of awls, punches, heavy thread, needles, blades, and scissors, finding what he needed. Another box contained bottles of conditioning oil, wax, and rags. He tackled the next bridle on the pile. Awkward at first, because of the splint on his arm, he fell into the familiar pattern as he stitched and mended gear, setting aside a bridle and one of the saddles for his own use. He wanted his equipment in good shape when he rode into Dennison. Maybe he could buy back his own things. Sam would wire him money.

He felt more of his anger ease as he worked. It couldn't be easy for her, running a spread like this. She held a prime piece of real estate, but unless he was reading things wrong, she was having more than her share of troubles. He planned to take his meals in the cookshack from now on, listen to what the hands had to say, and try to figure out what was going on.

He arched his back, stretching the tight muscles. A man shouldn't be idle, it left him too much time to think. He wiggled his fingers and flexed the muscles in his broken arm. There was very little pain now, and the splint could come off soon. As the day wore on, he became tired and more than sore, but felt good about being out of bed and working.

Hannibal stuck his head in the door. "You hungry?"

"You bet." Actually his stomach had been growling for over an hour, not surprising since he only ate half his breakfast due to that unsettling proclamation by Miz Holman about her daughter.

He stood and stretched out the kinks, then followed the wrangler out of the barn and over to the cookhouse. Hannibal motioned to a grizzled old man hauling a huge pot of chili off the stove. "Poison Joe."

Wes nodded at the old man. "Good handle for a cookie."

Poison Joe grunted.

"Gots nothing to do with his cooking." Hannibal picked up a bowl and served himself out of the pot.

Wes followed suit. In spite of his name, the man produced a mean bowl of Texas style chili. "Great grub." The compliment earned another grunt from Poison.

As they were eating, another man came into the cookhouse. Hannibal scooted down the bench to make room. "This here's Tully."

Wes nodded at the new arrival, noticing how gingerly the hand moved. He had a knot on his forehead and two black eyes.

Tully spoke to Wes. "You sure look a heap better than you did when you got here."

Wes had no memory of his arrival at the ranch. "That so?" He wondered how much these men knew of his situation.

"Yep. Me and some of the boys helped carry you up to the house." Tully put both elbows on the table and, head down, attacked a bowl of chili con carne.

Wes knew he didn't make the statement expecting thanks, and he would offer none. The man was only stating what had happened. If Wes were to thank him, Tully would take it as a sign Wes thought Tully had gone out of his way, and that meant Wes owed him a favor. No cowpuncher wanted to be beholding to anyone, or have anyone beholding to him.

Wes decided to change the subject. "What happened to you?"

Tully shook his head. "I was out nightriding, after they killed those steers, and somebody shot my horse out from under me. The night they made off with some stock."

Wes stared at Tully. Killed steers? Lost stock? The little lady who had saved his hide had more trouble than Wes knew. He realized that because he was living in the house the hand assumed he knew what was going on. It sounded like the kind of thing that Watson and his gang might do. "Rustlers?"

Tully gave him a long hard look. "That night, yeah. They took some breeding bulls. But not the time before. No rustler kills steers, cuts up the hides, and leaves them to rot. Still can't make no sense of that one."

Neither could Wes, but it sounded like Miz Holman had run into a heap of trouble. It sounded like someone was trying to scare her, or warn her about something.

He finished a second bowl of chili and headed back to the barn. He couldn't stop thinking about the two incidents Tully had mentioned. They must be connected in some way, but neither made much sense. He worked until his arm ached before deciding to quit. He had made a fair dent in the mending, as well as conditioning all the bridles he had repaired.

As he screwed the top on the tin of wax, he heard a buggy pull in. He stood and tossed the tin into the open box, then waited just inside the door of the tack room, watching down the length of the barn as Hannibal helped Katherine Holman from the trap. From where Wes stood she looked ill, her face drawn and gray. His anger turned to concern and he suppressed an impulse to hurry to her side, deciding that the feisty, independent woman would not appreciate his gesture.

Katherine thanked Hannibal for his inquiry about her health, assuring him she would be fine. Actually, she felt terrible. On the ride back from Miles City her head had started to ache, and now she could hardly see from the pain behind her eyes. The walk from the barn to the house seemed to take forever.

She stumbled on the second step on the porch, and caught herself by grabbing the railing. Carefully she gathered up her skirt and climbed the rest of the stairs. Consuela was in the front room dusting, and the housekeeper looked up from her chore when Katherine entered.

"*Mija*!" Consuela dropped the feather duster and rushed to Katherine's side.

"Consuela, I have one of those terrible headaches." Katherine's steps faltered and she felt the Mexican woman's arm come around her waist. Gratefully she accepted her help up the stairs.

"Where's Hannah?" Katherine asked the question as they entered her bedroom.

"Napping, senora, as you must do also." The old woman eased Katherine down on the side of the bed. "You sleep and the pain will go." Consuela helped her undo the small buttons down the front of her jacket.

She took Katherine's clothes and laid them across the overstuffed chair, and then brought her a nightgown out of the dresser drawer. Katherine caught a glimpse of herself in the oval mirror over the dresser. What a sight she was, all pale and drawn. The thought flashed through her mind that she was glad she had not run into Mr. Merrick looking like this.

After Katherine crawled into her bed, Consuela pulled the curtains closed and left the room. The white lace did little to shut out the light, and Katherine closed her eyes against the late afternoon sun.

Consuela returned with a glass of dissolved headache powder and a damp cloth. Katherine drank the bitter liquid and lay back, her eyes covered by the cool towel, trying her best to relax and not think about the deed to the ranch. She was not very successful until the medicine finally eased the pain and she drifted off to sleep.

When Katherine woke it was pitch dark outside. Something had awakened her, but she didn't know what. A noise perhaps. She lay very still and heard nothing. She had no idea of the time, but it must be late, for the house was very quiet. She tried to go back to sleep, but her grumbling stomach nagged her into full wakefulness. The headache was gone, but she hadn't eaten since breakfast, and that hadn't been much of a meal after her nasty run-in with Merrick.

She swung her legs over the side of the bed, and winced when her feet hit the cold floor. Feeling her way to the dresser, she lit the lamp and hurriedly slipped into her knit slippers and woolen robe.

Katherine picked up the lamp and opened her door, hesitating just outside in the hallway. She had the oddest feeling something wasn't right, but she couldn't put her finger on what that might be. Perhaps the unfinished business she had with Merrick was heavy on her mind. She looked over at his closed door, promising herself to speak with him in the morning.

She tiptoed down the hall to Hannah's room, and opened the door, holding the lamp high so it cast a pool of light on the child, sleeping curled up in her bed. Katherine backed out of her daughter's room and closed the door. She backtracked down the hall and then quietly down the stairs into the kitchen. She didn't want to wake Consuela, sleeping in her room next to the kitchen. The housekeeper would feel she had to get up and fix her a meal, even if it was the middle of the night. All she needed were some leftover biscuits and a glass of milk. That would hold her until morning.

The clock on the mantle in the living room began to chime, and Katherine counted twelve. Midnight. She had slept straight through from this afternoon. With the aid of the lamp, she found a plate of biscuits on the dry sink, covered with a damp towel. She put the plate on the table and got a glass out of the cupboard. With any luck there would be some milk left in the can on the back porch. She left the lamp on the table and opened the back door. A blast of cold air made her catch her breath.

A strange flickering light came from the barn. She froze in place. Fire! The barn was on fire. Oh sweet Mary, if she lost the barn, they wouldn't survive the winter.

Katherine dropped the glass she was holding and raced out the porch door. She started screaming for the hands as she headed for the iron triangle hanging on the porch of the cookshack.

She reached the cookshack in no more than a minute, and beat on the iron triangle until it sang in the cold, still night air. She kept pounding the iron until she could hear shouts from the bunkhouse. Jumping off the porch, she headed for the barn. On the way she stopped at the horse trough, and with her fist, broke the thin film of ice that had formed on the water. She struggled out of her robe and dunked it in the water, then dragged the sodden fabric around to the burning end of the barn.

The flames started at the ground and reached ten feet up the wall, hissing and spitting as they bit into the painted wood. She swung her wet robe and beat at the flames, which seem to leap away from her and mock her efforts by spreading. She heard Wade and Tully shouting to some of the other hands to get the stock out of the barn. Thank goodness they had come. Again and again she swung her wet robe, hitting the flames with a sizzling sound.

Tully came up beside her with a feed bucket full of water, and threw it on the worst of the fire. Soon, two other men took his place, and then a whole line formed beside her, buckets passed from hand to hand.

Panting for breath, she clutched the robe, resting her shaking arms for a moment. Then she pulled back, ready once again to beat at the flames. She shrieked as an arm came around her middle, yanked her back against a warm, hard body, and lifted her off the ground. She looked back over her shoulder in surprise and saw Wes Merrick, his face set in a hard expression.

"Put me down," she struggled against his strength.

Merrick swung her around, and deposited her on the ground. "You go back to the house." He pulled the soggy robe out of her hand.

"How dare you!" She glared at him, furious at his high-handed behavior. No way was she going back to the house with her barn on fire. He ignored her and went to work on the flames, rhythmically swinging her wet robe. His reach was far higher and more effective at smothering the flames than hers. When she saw how efficiently he beat out the fire, she bit down on her anger and left him to it.

She would deal with him and his arrogance later. Katherine ran to the front of the barn to see how things were going, stopping on her way to check on the amount of water left in the trough. The low level made filling buckets difficult. Furiously she pumped the handle until water flowed into the trough. She grabbed one of the hands who had come to fill a bucket, and told him to keep pumping.

At the main doors, she peered into the interior of the barn, but all she could see was thick black smoke. The animals that hadn't immediately bolted milled around outside, and the cowboys herded them toward the corral. One of the milk cows, confused by all the commotion, tried to reenter the barn. Katherine caught her by an ear, and tugged until she changed direction.

A man, his face so blackened by smoke she wasn't sure who he was, took the other ear of the cow and shouted over the animal's head. "Hannibal says that's all of them out of the barn, Miss Holman."

She could see one of the wranglers over by the gate, supervising the handling of the stock. "Good, take her to the corral." She left the cow to the hand, and shoved the big door closed, then raced back around to the rear of the barn.

The flames were out. Plumes of hissing white steam mixed with the black smoke. Gibby and Merrick took buckets from the hands and emptied them on the charred wood.

From what she could see, the damage didn't appear to be very extensive. She shuddered. A few more minutes and the flames would have burned up through the wall and into the hayloft. Then they wouldn't have been able to put it out, and she would have lost the barn and the animals.

She tried to calm herself, not wanting her men to see her alarm. Then the thought occurred to her. Whoever had set fire to the barn could have just as easily torched the house. She had a vision of Hannah, curled up, sleeping in her bed. The fear she had felt after the slaughter of her cattle and the attack on Tully was back, tenfold.

Consuela appeared at her side with a lamp and an armful of blankets. Numbly she watched Merrick take two blankets out of Consuela's hands. He moved behind her and draped one around her shoulders. "I thought you were going up to the house." He threw the other blanket around his own shoulders.

"Well, you thought wrong." Her retort sounded loud and sharp in the cold night air. Several of the men looked up in surprise. Gibby's gaze shifted from Katherine to Merrick, then back to Katherine.

Katherine took a deep breath, trying to calm herself, and turned to Consuela. "Thank you. Please, go back to the house in case Hannah wakes." Consuela nodded and turned to go.

She watched Merrick go after Consuela, say something to her, and take the lamp out of her hand. He returned and placed it on the ground by the burnt wall and knelt down. Still trying to control her feelings, Katherine could see him study a lump of something charred lying on the ground. Curiosity overcame her and she moved closer.

"My robe?" The fabric was so burnt she couldn't recognize it.

Merrick looked up at her "No. Your robe's over there." He pointed to a place on the ground about ten feet from where they stood. He lifted the mess of burned rags in his hand to his nose, then passed it on to Gibby.

Gibby sniffed, then looked at Katherine. "Kerosene." Merrick held it out and she leaned over and inhaled. The charred bit of cloth smelled strongly of the oily fuel they used in the lanterns in the barn.

Merrick straightened and stood up, turning to Katherine and fixing her with those cobalt eyes. "Who wants to burn you out, Katherine?

11

Katherine pulled the blanket closer and looked around at the silent watchful crowd of hired hands. She had no intention of having a discussion about who might want to burn her out here in front of all her men. Besides, she had no idea who might have started the fire, any more than she knew who had slaughtered her cattle or shot at Tully.

Katherine felt a wave of exhaustion as she turned to face her men. "Thank you, all of you. I appreciate what you did to save the barn. I don't know what we would have done with winter coming on if we had lost it. Go back to the bunkhouse and get some sleep." Her voice felt rough from the smoke.

Some of the hands looked from Katherine to Merrick. He nodded at them, and they drifted away, curiosity written all over their faces. She realized that word must have gotten around about who Merrick was and why he was living in the house. This was the first time the hands had seen the two of them together, and already they looked to him for the final word.

The fact that the men looked so quickly to Merrick stung. She was the one who paid them wages to work the ranch.

Merrick wore his blanket Indian-style around his shoulders over his bare torso. She noticed he had gotten into his pants and boots. Most of the hands wore only their long johns and boots. Her feet were numb with cold in her wet yarn slippers. The efforts to fight the fire had made a muddy mess of the ground, and now the mud was starting to freeze. She wished she had had the time to put her boots on too.

Merrick and Gibby fell into step with her as she turned and headed for the house. Gibby's breathing sounded wheezy as they climbed the steps.

Katherine stopped on the front porch to peel off her muddy, ruined slippers. Her nightgown, wet and smeared with soot, clung to her bare legs. She would have to see to new yarn and yard goods for a pair of slippers and a new robe for herself. Her brain must be as numb as her feet. Someone had just tried to burn down her barn and all she could think about was her slippers. She clutched the blanket around her shoulders as they went inside.

"Thanks, Sawyer." Merrick's voice held a note of dismissal. Gibby touched his hand to his hat, turned and went down the steps.

Katherine, mouth open, watched her foreman leave. She slammed the heavy front door. Still furious at the way her men had turned to Merrick, she was amazed that he had the gall to dismiss her foreman. "Just who do you think you are?"

Calmly, Merrick faced her. "Katherine, he's an old man, and he swallowed a lot of smoke fighting the fire. He needs to rest."

She felt a stab of guilt. "Of course." She should have thought of that. Gibby would never admit that he felt unwell. Merrick had smoothly saved Gibby from that embarrassment.

In the parlor the lamp glowed, shedding a mellow light on the comfortable furniture. The fireplace blazed, throwing warmth into the room, drawing Katherine like a moth. Consuela entered the front room through the dining room. She carried a pot of fragrant coffee and two mugs on a tray. Bless the woman, Katherine thought. She always seemed to know just what comfort was needed.

Consuela set the tray down on the little table near one of the overstuffed armchairs, and poured two mugs of fresh black coffee. Katherine gratefully wrapped her chilled fingers around the cup.

"Thank you, Consuela. Please go to bed now. One of us has to be able to keep up with Hannah in the morning."

Consuela ignored what Katherine said in favor of a scolding as she offered the other mug to Merrick. "You go now and get dry clothes."

"I will, I promise, as soon as I speak to Mr. Merrick."

Consuela nodded, turned and disappeared through the dining room door. Katherine sank down into the chair, and moved her chilled feet closer to the blaze. She gestured to Merrick to sit in the matching chair opposite her.

She didn't like the way he had taken charge, but she did owe him her gratitude. "Thank you for your help." Katherine pulled the blanket more closely around her shoulders, and lifted her bare feet to the warmth of the fire.

He stared at her for a long, unnerving moment before he spoke. "Seems like someone is trying to scare you off. I would think anyone around here would know that a few things like what they been doing wouldn't be enough to get a woman like you to go."

She was glad he acknowledged her courage. He couldn't know how scared she really was. "Burning the barn down wouldn't have been just a little thing, especially with winter coming on. We wouldn't have time to rebuild before the first snow." She took a sip of the hot black coffee.

"Well, if they really meant to burn you out, they sure went about it in a stupid way. Why put burning rags on the outside where they were slow to catch and could be seen, when you could throw a little kerosene in the loft, and really burn the place down?"

Katherine had no answer. It didn't make any sense to her either. Maybe she could think more clearly in the morning. Her brain seemed sluggish and slow. "You're right."

Merrick nodded. "Excuse me." Abruptly he stood and left the room. She heard him go up the stairs.

Still annoyed at the high-handed way he had taken over, she told herself she was glad to see him go. Katherine pushed the blanket off her shoulders and pulled the big chair over to one of the front windows, then picked up a lamp and went to the gun case in the office and picked out a Winchester rifle. She checked to see that it was loaded, and then took a box of ammunition, blew out the lamp, and returned to the parlor.

Carefully she laid the rifle on the floor under her chair, then placed the extra ammunition on the windowsill and sat down, pulling the blanket back up around her shoulders and curling her cold feet up underneath her. She had promised Consuela she would change, but dry clothes would have to wait for later. She planned to keep watch and see if anyone would come back, and try to finish the job on the barn.

The fire had died down, and she was cold, but she figured she would stay until dawn. She heard Merrick come back down the stairs. "I thought you went to bed."

"Nope. Just went to get a shirt." He flipped his blanket into the other chair, then pulled it over beside hers, and sat down.

She turned and looked over at him. It was hard to see his features in the dark, but she noticed by the glow of the fire that he had a fine profile.

He turned and met her gaze as he spoke. "Who wants you out, and why?"

She pulled the blanket closer around her shoulders. "I don't know. Maybe it has something to do with you." There was no point in beating around the bush. The thought that he had something to do with her recent troubles had bothered her since the stock had been slaughtered right after she had hauled him to the ranch in her wagon.

"Me?" He sounded genuinely surprised. "Why do you think that?"

"Things started happening when I brought you here. How many men were in Watson's gang?" She knew she was grabbing at straws.

"By the time they got here, to Montana? Four. How many did they hang in Dennison?"

"Four, not counting you."

He slapped the arm of the chair with the flat of his hand. "I told you I wasn't part of the gang." He sounded angry.

"I know you did. Several times." She didn't care if he disliked what she said. Nothing that happened made sense, and it bothered her.

"I came back down here to see if I could help."

She twisted around so she faced him. "Well, don't do me any favors. And don't ever order me around like that again in front of my men." Now that she had said it, she felt better.

He didn't say anything for a long time, just stared out the window. "Why did you save me from hanging?"

She had to tell him sooner or later. Now in the dark, this seemed as good a time as any. "I needed to be married."

He didn't speak for a moment, and she could feel him staring at her. Then came the inevitable question. "Why?"

"Because I can only inherit if I'm married." It galled her to have to tell anyone that her father didn't think she was up to the task of running the ranch by herself.

He leaned forward in his chair. "Inherit what?"

Silently she thanked him for not just assuming she spoke of her land. "This ranch."

He paused again before he spoke. "Why me? Why marry a man you thought was an outlaw?"

"Because I knew I could get you to leave. I needed to be married. I didn't want a husband."

"Well, that really clears things up." His voice held a touch of dry humor.

She remembered what she had said to him this morning, and felt she needed to apologize. "I'm sorry about the way I talked to you this morning, in front of my daughter."

He nodded. "It really bothered me until I realized you were protecting your young'un. I should have known better than to get between a she bear and her cub."

Katherine wasn't sure how to take that statement, but she was relieved he seemed to understand how she felt.

She hesitated a moment, then turned toward him. "I have a favor to ask. If you'll do one thing for me, I'll help you get your name cleared so you can go, legally."

"What?"

"The attorney insists on meeting you. Will you pretend to act like a husband?" She truly needed his cooperation.

"Pretend?" Again she could hear the smile in his voice.

He was teasing her, and the knowledge sharpened her reply. "You know what I mean." This change in him unsettled her. She found dealing with him had been easier when she thought of him as an outlaw.

"I think I can manage." The room was quiet for a long time before he spoke again. "What kind of a rifle do you have under your chair?"

The man had good eyes. She was relieved to change the subject. "A Winchester. Loaded and ready." Her thoughts went back to the gang. If it wasn't a crony of Watson's, then who could it be? And more puzzling, why?

"You having any trouble with neighbors? Over water or fencing or changed brands?" His voice was tentative as he asked the question.

What was he implying? "No one on the Rocking H has ever changed a brand!"

"Never said you did." His voice was low and smooth, like warm molasses. It kind of flowed over her, smoothing down her ruffled feathers.

Her voice sounded calmer when she spoke. "No trouble. My only real neighbor is to the south. His name's Eckhart, and we've always gotten along. He has a different source for water than we do, and we put up the south fence together."

Merrick didn't say anything, but she noticed he nodded, so she kept on talking. "Beyond that is the old Chapman place. The sheriff in Miles City just bought it."

He turned his head in her direction. "What's his name?"

"Denty. Martin Denty."

"You know him very well?"

"Well enough." The room had grown quite cold. She pulled the blanket tighter around her shoulders, and the heavy woolen cloth snagged on something at her elbow and it hurt when she tugged on it. "Ouch."

"What's the matter?"

"I'm not sure. The blanket snagged on something." She unbuttoned the cuff and ran her hand up under the full sleeve of her nightdress. The sleeve had a tear in the fabric, and she could feel something lodged under her skin. "I think I got a splinter."

Merrick scooted his chair around to half face her and perched on the edge. "Where?" He sounded concerned.

"On my arm, just above my elbow." He grasped her hand in his big warm fist, and ran his other hand up her arm until he hit the splinter.

His movement drove it further into her skin and she flinched. "You're not helping." She jerked her hand out of his grip and pushed the sleeve up around her upper arm. Even if she twisted her arm around, she couldn't get a good look at the spot.

He spoke up while she was trying to see what had happened to her arm. "It's too dark in here to see anything. Where's the lamp?"

"I don't want to light it. You can see it from outside."

"You think whoever torched the barn will come back tonight?"

"You don't?"

"I doubt it. They'd figure you'd post a guard, or at least let that dog loose."

She had certainly thought about keeping watch, but hadn't considered the dog. The hands routinely locked Hamlet in the bunkhouse at night. If they didn't, he barked at every noise and creature, real and imagined, and woke everyone up. "The lamp is on the table by the fireplace. Matches are on the mantle."

When he got up, he picked up the Winchester and rested it against the wall by the fireplace before he threw a log onto the hot coals. A flare of sparks lit the room. She watched as Merrick found the lamp. Suddenly the room seemed warmer with the light. He came back and pulled her high-backed chair around with her still in it.

The sudden movement startled her. She grasped the arms of the chair and held on as he swung her about.

His smile reminded her of a mischievous little boy, and her annoyance at him melted a little. Her brother, Farley, used to do things like that to her.

Then he took her hand again and pushed her sleeve out of the way, holding her arm up to the lamp. He whistled. "Whew. Look at that. You didn't feel it?"

She tilted her head back and could see the end of a huge splinter sticking out of her flesh. "It must have happened at the water trough. I had other things on my mind."

Without any warning, he grasped the end of the sliver and yanked it out.

"Ow!" She yelped at the stab of pain and pulled her arm out of his grasp. "Why didn't you tell me you were going to pull it out?" She held her hand over the spot. Now she could feel it, and it burned like crazy and bled onto her hand.

He smiled at her again, and held up an ugly jagged splinter of wood about two inches long. "And let you fret first? It's easier to just get it done." He tossed the splinter into the fire. Gently he took her arm back.

"I don't fret." She dropped her other arm limply into her lap at his touch. He pushed the sleeve back up over her elbow, holding her arm up to the lamp.

"No, I guess you don't." He stared at her for a disconcerting moment, then reached into his back pocket and took out a handkerchief, and held it firmly to the small wound until the bleeding stopped. When he pulled the cloth away he stroked and probed the skin around the hole left by the piece of wood. His warm rough hands felt pleasurable against her skin, making every place he touched tingle. "Looks like it came out clean. If it didn't, you'll know in a few days. It'll start to fester."

Katherine had trouble listening to what he said as his warm fingers glided over her skin. He bent so close she could smell the lingering scent of smoke in his hair. The room seemed to grow much warmer all of a sudden.

"Thank you." Her voice sounded a little shaky. She pulled her arm away from the sensations he caused with his touch and pushed down her sleeve to button it. She kept her head down because she knew she was blushing. She could feel the heat on her cheeks.

She glanced down at the blanket around her shoulders to be sure she was decently covered. In the light of the lamp and fire she noticed that her white nightdress was filthy, smeared with soot and mud. The hem had dried and the caked dirt fell off in little chunks on the chair and floor. She could only imagine how her hair must look. Self-consciously she took the thick braid that hung down her back and smoothed it over her shoulder as she glanced over at him.

Merrick sat back, his spine low in the chair, his fingers laced loosely over his lean stomach. He stared at her, making her even more uncomfortable. His voice sounded low and rough when he finally spoke. "I want to go to Dennison. As soon as possible."

The clock on the mantle chimed two, making both of them start.

She felt unsettled by what had just happened here in her front room. She spoke quickly. "I'll take you the day after tomorrow." Perhaps it was best for him to be gone, especially if his touch could make her feel like this.

Wes stood up and pulled his chair back into its original position. He looked at Katherine for a moment, wondering at his reaction to her. He needed to put some distance between them. "You go up to bed."

She looked startled. "No."

Stubborn female, why wouldn't she listen? She looked exhausted. He softened his voice. "Go ahead, I'll stay up."

She turned toward him, looking him in the eye. "No! It's my ranch, and I'll decide who takes a watch."

One thing was certain. He wasn't going to leave her down here by herself. He'd offer her a compromise. "All right. We can both stay up." He said, sounding calmer than he felt.

She didn't answer him, just settled back into her chair. He'd have to sit on the other side of the room. Being close to her did funny things to him. He had never reacted to touching a woman casually the way he had just reacted to Katherine Holman.

What a changeable creature she was. Out by the barn, during the fire, she was hell-bent, yelling orders and beating out the flames with her own dressing gown, getting so close she could have set her nightgown on fire. Half an hour later she's curled up in that big chair, looking like a little girl and acting like one too, when he pulled the splinter out of her arm. He wondered how old she was. He might just give in to his impulses and kiss her, just to see what those lips of hers tasted like. He groaned, as the thought of touching her caused his body to react.

"What's the matter?" Her sleepy voice came from deep in the chair.

"Nothing." His life the last few days had been like a strange dream. He recalled her explanation for rescuing him. She needed to be married but didn't want a husband. Perhaps she still loved her first husband too much to willingly remarry. Wes wondered what kind of man that husband had been to insist his wife remarry in order to retain property that was hers by right. Could the man have been such a poor judge of her character?

Wes could only see the top of her head. He had never met a woman with her kind of determination. There was no doubt in his mind she was capable of keeping a ranch like this going. It certainly was a puzzlement.

The subtle change in the sound of her breathing told him she had drifted off to sleep. All he could see of her in the wing-backed chair was the top of her head. Legally he was her husband. As he stared into the dying embers of the fire he thought about carrying her up to his bed, imagined making love to her. The vision of the two of them, naked in his bed, was as clear and as startlingly as a punch in the gut, and stayed with him for the rest of the night.

When the morning sunlight came through the window, he stretched and felt the effects of last night's fire-fighting efforts on his half-healed body. He looked over at her, still curled up, asleep. She had agreed she would take him into Dennison.

He didn't feel as strongly about leaving today as he had yesterday, even though every ounce of common sense told him he should. He had business at home. And, he argued with himself as he watched her sleep, plenty of brothers to see to it. His father's ranch was profitable enough for all of them to work there, but the ranch really didn't need him. Any hired hand could do the work he did. Katherine Holman had troubles. Could he leave her now, when someone was trying to scare her out?

He did need to clear his name. As soon as possible. He couldn't live with the fact he had put a blot on the Merrick name, no matter how unfair it might be. He had to clear up the misunderstanding as soon as possible.

Wes pushed himself off the chair. He looked out the window and saw the foreman, Gibby, down by the barn, looking at the burned area. Who would have set the fire, and why? Maybe she had held back and hadn't told him everything. What she had revealed hadn't made much sense.

Hannibal had told him about the cattle they had found all hacked up, and he had seen for himself what had happened to the hand named Tully. Then the fire. Last night she had voiced the thought that her troubles might have something to do with him. He definitely needed to clear his name and then remove any doubt from her mind that he had anything to do with all this.

The smell of fresh coffee drifted in from the kitchen. He headed toward the delicious aroma, then stopped in the dining room when he heard the child's voice. Despite what she had said last night, Katherine's demand that he stay away from her daughter still stung. Deciding to avoid the kitchen and any possibility of another unpleasant run-in, he turned and tiptoed past the chair where she slept, then out the front door. He could find a cup of coffee in the cookshack.

Cold morning air hit him when he stepped onto the porch. The chill wiped the last of the fuzziness out of his head. He wanted to get a look at the barn. It had been a little hard to tell how extensive the damage was in the dark last night.

He thought about her as he walked across the yard. Katherine. Her name didn't feel right. And her last name wasn't Holman anymore. Legally it was Merrick. He pondered that thought for a while. It certainly gave him something to chew on. In the past he hadn't given much thought to when he would marry. What a ribbing he would take when his brothers found out what had happened.

A thought struck him. As innocent as he was in the matter of rustling, the fact was she had saved his life. Katherine Holman. She called herself Katherine. He had heard Gibby call her Kate. Katherine was too formal for her. The name Kate was too short and abrupt. Katie. Now that name fit her. Sassy and cute.

The sun, bright on the eastern horizon, cast more light than warmth. Gratefully he entered the cookshack and poured himself a cup of coffee. Several of the hands he had met yesterday and seen last night fighting the fire were still there. Tully nodded and greeted him. So did several of the others. He knew why they seemed to treat him with more deference than a new hand could expect. They didn't know quite what to make of him. He was staying at the house and they had probably heard he was married to the boss, but he had almost been hung for rustling. If his position here puzzled him, it must confuse the heck out of them.

Merrick left the cookshack and saw Gibby at the barn door. He tipped his hat to the foreman. "Morning. I was just going to take a look at the damage."

"Good job last night, Merrick."

Wes peered into the dimly lit barn. "Sorry work for the middle of the night."

Gibby nodded in agreement. "Stinks of smoke inside and the animals are a little spooky. We'll keep them in the corral for the day. Tack room is kind of a mess. Hannibal and a few of the boys are moving the stuff out to an empty stall."

Together they walked around to the back of the barn. The wood was badly charred about five feet up the side.

Wes eyed the damage, then spoke to Gibby. "If we cut the boards at about six feet up and replace the charred wood with new stuff, and after a coat of paint, the damage would hardly be noticeable."

"I'm going into Miles City to order the wood. If we're lucky, Hiram will have boards in stock, and I'll bring them back today."

Wes considered the amount of work involved in getting the old wood down. "If you think the weather will hold, I'll start taking the damaged boards down now, so it'll be ready when the wood arrives."

"Don't matter too much about the weather. We can just close off the tack room while the wall's down. You up for that much work?"

"Sure. Just point me in the direction of the tools."

"Want anyone to help you?"

"Nope." Wes liked to work alone. This was just enough work for one man anyway. Anybody else would get in his way.

"You'll find everything you need in the room next to the tack room." Gibby tipped his hat and left.

Wes went into the barn, said hello to Hannibal, and found the tools he would need, plus a ladder. He carried the implements around to the outside of the barn.

When he tried to climb the ladder and use the saw, the splints on his arm got in the way. He had to wrap his bad arm around a rung of the ladder and hold on. It was an awkward way to work, but he kept at it doggedly, and saw progress through the morning. He stopped at noon and ate a bowl of Joe's chili.

As he came out of the cookshack, he saw Katherine in the wagon, headed alone toward Miles City. Fool woman should know better than to ride off alone, especially after last night. He also knew after last night that telling her so wouldn't do a wit of good.

He threw himself back into his work. It felt good to be outside, using his skills to accomplish something after all the time he had spent in bed. After working all day, he expected to get a good solid night's sleep, and be ready to ride into Dennison tomorrow.

He saw someone come around the side of the barn, and he used his sleeve to wipe the sweat out of his eyes. He didn't know the man, hadn't seen him on the ranch. Not quite as tall as Wes, but heavier, the man had a powerfully built chest. He wore a gun on his hip, and just under the front of his open jacket Wes could see a badge pinned to his shirt.

Wes climbed down off the ladder and stuck out his right hand. "Name's Merrick. Wes Merrick." For a moment Wes thought the other man was going to refuse to shake his hand.

"Martin Denty. I'm sheriff over to Miles City, and Katherine's neighbor." He finally took hold of Wes's hand in a quick powerful grip, and looked him up and down.

Wes didn't like the proprietary tone he used when he spoke Katie's name. He also didn't like the way the man looked him over, as if he was judging him.

Denty turned and glanced at the barn, the worst of the charred wood now down, a gaping hole leading into the tack room. "Bad business, this." He indicated the wall with a jerk of his head.

Wes watched him, and noticed he paid little attention to the damage, but seemed very interested in Wes. "Any ideas who might have done it?"

"No. Thought maybe you might know." The sheriff picked up a piece of straw and stuck it in the corner of his mouth.

"How would I know?" Now Wes really didn't like this fellow.

Denty shrugged. "Just thought I'd ask. You planning on staying long?"

"For a while."

"I know who you are and how you got here. I know you came up from Texas."

Wes assumed when Denty said he knew who he was he referred to the charges of Wes being a rustler. "I'm no rustler. I plan to clear my name." Wes waited, expecting a negative remark from the lawman about his own asserted innocence.

Denty shifted the bit of straw to the other side of his mouth before he spoke. "Good idea. A man can't rest easy with a cloud hanging over his name. You could ride back to Texas, and send proof."

That struck Wes as an odd comment, considering that Katie had told him if he left the ranch he would be arrested again and hung on the original charge. What she had done in marrying him didn't make sense, but he had no reason to doubt she told the truth. It sounded to him as if Denty was anxious for him to leave. Why would the sheriff want him gone?

Wes decided to keep his doubts and his plans to himself, and agree with Denty for the time being. "Sounds like a good idea."

"Seems to me if you're fit enough to work, you're fit enough to ride."

It wasn't a threat, exactly, the way he said it, but the meaning was clear. Wes smiled and commented. "Just trying to pay Katie back." He repositioned the ladder, hooked the saw with his arm and climbed back up to his work.

Denty's lips thinned out. "I'm sure Katherine would understand if you were to go." He shoved his thumbs into his gun belt, as if to emphasize what he said.

"Thanks for the tip. I'd like to get going before the snow falls."

"That's bound to be real soon." Denty turned and left without saying anything else.

Wes continued to pry away the damaged wood until he had it all down. As he worked, he thought about the sheriff. Could be he just had Katie's best interests at heart, but for some reason Wes couldn't put his finger on, he didn't think so.

He saw her coming up the road in the middle of the afternoon. Something inside him he didn't even realize had been tensed up relaxed at seeing her home safe. He waved to her and she nodded in response, then he went back to his work.

He finished sawing up the charred wood and stacked it by the cookshack to be used in the stove. Then he cleaned off the tools and put them away, along with the ladder. The sun sat low on the horizon when the cook started beating on the triangle of iron that hung on the porch.

Wes's clothes were covered with soot and grime. He decided to wash his hands and face, eat with the hired hands, and clean up after supper. He hadn't really seen Katie to talk to her since he had left the house this morning, and he wanted to firm up plans for tomorrow.

Exhausted after his long day of work, he borrowed a clean shirt from one of the hands, and bathed in the cookshack. For his own peace of mind he thought about moving out of the big house and into the bunkhouse, but the hands would talk. He didn't want to put Katie in the position of having her men gossip about her. Things were bad enough for her now, what with everything that was going on, she didn't need the hands speculating over her private life, too.

He took off his hat as he went up the front steps of the main house. He could see through the curtains of the front room window into the room she used for an office. The lamp was lit. She must be working at her desk. He knocked lightly and opened the front door, heading for the office to tell her good night. She must have heard him, because she appeared in the office door, the lamp back-lighting her with a soft glow.

"I wondered where you were." She smiled at him.

"I was so dirty at suppertime I ate with the men." She had smudged purple shadows under those big brown eyes. Last night had caught up with her, too.

She glanced at his clothes. "Oh."

"I borrowed some things from Olsen, and cleaned up. We still going to Dennison tomorrow?" Anxious to get his saddlebags and his horse back, he hoped they hadn't been sold.

"Yes. There wasn't wood for the barn in Miles City. I'm hoping they have some cut lumber for sale in Dennison." She leaned tiredly against the door jamb. "I saw all the work you did. Thanks." She stifled a yawn behind a small white hand.

He had an impulse to pull her into his arms and cradle her head against his chest. That thought had come quickly, same as last night, like a punch he wasn't ready for. Surprised, he said an abrupt good night and hurried up the stairs.

Katherine stood blinking in the doorway, wondering at his hurried departure. She hoped he hadn't overdone the working today. He looked all right. In fact, he looked much better than all right.

She had held dinner for him until she got too hungry to wait, and then chided herself for being disappointed when he didn't show. It was her own fault. She had practically thrown him out of the kitchen when she had found him alone with Hannah. Somehow that incident seemed like a long time ago.

She recalled the way he had touched her arm last night, and how his touch had made her feel. She dismissed his actions as anything personal. He was just being kind. He would have done the same for Hamlet if the creature had had a splinter. His touch wasn't the problem, she reminded herself. The problem was her reaction to the feel of his hands against her skin. She decided she had reacted the way she did because it had been so long since anyone had done anything caring for her. It was not the man she responded to, she convinced herself, but the act of kindness.

Exhausted, Katherine decided to call it a night. She

picked up the lamp and went up to bed, longing for a decent night's sleep. This morning she had had Gibby give two of the hands a free day, so they could stay up tonight and watch for trouble. She planned to sleep.

No sounds came from Merrick's room when she passed by, and no light showed under the door. She hurried into her nightgown and burrowed under the covers. She lay awake for a long time, listening to the creak of the bedsprings in Merrick's room, and wondering what her life would be like if he decided to stay in Montana.

12

Katherine stood on the porch and tipped her face to the early morning sunlight like a flower, soaking in the warmth as it stole under the broad brim of her straw bonnet. She knew this rare autumn day might be the last time they felt any heat from the sun until the spring, and she meant to enjoy it. Her muslin dress had long sleeves and a high neck, so she might not even need the knitted shawl she carried in her hand.

She watched Wes come out of the cookshack and stop at the barn to pick up the buckboard. He climbed into the seat and took up the reins, turning the horse and heading for where she stood waiting on the porch. There was something different about Wes this morning, but she couldn't decide what it was. He wore the same blue plaid shirt he had borrowed from Olsen, and the only pair of pants he owned. No, it wasn't the clothes, she decided. It must be something else.

He handled the horse well, and as he drew up to where she stood, she came down the steps.

"Morning," he tipped his hat with his greeting, and jumped down from his seat to escort her around the vehicle. He put his hands on her waist and helped her up. She laid her shawl over the back of the seat, and leaned against it.

"Thank you," she said. If he could be polite, so could she. It was obvious he planned to drive. She would watch him, she decided, and when he tired, she would take over. She knew how difficult it was for a man to give the reins over to someone else, especially a woman. She had never been allowed to drive when her father and brother were alive.

The buckboard rocked under his weight as Wes climbed up and sat beside her. His sleeve brushed hers as he flicked the reins, and she leaned a little to her right, unwilling to sit too close to his big warm body.

He clucked to the horse, and as they pulled away from the house she realized what it was about him that was different. He had rolled his sleeves up, exposing his forearms, and he no longer wore the splint on his broken arm.

"When did you take the splint off?"

He passed the reins to his right hand and held up the left, flexing his fingers. "Last night. I'll put it back on if I'm working or riding."

The movement of his hand defined the muscles in his forearm and she quickly averted her gaze, but not before a warm feeling crept over her. She associated the sensations he aroused in her only with him. She did not remember warm tingly feelings like that, even when Gerald had made love to her. Perhaps she had only forgotten. Gerald seemed like such a long time ago.

She had loved Gerald, had agreed to marry him, had given herself to him. That night seemed like another lifetime. Looking back, she realized how young she had been. Her notions of romance and love had affected her judgment.

"Penny for your thoughts." His voice, low and quiet in her ear, rattled her. She could never tell anyone what she had just been thinking.

A flush worked its way up her neck and onto her face. "I was just thinking about how much lumber I need for the barn." She felt so warm, she had to resist the urge to unfasten the top two buttons at the neckline of her dress. Her thoughts wandered again as she smoothed her hands down the sides of her skirt. The little gun she always carried was not in her pocket today. She tried to convince herself she had forgotten it, but in truth, she felt safe up on the wagon seat with Merrick, relieved that she did not feel the need to carry a weapon. To her surprise, she liked the feeling that she trusted him to protect and watch over her.

His eyebrow cocked as he watched her face. "Right," he smiled and looked out over the rump of the horse.

She had lost her train of thought.

"About a hundred and twenty board feet." He flicked the reins.

"What?" Her attention had wandered again.

"You were thinking about the lumber. I figure you need about one hundred and twenty feet of twelve-inch board." He glanced at her face again, then turned back to the road.

"Of course. That's what I had figured." And that *was* what she had figured, yesterday, when she hadn't been sitting so close to him that she could detect the faint aroma of shaving soap.

She decided to concentrate on a conversation and keep her errant thoughts from wandering. "Thank you for taking all the burned wood down yesterday. You don't have to work, you know."

He laughed, a deep pleasant sound from down in his chest. "I'll go crazy just sitting around. If you can get the lumber today, I'll put it up tomorrow."

"That would be wonderful. I want to get the job done before the weather changes." Again she turned her face up to the sun.

"How long do you think it will hold?" He too faced the sun and its warmth.

"That's always the big question around here. The best answer is never as long as you might think." Katherine shifted on the seat just as Wes brought his arm up to flick the reins over the back of the horse. His arm brushed the side of her breast, and the tingle of sensation from the other night was still there. With a quick sideways glance, she caught a little smile hovering at the corners of his mouth, under his mustache. She tried to sit still and not fidget on the narrow bench seat.

He cleared his throat. "I like your Montana territory. Beautiful country." His comment warmed her, like the sun.

She found conversation with him easy, and decided to chance asking a personal question. "What was it like, growing up with so many brothers and sisters?"

Wes laughed. "Noisy. There were always people in and out of the house. Even with all those kids, my mother kept taking in anyone who came along." He shared some stories about growing up in Texas with all his brothers. The Merricks sounded like a close family. "Didn't you have a brother?"

"Farley died when I was ten. He was so much older that we never spent too much time together. After he passed on, my mother became ill and took to her bed.

She died when I was thirteen. My father sent me off to school in Chicago."

"What was that like?"

"Lonely. I hated the city. It was smoky and dirty. I lived for summers when I could come home." She still remembered the loneliness. Perhaps that was why she had been so open to attention from Gerald.

They stopped once to water the horse and stretch their legs. She offered to take over the driving, but he refused. Before she knew it, they could see the buildings of Dennison in the distance. The good-sized town dwarfed Miles City in comparison. The main street was twice as long, and some of the side streets sported businesses as well. Four roads led into the town square, a large area planted all the way around with trees.

Wes pulled up on the reins and stopped the horse on a small hill overlooking the town. Katherine looked over at him, wondering why he had stopped here. She could see that the scaffold still stood in the square in the middle of town.

He took off his hat and wiped his arm across his forehead. "I was here, wasn't I."

"You don't remember anything?" She found it hard to believe he had lost so much time. It must be unsettling for him. He couldn't miss seeing the scaffold, it was huge.

"Nope, nothing." He replaced his hat and released the brake. The horses started moving on their own. The animals were smart enough to know there would be water and feed in town.

Katherine directed him to the livery stable on one of the side streets, and they dropped off the buckboard. They could walk around town and place their orders for wood and supplies, then come back for the wagon later.

Katherine shook the dust out of her full skirt, and retied the ribbons of her bonnet under her chin.

He offered her his arm, and after a small hesitation she accepted, hooking her hand through the crook of his elbow, her palm resting on the hard muscle under the flannel of his sleeve. The warmth she felt through the fabric made her feel a little giddy. What a ninny she was, she scolded herself, to have such a reaction to a simple polite gesture on his part. They walked down the alley away from the livery until they came to the main street.

"Are you hungry?" He scanned the street as he spoke. Very few people were about in the middle of the day.

Pleased that he had thought to ask, and at the same time a little annoyed that he seemed to take charge of the outing, she answered, "Yes, and thirsty, too. There's a cafe across the square." She pointed to a wooden false-fronted building painted red with yellow trim. At least she would decide where they would eat. Once, when she was a child, her father had taken her to eat at Estelle's when he brought her to Dennison. The cook there was famous for his doughnuts. Her mouth watered when she thought about the yeasty fried pastries.

Katherine and Wes cut across the dusty square. At the far end of the open area stood the scaffold. Wes stopped walking when they drew even with the wooden structure, and stood very still. The wood had weathered and no longer had that new look, or the sharp smell of sap. She glanced up at him and saw the taut lines of his face, saw the muscles move in his throat as he swallowed.

The clock in the church steeple chimed twelve. How strange that she should be standing here with him, arm in arm. How different today would have been if she had chosen one of the other rustlers that day. She certainly wouldn't be standing here looking at the scaffold.

She looked away from his grim expression before she spoke. "The weather was clear, like today. Hot and dusty. The square was full of people."

He pulled his gaze from the raw wood of the structure, and his eyes rested on her face. He studied her intently for a moment. "Why did you choose me?"

The reality of how close he had come to dying was hitting him just now, she thought. She smiled at him, remembering how she had evaluated each member of the gang as they climbed up those steps. "I watched each man being sentenced. The deputies had to hold you up. You looked like you would cause the least trouble of all of them. You couldn't even stand up by yourself. I figured it would be hard to drive all the way to the ranch and hold a gun on someone at the same time, so I picked you."

The humor in her voice seemed to break his grim mood. He smiled and squeezed his arm against his side, catching her hand tightly against his body. "Thanks. I owe you."

She shook her head. "No. I think we're even. I'll have my ranch, and you can go on with your life." She was sure now that his life was his by rights, too. She couldn't put her finger on the exact time it had happened, but she could no longer believe he had been a rustler. He had too many fine qualities.

He gave her another long, intense look that made her uncomfortable. "Come on." She tugged a little on his arm to get him moving.

They paused in the door of the cafe, and inhaled the smell of fresh doughnuts. The scent wafted over her and brought back memories of standing in this very spot as a child, her hand firmly held by her father. She felt a wave of nostalgia at the thought. Life had been so uncomplicated then.

He took her hand out of the crook of his arm and held it in his. "You all right?" His question brought her back to the present.

"Of course." With a little start she slipped her hand from his and made her way to a table in the back. She didn't want to be seated by the front windows. The view of the scaffold would be hard to avoid.

The special of the day turned out to be pot roast with carrots and potatoes. It seemed like a heavy meal to her on such a warm day, but he finished all of his and part of hers, too. They ordered coffee and doughnuts for dessert, then sat back in their chairs and relaxed for a few moments.

She felt so sleepy. If she didn't move, she might just doze off. "We had better be going."

Wes leaned back in his chair and reached into his pocket. He stopped and looked at her with chagrin. "I don't have any money."

Katherine pulled a dollar out of her pocket and left it on the table.

Wes stood and came around to help her out of her chair. "Where are you headed?" He held the door for her.

His mother should be commended. He had fine manners. She didn't even know if his mother was still alive. He hadn't mentioned her. In fact, there was a great deal about him she didn't know.

"I need to go right here, to the dry goods store." She indicated the building next to the cafe.

"While you're in there, I'll see the sheriff." He escorted her to the door, then turned and headed toward the sheriff's office.

She watched him walk away and realized he no longer looked thin to her. In just a short time he must have put on the weight he had lost on the trail and in jail. His trousers no longer gathered around his waist. She remembered his bare, bruised chest, and the way his ribs had shown through his skin. Those bruises had probably faded to yellow by now. Even before, when she had first brought him home and he was so sick, he was beautiful.

The signs of his recovery should have cheered her because they meant he would be leaving soon, just as she had planned all along. In reality, they had the opposite effect on her. She didn't want to face the prospect of letting him go. He would be well enough next week when the drovers took the fall calves to the railroad station to ride with them, and then keep on going home to Texas. She tried to convince herself it was for the best, and she really didn't need him around to complicate her life, but it didn't work.

She felt as if he had reached inside her and grabbed hold of her heart, giving it a painful little twist. She liked being with him. She wanted him to hold her, to kiss her, to want her. She wanted him to make her feel like a desirable woman. She was falling in love with him, and it was one of the last things she needed.

Love had not entered into her plan at all. Katherine could feel a headache coming on. She rubbed her temples and decided to stop thinking about what was going to happen in the future, and concentrate on what needed doing today. Maybe she couldn't help falling in love with him, but she could try to ignore how she felt. She suspected that that might be harder than it sounded.

She entered the cool interior of the dry goods store, and asked the clerk where she might find yardage. He directed her to the rear of the store, where bolts of fabric were stacked on a long table. She hunted among the bolts until she found a suitable piece of green wool to replace her burnt robe. While the clerk measured off the amount she requested, she picked out some calico for a new dress for Hannah, and a piece of blue muslin for Consuela. The selection here was so much better than in Miles City that she decided to splurge. She added white sheeting to the stack for aprons and pinafores, and picked out buttons and thread to match the fabrics. Both she and Consuela would have plenty of time to sew when the snow made outside activities all but impossible. This winter she planned to master the new treadle machine she had bought from the Singer Company last spring.

While a clerk finished cutting the lengths of fabric for her, she wandered around the rest of the store, stacking the items she needed on the counter.

Near the fabrics, in the far corner of the store, behind a freestanding mirror, stood a narrow row of shelves filled with ready-made clothes. She hesitated for a moment, then picked out a lightweight blue denim shirt with bone buttons that looked to be the right size for Merrick and added it to her pile on the counter. He would have to return Olsen's shirt. The hired hand was one of the men who would not stay on for the winter.

An open case behind the table of cotton fabrics held bolts of finer cloth, silks and satins that shimmered in the dim light. One pale yellow piece caught her eye, and she pulled it from the shelf. The thin silk felt like cool spring water when she ran her hand over the surface of the material. She walked to the mirror and unfolded the bolt, draping a length of the silk over her shoulder and holding it up under her chin.

Wes appeared behind her in the reflection in the mirror. For a moment, before his eyes met hers, the look on his face made her feel as if she needed to cover up, a hot look she imagined she felt scorching her back. His hands came around her sides to the front of her without touching her. He stroked the fabric wound around the bolt. She imagined what those hands would feel like on her body and her knees went a little weak.

He leaned toward her so his mouth was up against her ear. "I like it, it suits you."

The heavy bolt began to slip through her hands, and with one fluid motion he reached to catch the fabric and lay it on the table where the clerk was cutting.

"And this one too." He turned to her. "How much do you need?"

She stammered as she gave him the yardage she would require for a gown, and moved away toward the part of the store where tools were displayed. It seemed like a safer place to be. Goodness, he could certainly unnerve her easily.

"Will we need nails for the barn?" He acted as if nothing had just happened over there in yard goods.

She gathered her thoughts. "Ah, yes. All we have are roofing nails." The clerk cutting the yard goods caught her eye and motioned. He was finished with her order. The fabrics lay on the counter, ready to be wrapped in neat bundles.

Wes added the bag of nails to the purchases, and Katherine pulled out some bills to pay for everything. She left instructions that they would pick up the order soon.

Wes offered his arm, and she took it a little reluctantly, remembering the incident in yard goods. Perhaps she had read too much into his look and she was just being fanciful.

They walked out onto the boardwalk. She wondered what the sheriff had said. Wes didn't make her wait long.

"Sheriff here didn't recognize me when I walked into his office." He looked bemused.

Katherine turned and looked at him. "I'm not sure I would have either. Your face was so swollen, and you had a beard."

"And I had spent weeks in the saddle, too." He fell silent.

They just stood there on the boardwalk in the sun. Finally she couldn't stand the silence. "Well, what did he say?"

Wes hesitated before he spoke. "He said I might have a hard time proving I was innocent, considering all the other members of the gang were dead. But he'll bring it up with Judge Casey. Maybe I can file an appeal. I'm going to send a telegram to my brother in Texas and get him to write a letter. That should help."

"There's a Western Union office next to the bank." There was no sense wasting time, she thought reluctantly. She wanted him to clear his name because it seemed so important to him, but if he did he would be free to go. She knew he could leave her ranch any time he wanted, and be well out of the territory before the sheriff here in Dennison ever knew about it, but she suspected that what Wes had told her was true. He was an honorable man. Knowing the only hold she had on him was the black mark on his name made her want to cry.

"Sheriff also said no ranchers around here are having any problems like you've been seeing."

"Thanks for asking him." She wasn't surprised she was the only one, but it bothered the dickens out of her trying to figure why anyone would cause her trouble.

His voice broke into her thoughts. "I have to ask you for a favor." He looked uncomfortable.

"What?" She watched him, curious to know what could make him so uneasy.

"I need money to send a telegram."

It must have been hard for him to ask her for money. She remembered the look on his face at the cafe when he had automatically reached into his pocket. She pulled out two bills. She saw people walking toward them on the boardwalk and didn't think he would appreciate being handed money, so she slipped it into his palm.

"Thank you." He pocketed the bills.

"It's over there." She pointed to the telegraph office. "While you do that, I'm going to go and check on the lumber. The office for the lumber yard is beside the livery. I'll meet you there."

He offered her his arm. "Wait for me, and I'll walk you."

She ignored his chivalry. She didn't want to watch him send a telegram that could eventually clear his name and take him back to Texas. "I am perfectly capable of walking to the lumber yard by myself." She had come to Dennison alone before. A little voice reminded her that the last time she had not gone home alone. She had had Wes in the back of her wagon.

Wes stiffened at her curt response and tipped his hat. Katherine hesitated, wanting to tell him how she felt about him leaving, then pushed the thought aside. She would live by the bargain they had made, and not complicate either of their lives.

Feeling his eyes on her back, she started back across the square alone, and avoided looking at the scaffold. She met with the owner of the saw mill, and he assured her he would have the wood loaded in the back of the buckboard. He sent a man to the livery. By the time she had paid for the lumber, Wes was waiting for her outside the office.

"Ready?" He again offered his arm.

She thought him brave to extend the courtesy after she had rebuffed him, and accepted his gesture. "The wood is being loaded now. We can stop at the dry goods store and pick up the order, and head for home." It was a long trip for one day, but Katherine had no intention of being away from the ranch overnight, not with all the trouble she had been having.

Within minutes, a driver brought the wagon out to them. Wes handed her up into the seat. She would offer to drive later, out on the road. She wouldn't embarrass him by suggesting she drive while they were still in town.

They stopped in front of the dry goods store. He came around and handed her down. "Why don't you have them load up, and I'll go into the cafe and get us a sack of doughnuts for the ride home."

"All right. I'll meet you here." She climbed the steps, and saw to the loading of the supplies. The clerk handed her up into the buckboard, and she had a few moments to think before Wes returned. She had enjoyed this outing, just being with him, having him to talk to and be with. She felt safe on his arm, and she knew that when he left she would miss him terribly. Her feelings certainly hadn't been part of her plan for Wesley Austin Merrick. Instead of being relieved that things had gone as well as they had today for Wes in Dennison, she fought back the urge to cry.

13

The wagon bounced east along the road on the way home from Dennison, throwing up a cloud of dust in its wake. In the bed of the wagon, the pieces of lumber slapped together every time they hit a rut. Katherine tipped her head back and to the side, loving the feel of the afternoon sun on her cheek. Out of slitted eyes she watched Wes drive. His forearms rested on his knees, and he held the reins loosely in his big hands.

His voice startled her. "You remind me of a cat. We had a big yellow mouser who lived in the barn. On a sunny day she would sit and face the sun like that."

Katherine wasn't sure she liked being compared to an animal that ate rodents for supper. She changed the subject. "What did the sheriff say about your gear?"

"Sold it to pay for the trial and the hanging. I pointed out to him that I hadn't used my fifth of the scaffold, but he wasn't amused."

Katherine remembered the look on the sheriff's face when she had stepped forward to claim Merrick. "Yes, well, he wasn't very amused the day of the hangings either. He took it real personal when I claimed you. I'm sorry now I didn't think to ask about your saddlebags."

He flicked his wrist and urged the team along. "There's nothing in them that can't be replaced. When I sent my brother that telegraph, I asked him to wire me some money. I'll pay you back as soon as it arrives."

"I told you not to worry about it." Once he had the money, he would leave. She needed to tell him Anderson and his wife were coming to dinner on Saturday.

His voice broke in on her thoughts. "Do you mind if I keep using your father's razor until I can get a new one?"

She liked the idea of him using her father's things. "Of course not. Use anything you find in the room." He wasn't a prisoner, he was a guest.

Katherine wanted to know more about him, personally. "What is your spread like, in Texas?"

"Not mine. The ranch belongs to my father. My brothers and I talked about splitting it up, but decided there wasn't enough land to go five ways. Texas is getting a little crowded, but here, in Montana, there's still plenty of room." He gestured at the open grasslands.

He was right. Land wasn't free for the asking the way it had been when her father had come up from Texas, but there was land still available. She worried sometimes that the territory was getting too crowded. Her father would hate the fact that more and more wire was being strung every year, but now it was by necessity. Good fences did make good neighbors.

"Do you run longhorns on your land?" He had rolled his sleeves back up when they left town. She watched the play of muscles in his forearms as he held the reins.

"No. They're ornery and too stringy for most people's taste. Our stock is mostly Hereford mix. We imported breeding stock from a fellow down near Abilene."

"We have two longhorns left. They came up the trail with my father over twenty years ago. He claimed they were too mean to die. I tried to put them in the barn last winter during a blizzard and they almost wrecked the place."

Wes whistled. "Twenty years. That's two tough steer."

"Actually, a tough steer and a tough cow. They're like an old couple who have been married for years. You always see them together. I can't tell if they like being by themselves or the rest of the herd shuns them. They're both so old and stiff they can't get through the deep snow to graze. I should put them down I suppose, but I can't bear the thought." Katherine took off her straw hat and let the breeze ruffle her hair. She noticed that he shifted the reins to his right hand and rested his left across his thighs. "Is your arm bothering you?"

"A little."

She could tell by his tone that he was impatient with his progress. He'd come so close to dying, she marveled that he was even up and walking around.

"I'll drive the rest of the way," she offered. She wondered if he would resist handing the reins over to her.

He studied the position of the sun. "How about I pull over and we give the horses a rest?" he said, guiding the team off the road into a grassy area under a stand of oak trees. "We're about half way, I reckon. We can rest and still make it back before dark."

Stopping was fine with Katherine. She had some personal business she had to attend to that she'd rather not wait two more hours on a badly sprung buckboard seat to do. He didn't give the awkward situation a chance to develop. Wes pointed behind the trees and said, "I'm going over there for a minute."

Katherine headed to the opposite end of the stand of trees, and by the time she got back, he had spread an old blanket in the shade and was unhitching the horses.

Katherine sank down on a corner of the blanket, curled her legs up underneath her and watched him with the animals. The man had a fluid motion when he worked that reminded her of poetry. Spare words that told a story with no wasted space.

He hobbled the horses, stopped to pick up the sack from the cafe, then came over and sat on the opposite corner of the blanket, keeping a respectful distance. They ate doughnuts and sipped lemonade out of a jar. Katherine couldn't think of anything to say, and Wes was equally quiet. The silence, filled with the hum of insects, stretched between them. A flock of geese, flying south and honking loudly, broke the quiet afternoon.

After a while Wes flopped on his back and closed his eyes. She knew he was asleep by the deep rhythmic breathing and the steady rise and fall of his chest. He had overdone himself the last two days, with the work on the barn and the trip today. Tomorrow he would probably want to put the new wood up, too. She decided to let him rest now. He was right, they still had enough time to get home before dark, and if they were late, it didn't really matter. She knew the road to the ranch in the dark and there should be a moon tonight.

She studied his face, dappled in the shadows of the leaves. He looked younger without the beard, but she was glad he had left the mustache.

Katherine's eyes traveled down over his chin and stopped on the open collar of his shirt. A tuft of dark hair peeked through the opening. She knew about the hair on his chest, thick and black. She remembered it had felt surprisingly soft that first night when she and Consuela had wrapped his ribs. Her eye traveled down his broad chest to the buckle of his belt. The buckle looked like a rectangle of bone, with a building carved into its surface, but she couldn't tell what it was. She looked at the fly of his denims, and for a moment, she focused on the obvious bulge there, straining at the front of his pants.

He cleared his throat and her eyes flew to his face. He wasn't asleep after all, and he had been watching her looking at him. This was the second time he had caught her.

"What's the matter, Katie?" She felt her face color as he grinned at her.

She turned away from him. "Nothing. Nothing's the matter." No one else had ever called her Katie. She liked the sound of it, coming from him.

She heard the rustle of the leaves under the old blanket and knew he was sitting up. She wished she could just dig a hole and jump in, she was so embarrassed.

"Turn around." His voice sounded low and husky.

"No."

"Katie, turn around." She felt his hands on her shoulders as he tried to pull her around to face him. She resisted him and lost her balance, then grabbed for his arm trying to steady herself. As she struggled to right herself, he slid his other arm around her waist and came up on his knees, bringing her with him.

There she was, plastered up against him, matched thigh to thigh, belly to belly. She felt a warmth creep into her limbs, making them feel slow and heavy. His arm tightened around her waist and his other hand came up to cup the back of her head. He tilted her head back, and she watched with open-eyed fascination as he lowered his mouth to hers. His mustache pricked the sensitive spot under her nose just before his lips touched hers. Then she forgot all about his mustache. Every bit of her mind concentrated on the sensation his lips were causing, moving back and forth over her mouth.

She felt herself start to melt, and she brought her hands up and clutched at his arms. He increased the pressure against her lips and she slid her arms up to his shoulders. He coaxed her lips apart and his tongue tasted the inside of her mouth, gently seeking her warmth. The combination of his lips and tongue caused a curious tingling in her breasts and belly. She swayed and he increased the strength of his grip around her waist.

She moved her hands up to his neck until they tangled in the hair that hung over his collar. It was soft and warm to her touch. She moved her mouth against his, and after a small hesitation, her tongue went seeking his. As soon as she found her target, he shifted her weight and wedged his thigh between her legs, pulling her up against the warm muscled length of his leg. His hand left the back of her head and sought out her breast. She could feel her nipple harden against his tentative touch, even through the fabric of her dress and camisole. She leaned back into his arm that gripped her around her waist, giving him better access, and moaned into his mouth.

He tore his lips away from her mouth, and spoke low and ragged into her ear, his breath fanning warm against her neck. "Oh, God, Katie. I want you so much."

She couldn't think, her whole body buzzed with sensation. All of a sudden they tumbled sideways to the blanket, and his big frame was draped over her, his weight supported on his elbows, and his mouth once again worked its magic against hers. Her hands moved up his broad chest, her palms sliding over firm, warm muscle.

She felt a tug on the hem of her skirt and then felt his hand stroking up her leg, rubbing the sensitive skin at the inside of her knee through her cotton stocking. When his hand moved up over her garter, and on to the bare skin of her thigh, a warning bell went off in her head. She was no blushing virgin, and she knew exactly where he was headed.

She pulled away from his mouth, and tried to roll out from under him. He had her trapped and wouldn't let her go.

"Whoa. Just a minute. Where are you going?" His voice sounded rough.

"I can't." She closed her eyes and braced for the tirade she expected from him.

He lifted himself off her, and said nothing for a moment. When he finally did speak, his voice sounded more normal than it had a few moments ago. "I'm sorry that happened."

His apology wasn't what she expected. She didn't know what he was sorry for, starting what had just happened, or the fact that she had stopped it. She sat up. Actually, she wasn't sure herself how she felt about the whole thing. When she went to smooth down her skirt, her hands shook.

She glanced over at him, and he smiled at her, a bemused sort of smile. She vividly remembered the night she and Gerald had vowed to marry, despite her father's feelings. They had been kissing and carrying on, and Gerald hadn't wanted to stop. He had told her it was cruel to leave a man all worked up, that it caused a man pain. She had loved him and felt guilty, so she let him go ahead. Against her better judgment, she had given herself to Gerald. A few months later she found herself pregnant with Hannah, and Gerald was dead. She wasn't going to repeat that mistake.

She knew from firsthand experience how painful the consequences of leaping before you looked could be. She and Hannah would pay for her mistake for the rest of their lives. She didn't mind so much for herself, she could handle what people said and how they treated her. But she ached for Hannah, an innocent child who had had no choice in the matter. That was why she needed the ranch, needed a safe place for her child.

"I think we better get going." Katherine started to get up.

"Wait." He put a gentle hand on her arm. "Tell me what happened just now. You wanted it too. Why did you stop?" His low warm voice failed to soothe her.

"Because I don't need that kind of trouble!" She shook off his hand as she got to her feet.

"What do you mean, trouble?" He followed her up.

She had been wrong. He was probably as angry as Gerald had been, he just didn't show it the same way. She turned and faced him, looking him square in the eye. "Look, I got talked into doing that once before, and now I have Hannah. Don't get me wrong, I love my daughter, but I'm not going to be a fool again."

He looked confused. "So you and Hannah's father weren't in love? The marriage wasn't happy?" He sounded sincere, like he really cared.

She gave a short bitter laugh. "There was no marriage!"

Wes studied her face, his mouth settled into a grim line before he spoke. "You mean he refused to marry you?"

He watched the tears pool in her eyes. One broke loose and ran down her cheek to her trembling lips. Her voice was so quiet he had to lean toward her as she spoke. "No, he died. Before I could tell him about the baby."

So she hadn't been Mrs. Holman, he thought. Her name was Miss Holman. She was crying in earnest now, and Wes didn't know what to do for her. He had seen the pain on her face. He did the first thing that came to mind, and reached for her and pulled her into his arms. To his surprise, she nestled against him and sobbed into the front of his shirt. He rested his cheek on the top of her head and smelled the faint lavender scent of her hair.

Unfortunately his body didn't seem to understand why she was in his arms this time. The kiss they had just shared had set him on fire. He was mighty attracted to this woman. He'd realized that the night the barn burned, when he had pulled that splinter out of her arm. Now he knew she had some of the same feelings for him. Being this close to her was a trial after feeling that rush of passion from her just now.

She must have felt his body's reaction to having her close again, and she pulled away from him and self-consciously wiped at her eyes with the back of her hand. She drew a hankie out of her pocket and blew her nose.

"I'm sorry for all that. I usually don't cry." She blew her nose a second time, and stuffed the hankie back in her pocket.

"I didn't mean to hurt your feelings by asking those questions. What was his name?" Wes felt a curious little stab of jealousy for the dead man.

"Gerald. My father didn't like him, so we waited to get married hoping Papa would come around. And then, well, Hannah happened."

"Why didn't your father like him?" Wes was ready to agree with the late Julius Holman, and dislike this Gerald person.

"Papa said Gerald was weak, but he wasn't. He just didn't like the same things Papa did, like being outdoors. He was a teacher, and he loved poetry. He didn't like to ride or hunt. I'm sure my father thought he wouldn't be able to run the ranch. It was a silly reason not to like him, because I could have run the place, but Papa didn't believe that a woman could do the job. That's why you're here."

She could tell by the expression on his face she had lost him with her explanation. "Excuse me?"

"My father died five months ago. I'm his only heir, but he put a clause in his will that I couldn't inherit unless I was married by the time six months went by after his death. And not to just anyone. The man I married had to know the cattle business."

Now he understood what she had meant the night the barn had been torched. He had assumed her husband had put the clause in the will. Her father probably had her best interests at heart, even if his ideas were a little old fashioned.

Her choice of him for a husband still had him puzzled. "He had to know the cattle business? And you thought I was a rustler." He laughed.

She gave him a sad smile. "Like I said the other night. I need to be married, but I don't want a husband."

Now that statement had him puzzled. "Tell me why don't you want a husband."

She looked uncomfortable, and for a moment he thought perhaps she wasn't going to answer. Finally she fixed her gaze on a spot somewhere over his shoulder. "The men around here know about me, and they don't treat me the way I want to be treated."

He had an idea what she meant, but wanted to hear it from her. "How so?"

She looked him in the eye. "They all know I had a child and I wasn't married. They came calling after Hannah was born and acted as if I was, well, soiled. If I would do that with Gerald, I would do it with them."

He had a sudden impulse to ride into Miles City, and punch every man he met on the street. "Are they rude to you, in public?"

She shook her head. "No. It's nothing that shows, really. It's just a feeling I get by the way they look at me."

"How about the women? How do they treat you?" He found it hard to believe a woman as wonderful as Katie Holman could be chastised by a whole town because of one mistake.

"Well, I don't get many invitations to teas anymore. But I don't mind that so much." Her smile was back, playing around the corners of her pretty full lips.

He smiled too, then he thought of something else she might have had to endure. "How about your hired hands? How do they treat you?"

"Gibby is very protective. They wouldn't last if they said anything." She bent over from the waist in a graceful movement to pick up the blanket. She straightened, and folded the blanket over her arm. "I don't take Hannah into town. I won't subject her to scorn."

He nodded, understanding. He had already had a taste himself of how protective she could be about her daughter.

"That's why the ranch is so important. I need a safe place to raise Hannah."

"I understand. She's safe with me, you know. I'd never hurt her."

"I know that now." She reached up, and for a moment placed her hand briefly on his cheek. The tender gesture touched him. "We better be going, or we won't make it before dark." As she spoke she walked to the wagon and stashed the blanket under the seat. She helped Wes hitch up the horses, and then climbed up into the seat and took the reins. She turned to him and put a hand on his sleeve. "The attorney, Mr. Anderson, and his wife are coming to dinner tomorrow night to meet you. If he doesn't think you are really my husband, he won't change the deed into my name, and the ranch will be sold. Could you, I mean would you act like my husband tomorrow night at dinner? Just that one night is all I'll ask of you before you leave."

As she spoke he realized that one night with her would never be enough. He had thought more today about staying than leaving, but he didn't think the time was right to tell her that. Her future really did depend on him.

He regretted the sound of desperation in her voice, and wanted to reassure her. "I suppose that's a fair thing to ask, since I owe you my life. And besides, we are married." His comment seemed to hang in the quiet afternoon air. He took the reins out of her hands and cracked them over the back of the horses. This ranch of hers meant a great deal to her. He supposed he'd feel the same way if what she had was at stake for him.

They headed back to the Rocking H. He had plenty to think about on the way home. His body didn't let him forget how close she was sitting beside him on the seat of that wagon. The warmth of her body next to him felt good. He had never reacted so quickly to a woman as he had to her earlier. When he had awakened from his doze and found her eyes wandering down his body, he had thought about what it would be like if her hands touched all the places her eyes touched him. He could act like he was her husband, at dinner and as far into the night as she would allow.

She had wanted to marry this fellow Gerald, and had given herself to him without a wedding, and she then had married Wes, and held him off. As they rode toward the ranch he decided that even though Gerald was dead, so far the other man had gotten the better side of the deal.

14

Katherine stood back, casting a critical eye on the table setting. White candles in silver holders cast a warm glow over her best china and linens and crystal. The silver bowl in the center of the table held a big bouquet of the last of the yellow mums from the garden.

The end of the day's sunlight filtered in through the crisp lace curtains. Happy at last with the table, Katherine blew out the candles to save them until her guests arrived. Next she hurried back to the kitchen to check on Consuela and the dinner. The roast beef smelled heavenly, and the last of the potatoes were peeled. Consuela stood at the stove and carefully dropped them one at a time into a big pot of boiling water. Satisfied with the way the preparations were going, Katherine went upstairs to check on Hannah and change her own clothes.

The child was asleep in her bed, where she had been all day with a fever. She had refused to eat supper because of a sore throat. Katherine brushed the wisps of hair off her forehead and felt the skin there. The child was warm, but not alarmingly so. She worried about her daughter, but reasoned sleep was the best medicine for a sick child.

Katherine kissed Hannah on the forehead and quietly closed the door to her room. She knocked on the door of Wes's room, and heard no sound. She had hoped to have a few words with him before company arrived, but apparently he wasn't in. He had worked all day on the barn, repairing the damage from the fire. Katherine could tell when she went to check on his progress that Wes was skilled with tools. It would be hard to see where he had cut the old burned wood away and fitted the new wood in once it was painted. The men who worked for her had accepted him. She hoped Mr. Anderson would be at least as accepting of Wes tonight.

Nervous about the evening, Katherine laid her two best dresses on the bed. She had to decide between the green dress with the full sleeves and the modest neckline, and the gold gown, with its daring scooped bodice that buttoned up the front and bared her shoulders. She held up the gold gown and looked at herself in the mirror. It reminded her of the bolt of fabric in the store, and Wes behind her, whispering in her ear that he liked it. She felt a wash of warmth, and decided on the gold gown.

She thought about him as she brushed out her hair, and twisted it into a thick coil at the base of her neck. She tried three times before she could get the hairdo right. Her fingers just couldn't seem to work tonight, and her mind kept wandering to the upcoming dinner and what chances she had of convincing Mr. Anderson that she and Wes were truly husband and wife. If he had been in his room she would have talked to him about how she wanted him to act. She had tried to remember how her parents had acted toward one another, and all she could think of was that they were courteous and polite. Surely she and Wes could manage that.

Finally she got her hair in an orderly knot. She wondered if Wes's brother had already sent a letter to the sheriff in Dennison. What kind of response would satisfy the sheriff? In truth, Wes could leave anytime. She wouldn't report his going, and the sheriff in Dennison wouldn't find out until Wes was well out of the territory. From what Wes had said, she knew he was determined to clear his name before he left. He was an honorable man, and he would stay until he proved his innocence.

Everyone had misjudged him. Only her impulsiveness at his trial had saved his life. She shuddered at the thought of what would have happened to him if she had stayed home that day. The town of Dennison would have hung an innocent man.

Katherine finished doing up the buttons on the bodice of her dress, and looked at herself critically in the mirror. The dress fit well, and the golden color looked good against her skin. The dress sat off her shoulders a bit, and scooped low in the front, displaying more flesh than she was accustomed to seeing. Just the top swell of her breasts showed, so she felt the dress was decent enough for wearing in the evening. She hoped it was the sort of dress Mr. Anderson would think a married woman would wear.

She put on a pair of her mother's earrings, beautiful fiery opals set in gold that dangled from a filigreed flower. Her father had bought them in Butte and gave them to her mother in celebration of their fifteenth wedding anniversary. At seven, Katherine had thought them the most beautiful things she had ever seen. When her mother got them out to wear on some special occasion she would sometimes let Katherine clip them on and wear them while she sat at her mother's dressing table. Katherine wondered what her mother would have to say about her daughter's current situation. She had warned Katherine repeatedly as she grew up about the dangers of acting impulsively.

Katherine heard the clock strike six in the front room, immediately followed by a knock at the front door. George Anderson and his wife had arrived. The man was punctual to an extreme. She took one quick last look in the mirror, and blew out the lamp. Just as she left her room to answer the door, Hannah began to wail. Katherine called downstairs for Consuela to answer the door, and went to check on Hannah.

The child had had a bad dream, no doubt brought on by the fever. She rubbed her eyes and blinked at Katherine. "Mama, drink of water." Hannah said in a dry croaking voice.

Katherine poured from the carafe by the bed. "Here you go." She helped the child sit up, then held the glass for her.

Hannah took a long drink, then pushed the glass away. "Mama, you look pretty."

"Thank you, darling girl. Mr. Anderson and his wife have come for dinner."

"Can I come too?" Hannah reached out and touched Katherine's earring.

"No, you stay in bed and get well." Hannah made no complaint, but lay back down and snuggled into the covers. Katherine stood for a moment and watched the child. The outcome of this dinner could decide their future. She tiptoed out of the room, and left the door ajar so she might hear her if she woke again.

As Katherine went down the stairs, she heard voices coming from the front room. Wes and Mr. Anderson were standing in front of the fire, their backs to her, each with a drink in his hand. Katherine paused on the last step, and put a hand over her stomach, willing the flutters of nervousness there to cease.

Wes turned and greeted her with a smile. "There you are, dear. I was ready to come back up and get you when Mr. Anderson arrived." She noticed how he spoke very naturally about being upstairs in her house. Wes walked over to meet her, stopping in front of her and giving her a kiss on the cheek before offering her his arm. "You look lovely."

Katherine started at his smooth greeting and then regained her composure. Her husband looked pretty wonderful himself. He must have bathed at the bunkhouse, because his hair was still damp, showing the marks of a comb. He had shaved, and smelled faintly of bay rum. He wore the new shirt she had bought him in Dennison, and a jacket she didn't recognize. The deep shade of blue of the shirt was perfect on him, matching his eyes.

She smiled up at him and took the arm he offered. "Good evening, George. Where's Beatrice?"

"She's not feeling well. She sends her regrets."

Mrs. Anderson was a frail woman who suffered from a vague nervous disorder. "Please send her our regards."

Wes walked her over to the fireplace and took a crystal glass filled with amber liquid off the mantle, handing the drink to her. "Sherry."

She thanked him and accepted the drink with a hand that trembled slightly, and took a small sip. His smooth, polished actions suggested that such gestures were made frequently between them. Now was certainly not the time to inform him that she did not care for sherry. She could tell by the smell of the liquor in his glass that he was drinking bourbon. He must have found the bottle and glasses in the cabinet in the dining room. Bless him for thinking of it. Caught up in the details of dinner, she had forgotten it would be his place as host to offer Mr. Anderson a drink before dinner.

Anderson and Wes resumed their discussion. "The railroad will be quite a boon to our little town, and quite a convenience for you ranchers."

Anderson studied Wes's face as he spoke. "It should certainly simplify getting the stock to market," Wes replied. "The increased cost of shipping should be offset by the improved condition of the animals when they reach their destination."

He certainly sounded as if he knew the cattle business. Katherine watched Anderson's reaction. The attorney nodded, but Katherine could not tell if he was agreeing with what Wes said, or if he was being positive about Wes himself.

She jumped slightly when Wes turned to her, leaned down, and cupped her bare elbow in his big warm palm. "More sherry, dear?"

She looked at her empty glass with surprise. When had she finished it? "Please." She didn't like the taste of the wine, but it did make her stomach feel warm and seemed to help soothe her nerves. He set his drink back on the mantle as he refilled hers. She noticed his glass was still half full. He didn't appear to be much of a drinker.

The men talked for a while longer and sipped at their drinks. Many of his clients were ranchers and Mr. Anderson was knowledgeable about the cattle business. He asked several questions about running the Rocking H that Wes had no difficulty answering. Katherine bit the inside of her lip, forcing herself not to jump into the conversation. It was Wes who had to meet the lawyer's approval, and he alone should respond.

Katherine found it very difficult to keep quiet, but for the most part she agreed with everything Wes said. She breathed a sigh of relief when Consuela appeared in the doorway to announce that dinner was ready. She hoped it would be easier to keep quiet while she was eating.

Wes escorted Katherine right past her usual place at the head of the table, to the seat that would put her with her back to the kitchen door. This had been her mother's place at the table. He indicated to Mr. Anderson to take the place opposite Katherine. Wes pulled her chair out for her and waited until she was seated to help push her chair into the table. Without warning he leaned over the back of her chair and planted a warm kiss on the spot where her neck and shoulder joined. She swung her head around to stare at him, and he placed a quick kiss on her lips before he spoke. "You look very beautiful tonight."

"Thank you." Her voice sounded breathy and she knew that if she looked down at the front of her dress she would see the start of a blush that probably reached all the way up to color her cheeks.

"You do look lovely tonight, Katherine," Mr. Anderson held up his glass in a salute to her. "To your marriage."

She joined the toast and held her glass up while she nodded and murmured another thank you to the attorney. When she looked at Wes he winked at her. She felt elated. After tonight, the ranch was hers. She was glad she had chosen the gold dress, for this would be a night to celebrate.

Consuela came through the door from the kitchen carrying a platter holding a beautiful roast of beef. She set the platter down in front of Wes, and he thanked her. He stood and carved the meat as Consuela brought other steaming dishes from the kitchen. Mashed potatoes, gravy, carrots, and fresh rolls completed the table. It was a wonderful-looking meal. To Katherine's surprise, she had a huge appetite. She had thought she might be too nervous to eat.

After Wes finished carving and serving the beef, he took a bottle off the sideboard. It was Mrs. Moody's wine. He filled Katherine's glass, then Mr. Anderson's, then his own.

Before he sat down he raised his glass and looked at Katherine. "Now it's my turn. To my beautiful wife." Mr. Anderson stood and lifted his wineglass in her direction with a smile. Katherine just stared at Wes for a moment, knowing she was blushing again. He was playing the role of loving husband to perfection. They all drank and the men sat down. Katherine liked Mrs. Moody's wine much better than the sherry she had drunk before dinner. She relaxed and enjoyed the food.

Wes was the perfect host. He kept their glasses filled, guided the conversation, and made sure they had enough to eat. The food was delicious, and the three of them finished the bottle of wine. Consuela brought in a beautiful chocolate cake for dessert, along with fresh coffee. The meal had been festive, the conversation interesting, and Katherine knew they had been successful at their charade. Wes had played his part well, and the attorney didn't seem to notice how nervous she had been.

Just as they were finishing their coffee, Katherine heard Hannah cry from upstairs. "Excuse me." She stood and the room seemed to tilt just a bit. She quickly exited the dining room. She had caught the look of amusement on Wes's face when she stood, and she knew that if she looked at him she might start to laugh. Mrs. Moody's wine was more potent than she had realized.

Hannah needed another drink of water and a kiss. Her forehead felt just a little warm, and Katherine tucked her in. The little girl was asleep before Katherine left her room.

Mr. Anderson and Wes were on the front porch smoking cigars when she came downstairs. The attorney was in the process of saying good night when she went out onto the porch. The night had turned very cold. He thanked them for the dinner and said he would see to the filing of the new deed.

The news should have made Katherine very happy, but her joy was overshadowed by the thought that now Wes could leave. There was no reason for her to keep him here any longer. As soon as the sheriff of Dennison was satisfied that Wes was not one of the rustlers, and his name was cleared, he would be heading back to Texas.

They waved good-bye to Mr. Anderson and returned to the front room. The warmth of the fire felt good.

"Katherine?" She noticed Wes used her formal name instead of calling her Katie. She liked the nickname when it came from him.

"Yes?" She brought her thoughts back to the present. Katherine heaved a big sigh of relief. It was done.

The ranch was hers. Somehow she didn't feel as good about it as she thought she would.

"Anything wrong?" Wes watched her with concern.

"No, everything's fine. Thank you, you were very convincing."

"It wasn't too difficult." He leaned toward her and she knew he was going to kiss her. Just then she heard something drop in the kitchen.

She backed away from Wes. "I better see if I can help Consuela."

"Come back when you're finished. I want to talk to you."

Her stomach knotted up. He was going to tell her that he was going to leave. She had the silly urge to go up to bed and not talk to him, as if that might keep him here for a while longer. "As soon as I help Consuela."

Katherine hurried into the kitchen. Consuela was just finishing drying the dishes. "Consuela, dinner was wonderful. Thank you."

Consuela gave Katherine a tired smile. "It was good?"

The Mexican woman had been very quiet about Wes and why she had brought him here, but Katherine knew her housekeeper. Consuela probably knew what the situation was all about. "Very well. You look tired. Is there anything I can do?"

"No senora. All is done. I will go to bed now. I think I have the same throat as *mija*."

"Consuela, I'm sorry. You worked so hard today. Please, stay in bed in the morning. I'll be up with Hannah." The woman did look very tired. She nodded and walked into her little room beside the kitchen. Katherine watched her with concern and hoped that she would feel better tomorrow.

The kitchen was spotless, and Katherine had no excuse not to return to the living room. Wes had built up the fire, and turned the two overstuffed chairs around so they could sit and enjoy the warmth of the flames. He had taken his boots off and he propped his stocking feet on the bricks of the hearth.

He handed her a glass half full of amber liquid. "What's the matter?" He gestured to the chair and she sat down.

"Consuela is a little under the weather. I think she has a touch of what Hannah has."

Immediately a worried look showed on his face. He turned in his chair to face her. "Hannah's ill? Should we send for a doctor?"

She was pleased he showed concern for her child and sought to reassure him. "No. A little fever and a sore throat," she laughed. "Didn't you notice how quiet it's been around here?" Then she recalled the scene in the kitchen when she told him to stay away from her daughter. "I want to apologize again for what I said to you before about Hannah. I didn't know you then."

"I was angry, but you were in the right. You couldn't take a chance." He smiled and took a sip from his glass.

She held her glass up to the light of the fire. "What is this?"

Wes took a sip, obviously enjoying the liquor. "Brandy. Your father knew how to stock his cupboard."

She took a sip, and the stuff burned a warm little trail down to her stomach.

His voice broke in on her thoughts. "What will you tell Anderson when I go home?"

His question caused a stab of pain in the region of her heart at the thought of spending her days without him. "I'll tell him you had to go back to Texas on business.

People will assume you didn't like me well enough to come back."

He held his glass up to the fire and swirled the contents. "Only a fool would believe that. I don't think Anderson's a fool."

"It doesn't matter what people think. I'll have the ranch. I stopped worrying about what people thought a long time ago."

Wes didn't say anything for a moment, he just stared into the fire. Then he turned his head and looked at her. "Because of Gerald? Was he from around here?"

Katherine took another sip of brandy. "No, I met him in Chicago, when I was going to school. He was a teacher of English literature."

She turned and looked at him. He had the same look on his face he had had when he had kissed her senseless on the way home from Dennison. That look held her entranced and made her feel as if he were touching her in places she didn't have names for.

Without a word he got up and set his glass on the hearth, reached out and took the glass out of her hand to set it beside his. In one fluid movement he leaned toward her, took her hand, and pulled her out of her chair, wrapping his arm around her waist.

Tipping her back against his arm, he looked her in the eyes. "Do you have any idea how beautiful you are?" Without waiting for her to answer, he lowered his mouth to hers and kissed her, so gently their lips barely touched. Then he increased the pressure, and ran his tongue against her lips.

"Open your mouth and let me in," he murmured against her lips. She obeyed his instruction, with delightful results. He tasted of brandy and chocolate, an intimate touch that made her tingle.

She did a little exploring with her own tongue, and heard him groan from deep down in his chest.

"I've never seen your hair down." He reached up and pulled the pins from her hair, and she felt it unwind from its knot and cascade around her shoulders. He ran his fingers through her hair to her scalp and held her head still while his lips continued to move over hers.

Her head swam with the giddy feelings she got when he kissed her. She could stay like this forever, wrapped in his arms, kissing him. The fire warmed her from the outside, while Wes warmed her on the inside.

He turned and lowered both of them into one of the armchairs, draping her over his big body. His mouth continued to coax and tease. His lips left hers and moved across her cheek to her ear, and then down her neck, where he paused and nibbled for a moment. "You have perfect ears." The sensation of his warm breath and tongue was so heavenly she braced her hands against his chest and tilted her head to the side, to give him easier access.

While he continued to kiss her, he shifted her so that the arm he had around her waist could reach the underside of her breast. He rubbed his thumb back and forth across the fabric of her dress, and she could feel the heat from the friction against her sensitive skin. His free hand worked at the buttons on the front of her bodice.

She knew exactly what he was about, and she made no move to stop him. It just felt too good. She had married the man, and she wanted some memories of him to hold dear when he left. Just this one time she wanted to feel alive, to feel wanted.

Katherine ran her hands up his chest to his collar. As he unbuttoned her dress, she did the same to his shirt.

She wanted to touch his skin. She had imagined what it might feel like to touch him like this a hundred times. After she had his shirt unbuttoned, she spread it open and pushed her fingers through the hair on his chest until her fingertips rested against the warm, hard muscle. Her fingers tingled with sensation. The feeling was even better than she had imagined.

He had her bodice unbuttoned to the waist, and as he untied the drawstring on her camisole, and pulled it down, he kissed her skin as he exposed it inch by inch, until her breasts were bare.

His eyes never left her as he shifted her higher against the arm of the chair. "You're so beautiful." He traced around her nipples with his fingertip. "Hold still." Her head fell back as he took one of her nipples in his mouth. She arched her back as a shaft of pure pleasure shot from the spot where he suckled, down to the core of her, between her legs.

When she felt his hand pull at the hem of her skirt, instead of stopping him in a panic as she had before, she shifted her weight in the chair, granting him access. This time she wanted him to touch her, to make love to her. She had married him, and even the risk of another child could not stop her now.

She couldn't bear the thought that he might leave her forever and go back to his home in Texas without sharing this experience with her. She let herself be swept away with passion for him, and felt delightfully powerless against the feelings he was causing with his lips and hands.

His fingers caressed the inside of her thigh while his mouth moved back and forth across her nipples. She could feel the swell of his manhood under her bottom, and she shifted against him, pleased when his mouth left her nipple long enough for him to moan. "If you keep that up, I'll carry you up those stairs and into my bed."

She had to gasp for air in order to speak. "Is that a threat or a promise? If you don't touch me soon, I'll go crazy." She grasped the wrist of the hand he had run up under her skirts, and guided his fingers to exactly where she wanted them. Then she arched up into his hand again and it was her turn to moan as his fingers stroked her needy flesh.

She felt his breath catch in his chest. "Oh, God," he murmured. Without warning he stood up and took her with him.

For a moment, the room spun dizzily and she threw her arms around his neck. He took a few long strides to get to the stairs and then climb them. She felt secure in his arms and pulled his head down for a long kiss that involved a tangle of tongues. He hesitated for a moment at the top of the stairs, then he turned and carried her into her room, kicking the door closed with his foot. He set her on her feet by the bed, and she immediately reached out and pulled the shirt tails out of his pants, then began working on the buttons of his trousers.

He finished the buttons on the front of her dress, and pulled the sleeves down her arms, pushing the garment down past her waist and onto the floor. She worked at the tapes of her petticoat while he shucked his pants and in less than a moment, they stood facing each other, both of them gloriously naked, his throbbing manhood sticking proudly out from his body.

Katherine stepped into his arms, and their bodies met, bare skin to bare skin, his stiff manhood thrust up against her belly. She could feel him throb as she felt the beat of his heart against her. The texture of the hair on his chest rubbed against her sensitive nipples, and she reveled in the sensation.

She wanted him so badly she felt she could not wait, and when he pulled her down with him onto her bed, she went willingly. She rolled onto her back and he came up over her, poised, his knees gently parting her legs. She ran her hands down his back to his buttocks, and pulled him against her, lifting her hips and gasping at the sensation of him sliding into her ready, waiting body.

She savored the throbbing feelings as his body joined with hers, filling her. He went perfectly still for a moment and she pressed her head back into the mattress and looked up into his eyes. He gave her an intense look, and she smiled up at him, then she brought her hips back down ever so slightly and thrust back up against him where their bodies joined. He let out a low groan and drew back, answering her movement by thrusting into her. She ran her hands up his muscled back, and met him move for move. He set the pace, increasing the speed of his thrusts until she thought she might scream with the pleasure of it. Her senses started to fall away, until all she could think about, all she could focus on was the spot where their two bodies joined. She felt the pressure build and build within her, until she thought she might explode. And then it seemed she did, shattering into a thousand pieces. When she could think again, she marveled at the wonder of it.

He gave a final huge thrust into her body and then he stiffened, shuddered, and moaned into her hair. He took her face between his large warm hands, and kissed her very gently on the lips, then put his cheek to hers and sighed. He gathered her into his arms, their bodies still joined, and they lay there for a few moments, his form atop hers, sharing each other's warmth. Finally, as their breathing returned to normal, he rolled to the side, taking her with him, cuddling her up against him.

She wanted to say something, but she couldn't think what. Her head felt warm and fuzzy, and her limbs seemed to be made of jelly. She sighed and snuggled up against him, feeling safe and very thoroughly loved.

Wes shifted so that Katherine's head rested against his shoulder. He could feel her breath stir the hair on his chest. She felt so very right there in his arms. He had suspected any woman with the spunk and courage Katie possessed would prove to be an armful in bed, and he hadn't been disappointed. She had shown him what she wanted, and this had been the best bedplay he had ever had.

She sighed and snuggled closer. He pulled his arms tightly around her, holding her, loving the way she felt, the way she smelled. Gradually her body relaxed and her breathing deepened, and he knew she was asleep. He also knew he loved this woman like he had never loved anyone before. He watched her while she slept, and wondered what he would say to her in the morning, wondered if he could find words to express the way he felt just now. She said she didn't want a husband, but she would have to change her mind, because he wasn't leaving.

Just thinking about her aroused him, and holding her like this made him hard and wanting. He pulled the quilt down her sleeping form until her bare breasts were exposed. She fumbled for the bedcovers in her sleep, trying to pull them up against the chill in the room. He held them away, and propped himself on one elbow, holding her in the crook of his arm. He bent over her and drew one of her nipples into his mouth, sucking on the tip of her breast. She moaned in her sleep, and as he suckled her, he ran his hand down her belly, and into the nest of curls covering her mound.

Slowly she came awake and he felt her hands move up his arms and around his neck, holding him to her breasts. His fingers slid into her wet silky warmth, mimicking what his body had done to her earlier. Her knees parted as she welcomed him. He drew his hand back and turned her on her side, away from him, staying her sleepy protest with murmured promises as he moved his hand up behind her knee, pushing her leg up gently, until her female flesh was open to him.

He stroked her as he positioned himself behind her, then slid into her waiting warmth. He used his hands to fondle her breasts and her core, while his manhood pulled in and out of her silky sheath.

When her hips began to buck wildly, he grasped her by the waist and rode with her to a roaring climax. He lay, still inside her, and wrapped his arms around her, pulling her up against the warmth of his chest, her head resting on his shoulder. She murmured and settled against him, and he felt her relax as she drifted back to sleep.

He began to feel drowsy, and he decided reluctantly to leave her and return to his own bed. He pulled away from her warm body, being careful not to waken her. He found his pants and shirt, and slipped them on. He couldn't find one of his stockings, but he gave up looking in the dark.

Without his warmth to cuddle against, Katherine had rolled into a ball under the covers. He pulled the quilt up high over her, and tucked it around her sleeping form, then he kissed the top of her head and went to his room, and into his cold empty bed.

*   *   *

Katherine woke in the morning with a headache, and a driving thirst. She remembered the wine and the brandy from the night before, and then she remembered what they had done after the brandy, and she stretched like a cat in the sunshine. Wes must have gone from her room in the night, because the other side of the bed felt cold. Not knowing quite what she was going to say to him when she saw him, she was relieved he had left before the house awakened.

She squashed the beginning of a regret, and decided firmly that she would not be sorry for what she had done. Indeed, last night had been an incredible experience, and she refused to make excuses, even to herself. If she had to face consequences, she would do that without regret.

When word had reached her that Gerald had died, the pain had been so great that she had decided she would not hazard having feelings for anyone again. The cost had been too high.

Last night had changed her mind. She had felt so alive in his arms, and here in her bed. More alive, and certainly more complete than she ever had before. At the thought of the things Wes had done to her, her nipples hardened and she felt a tingling throb in the very core of her womanhood. Last night she had thought she might die of the pleasure of it.

She sat up and realized she was naked. When she peeked over the side of the mattress and saw her clothes all over the floor, she blushed.

Katherine stumbled out of bed and poured a drink of water from the pitcher on the wash stand. Quickly she put on clean underwear, washed her face, and cleaned her teeth, then brushed her hair back and twisted it into a knot at the back of her head. There were no hairpins on her dressing table, and she remembered his hands in her hair last night. The floor in the parlor would be the place where she would find them. With one hand holding her hair, she searched the top drawer for pins.

She hurried into a riding skirt and a clean shirtwaist, then scooped up the clothes from the floor. Underneath her petticoat, she saw one of Wes's stockings. He must have missed finding it in the dark. She grabbed it off the floor and stuffed it into the pocket of her skirt.

Katherine tiptoed down the hall and peeked in on Hannah, and found her daughter still sound asleep. When she passed Wes's door she was tempted to look in on him too, but she decided it would be too embarrassing if he should prove not to be asleep. Heaven knew she had certainly acted wanton last night, and she wasn't sure exactly what she would say to him when she did see him.

She had the most peculiar feelings about spending the night with him. After all, they were legally married. Perhaps she felt this way because they hadn't lived as man and wife, and Wes didn't even remember getting married to her.

Katherine went down to the kitchen to start the coffee and breakfast so that Consuela could sleep in this morning. She glanced around the front room, and noted that the overstuffed chairs were pulled in front of the fireplace, just where they had left them. She pushed them back into their usual places, and felt warm all over when she recalled the things Wes had done to her in that chair in front of the fire last night. She picked up the two glasses, still fragrant with brandy, from the hearth and carried them to the kitchen.

Katherine decided some coffee would go a long way toward helping her get rid of the persistent little headache that still plagued her. She hoped it was a sign of her monthly, and not just the wine from last night. She knew all too well the consequences of being with a man.

Katherine slipped on her jacket on the porch, took a basket, and headed out the back door to the chicken coop. The cold morning wind slapped her in the face when she stepped outside. Gray clouds hung heavy on the eastern horizon. They would probably see snow before nightfall. When she got to the coop, all the hens were still huddled protectively over their nests, and she had to shoo them out to collect enough eggs for breakfast.

Katherine stepped out of the henhouse and saw Wes coming out of the cookshack. He spotted her, and made a beeline for where she stood. She clutched the basket of warm eggs to her chest, experiencing a moment of awkward hesitation.

He didn't look the least bit reluctant as he approached, and that put her at ease. He tipped his hat back and smiled down at her. "Morning." Then he grasped the collar of her jacket in both hands and gave her a quick hard kiss, right there outside the chicken coop where anyone could see them. When he let go of her she almost dropped the basket of eggs.

"Someone might see," she protested feebly.

He grinned at her. "So?"

She smiled at him, loving the possessive sound of his answer, feeling warm all over and pretty wonderful, too. Her hesitation vanished. "How are you?" Her voice sounded breathy.

He leaned forward until she could feel his breath like a gentle caress on her face. His voice sounded low and throaty. "Well, I'd have to say I'm fine. In fact, I feel pretty special this morning."

Her heart went racing, and she knew she blushed, she could feel the heat on her cheeks. For a moment, she thought he might kiss her again. She groped for something to say. "Have you had breakfast?"

"Yup. 'Bout twenty minutes ago. Steak and eggs. Why are you in the chicken coop?"

"Last night I told Consuela to sleep in. I'm afraid she's coming down with Hannah's bad throat." She started to walk back toward the house and he fell in beside her.

Wes took the basket from her hands and she felt him staring at her. "How do you feel?"

She tucked her hands in the pockets of her jacket before she gave him a sidelong glance and answered his question. "I'd have to say I feel pretty special, too."

He stopped her with a hand on her shoulder, turning her toward him and studying her face. "You look a little pale."

She laughed, then brought her hand up to catch a cough that took her by surprise. "I think I drank too much wine and brandy last night. I'll be all right as soon as I get a little coffee."

They both turned their heads when they heard his name being called from the barn. Hannibal waved and motioned to Wes. With a look of regret, he handed her the basket of eggs. "I told Hannibal I'd help him this morning. I'll see you later."

She headed into the house, left her jacket on the porch, and entered the welcome warmth of the kitchen. Hannah was just wandering in through the kitchen door. Katherine set the eggs on the dry sink.

Katherine eyed her daughter's pale little face. "Well, little one, how do you feel this morning?"

The child heaved a dramatic sigh. "Not fine."

Katherine scooped her up and gave her a kiss on the cheek. "How about some breakfast?"

Hannah looked around the kitchen. "Where's Consuela?"

"She's still in her bed. She doesn't feel very well either."

Consuela appeared at the door in a wrapper, looking very tired. "I can cook, senora."

"Nonsense." Katherine was perfectly capable of fixing a meal.

Hannah held her arms out to Consuela, who took the child from her arms. Katherine had vague memories of being carried that way many years ago by the Mexican woman. "You two go into Consuela's bed and stay warm." She shooed them through the door, then fixed a tray with tea and toast. Hannah was enthralled with the idea of eating in bed.

Katherine returned to the kitchen and decided against cooking just for herself. All she really wanted was coffee. Her throat felt a little raw and she didn't like the thought of swallowing food.

Consuela and Hannah settled into Consuela's bed for a nap. Katherine decided to spend some time in the office and work for a while on the books. Later she might ride out with some of the hands and bring the bulk of the herd closer in to the barn. She sat in front of her books, but accomplished nothing. All she could think about was what had happened between her and Wes last night.

She gave up on the office work and attended to tedious chores all day, always on the lookout for Wes. She caught sight of him several times as he worked around the barn, finishing the painting and nailing patches to the roof of the cookshack, but there were always other people around, and they had no privacy to talk to one another. Katherine yearned to be with him, and wondered if being apart bothered Wes as much as it bothered her—wondered if she would be able to convince him to stay in Montana.

Katherine had not been able to coax Consuela and Hannah to eat supper, and she was becoming concerned about them. They were both running mild fevers, and just wanted to stay in bed. Katherine tucked her daughter in with Consuela for the night. The room Consuela occupied off the kitchen was much warmer than Hannah's bedroom, and her daughter would be more comfortable there, especially if she kicked her covers off as she slept.

Katherine returned to her office, and made plans for the spring. If the price of beef held—and the winter was not too severe, so she wasn't forced to spend more than she had planned on feed for the stock—she would make a nice profit. Placing the pen back in the inkwell, she rubbed her temples, wishing away her nagging headache.

She heard someone come in through the back door and knew it must be Wes. Her heart started to pound at the thought of seeing him. A few moments later she didn't even have to look up to know he was standing in the doorway.

15

Katherine glanced up from her desk. Wes leaned casually against the door frame. The look he gave her heated her blood. An expression of pure need, echoed instantly by the same feelings in her body. She didn't say a word as she stood and walked around the desk, her eyes never leaving his. Silently he waited for her with open arms, and she walked into his embrace and tipped her head back, aching for his kiss.

Wes didn't seem to need any prompting as to what she wanted, what she needed, what she felt she might die for if she didn't get. He kissed her hard, his mouth opening over hers, his tongue probing.

She ran her hands up his broad chest until her arms were twined around his neck, her hands buried in his black hair. As he deepened the kiss, his arms tightened around her, pulling her up against him until she straddled his thigh, her toes no longer touching the floor.

He pulled his mouth away from hers, and sighed into the hair above her ear. His warm breath sent chills along her scalp. "I feel like a drowning man, and your kiss is the air. I thought I'd die today thinking about you and not being able to do this. You don't know what it took to stay away from the house."

She cut off any more conversation with another kiss. If she could she would climb inside him, that was how close to him she wanted to be. She rubbed up against his leg, and she could feel his body straining the front of his denims. She knew she was ready for him, here, now, in her office. The intensity of how she wanted him amazed her, and she pulled back, trying to regain her equilibrium.

She saw the look of concern on his beautiful face, and loved him for it. He gripped her arms, then ran his fingers down to catch her hands. "What's the matter?"

She stared down at their joined hands for a moment, then looked up at him as she answered. "I, well, I've never felt like this." She lowered her gaze to their hands again. "I see you, and I get the most unladylike urges."

He laughed and pulled her back into his arms. "I plan to accommodate your urges." He nibbled up her neck to her ear, and whispered into it. "Where are Hannah and Consuela?"

She had to think for a moment, he was distracting her so much. "Asleep. I put them to bed in Consuela's room."

He started at her waist and ran his hands up and down her sides, stroking the outer curve of her breasts as his fingers moved over her ribs. Again her legs threatened to turn to jelly, and she wrapped her arms back around his neck.

"Then I suppose I should put you to bed, too." He pulled away from her long enough to blow out the lamp on her desk, then he kissed her all the way up the stairs.

She led him to her bed, and he pushed her into the middle of the mattress and followed her down.

Katherine unbuttoned her shirtwaist and skirt and had her outer clothes off in record time. She noticed that he was even faster. While she worked on the buttons of her camisole, he untied her bloomers and slid them down her legs, kissing her skin as he went, leaving a scalding trail.

Her fingers turned clumsy. All she could concentrate on was what he was doing to her belly with his mouth. Finally she got the buttons undone, and he leaned up and nudged the fabric aside and took one of her nipples into his mouth, while his hand worked its way down, and into the nest of brown curls between her thighs. Shafts of lightning shot through her limbs and her legs fell open, and she tugged at him to come over her.

"Not yet, darlin'. I've still got a little bit of tasting to do." His mouth closed over her other breast and he suckled until she thought she might go crazy with wanting him. She stroked her hand down his hard chest and flat stomach, through the hair on his groin and closed her hand around him.

He groaned and let go of her nipple. "Ah, not fair." His breathing changed as she stroked and fondled him.

"Come here, please, now." Again she urged him over her. His fingers inside her were making her wild for him.

"It's your turn." He startled her when he rolled to his back and pulled her over on top of him so she straddled his hips. Cupping his hands around her buttocks, he lifted her over him, easing her down, slowly, until the tip of his penis entered her. She braced her hands on his chest to steady herself. The length of his shaft slid up inside her and she almost called out with the pleasure of it.

"Oh, my," was all she could say as she settled on him.

She held still for a moment, savoring the incredible feeling of having him inside her, then his hands urged her to move, and she raised up a bit on her knees, then settled back over him. Nothing had ever felt as good as this. When she repeated the motion again and again, he let go of her bottom, and brought his hands around to her breasts, where he rubbed her nipples with his fingers until she thought she might go mad. He pulled her down and kissed her, his tongue mimicking in her mouth what his shaft was doing in her sheath. Then he took one of her nipples in his mouth and sucked on her.

She lost all control, bucking and riding on him like a wild creature. Her world shattered into a thousand golden shards, and she collapsed against his chest, gasping for breath. His chest heaved under her, and she knew he had hit the same heights she had. He stroked her back as their breathing returned to normal, and she relaxed under his warm hands.

As she slipped into sleep she thought she heard him whisper into her hair, "I'll never leave you. Never."

16

Katherine pushed the ledger away from herself in exasperation and stood and stretched. It was obvious she would not get any work done this morning. Every time she tried to add a column of figures, her mind strayed to last night, and Wes's whispered promise never to leave. He had been gone from the bed again this morning when she had awakened, and she had almost convinced herself that she hadn't dreamed those words.

Her face warmed as she thought about the way their evening had ended. They had done what she had been dreaming about all day, and she had enjoyed every moment of it.

Katherine rubbed at her temples. The headache that had plagued her yesterday had only gotten worse, and her throat ached. It looked as if she wouldn't escape the malady that had both Hannah and Consuela in bed. To her relief, her monthly flow had started this morning, too. All in all, she felt lousy.

She hated being sick, there was just too much to be done around the ranch with winter coming on. Katherine decided that if she had to stay in tomorrow because of a cold, she would get as much done as she could today.

She walked from her office to the front room, stopping to gaze through the front window. Low black clouds hugged the horizon, clouds that threatened bad weather. Probably snow, she figured. They had been fortunate so far to have a mild fall, and the herd was in good shape. She wanted to bring the animals even closer to the ranch, so that if this turned into a really bad storm, the hands could hitch up the hay sled, and take feed to the stock.

Katherine went to check on Hannah and Consuela. She found Consuela in the kitchen fixing the noonday meal.

"I thought you were going to stay in bed." She worried that Consuela's feelings of devotion to the family would endanger the woman's health.

"I am feeling much better. *Mija* still sleeps. I will make some broth and go back to bed."

"Don't do too much. I can go and eat with the men." Katherine liked the idea of seeing Wes at meals. When Consuela felt better, Wes could eat at the house.

Consuela looked horrified that Katherine would even consider eating in the cookshack. Katherine was aware of Consuela's opinion of Poison Joe's cooking. "I will cook for you," she insisted. Her tone brooked no argument.

Katherine gave in with a shrug. "I'm going to change so I can ride out this afternoon." She knew she would need her winter underwear if she was to remain comfortable out of doors. The temperature was dropping steadily.

Consuela looked concerned at her statement. "The weather will turn, senora." Consuela's joints had proved to be an excellent indicator of the storms over the years. On top of the sore throat, she must have aching knees, too.

"I won't be out long. We just need to bring the herd closer to the barn." Katherine went upstairs. From her bedroom window she watched the sky darkening as she changed.

She ate quickly, and in spite of Consuela's disgruntled attitude, saw that the woman got back in bed, and left Hannah in her capable care.

On the back porch she donned her heavy red plaid jacket, and checked the pockets to make sure she had her gloves.

She stopped at the barn, and let Hannibal know she needed Dynamite, then went to the cookshack to gather some of the hands. She stuck her head in the door, expecting to find Wes, and was disappointed when he was not among the hired hands finishing their meal. Gibby was also missing.

She knocked on the doorjamb to get their attention, and several of the men stood when they noticed her in the doorway. "Finish up, boys. We need to bring the herd off the east pasture closer to the barn. We've got weather coming." She retraced her steps to the barn, where Hannibal had her mount ready.

Curiosity got the better of her, and she had to ask, "Hannibal, have you seen Gibby or Mr. Merrick this morning?"

"Yes, ma'am, they ate early and rode out to the line shacks to make sure they was stocked before the storm." Katherine thanked the bent old man and took the reins of her horse from him.

Katherine slipped her foot into the stirrup and swung her leg over the saddle. She had her suede riding skirts especially made so she could ride astride with minimum fuss and maximum modesty.

As soon as she left the shelter of the barn, a biting wind coming in from the northeast stung her cheeks. Earlier she had thought the storm would hit around suppertime. She amended her forecast, and realized they had only a few hours to move the herd, or get caught in the open. As a matter of pride in her ability to run the ranch, she didn't intend to lose any stock in the first storm.

She called to the hands who were at the corral catching their mounts. "I'll go ahead. Head across the stream and up into the hills. I don't want any of the stock in those ravines when the snow hits, or they'll get caught. Drive them down across the stream, and have someone ride the perimeter until it gets dark." They nodded and she knew they understood what she wanted. Not one of them would waste words when a nod of the head would do.

Katherine rode over her land, eager to be out even in what promised to be miserable weather. She headed east, across the stream, at a fast clip as a few flakes of snow fell. In the springtime when the snows melted, the water could become a danger to cross. Now it barely came halfway up Dynamite's legs.

The wind became stronger and she pulled her bandanna up to protect her nose and mouth from the cold air. Turning her collar up around her aching throat, she pulled the brim of her hat down to shield her eyes. The chill made her eyes water and numbed her cheeks. She figured it would take about a half hour to reach the hills, and another hour to gather the animals they had moved there recently, and then a second hour to drive them back. With luck, she should be back at the house by late afternoon. Then she planned to build up the fire in her room and crawl into bed.

The first swirling flakes of snow blew into her face before she even made it to the hills. The going was slower than she expected as she rode into the wind, and the cattle had already started to move into the ravines for shelter. With practiced skill, she traveled up the first ravine she came to and guided Dynamite around behind the animals and drove them into the open. By the time she had routed seven head out of the first ravine, the hired hands had caught up with her. She turned the cattle over to two riders who would start to move them so the beasts couldn't return to the sheltering ravines.

She had to shout to be heard above the howling wind. "Jake, Tully, you go on east as far as the property line, and start there. Drive them toward the barn." The two men nodded and, shoulders hunched, turned their mounts into the wind.

"Olsen, go with them." The cowhand took off after his buddies, who had all but disappeared into the swirling snow.

She had to yell to be heard over the wind. "Wade, Danny, you clean out that deep ravine over by the hills. I'll finish here. I want them west of the stream." They tipped their hats and headed out to follow her directions. She brought a gloved hand up to her aching throat.

Katherine watched the riders take off, then headed back into ravine. Instead of finding respite from the wind, the low cut in the land acted like a funnel and intensified the storm. She found several head of cattle, including two half-grown calves, their backs to the wind, huddled about one hundred yards up the draw. The snow had turned to sleet, and cut at her exposed skin. She took off her hat, and waved it in the air, yelling at the beasts to move. Instead they huddled closer together. She pulled Dynamite in close to the cattle, and took her rope off her saddle, smacking the cows and steers on their hindquarters to get them moving.

The main group started down toward the mouth of the ravine, but one calf broke and got past her, running deeper into the cut. She'd have to go back for him after she herded the other animals out to the waiting drover. The sleet was so heavy, she wasn't even sure who the man was.

They might have to give up sooner than she had anticipated, and come back later, after the storm had blown by. When she was sure he had control of the cattle and they wouldn't bolt back up the ravine, she went after the calf.

The critter had worked his way back into an area at the head of the gully. The rock there was already covered with ice, and the footing was too treacherous for her horse. She dismounted and let his reins hang. Hunched against the wind, she worked her way on foot up behind the calf. He rolled his eyes at her and let out a pitiful wail.

Her head ached miserably, and she lost her patience. "You stupid beast, move. Get going." Katherine waved her hat, and tried to shoo the animal out, but he refused to budge. He was small enough that if she could get hold of his ear, perhaps with a good tug, she could get him moving. She came up beside him and just as she grabbed for him, he bolted. She lost her footing on the icy rocks, flailing her arms in a desperate attempt to regain her balance. Her booted feet flew out from under her and she went down hard, knocking the wind from her lungs, and smacking the back of her head against a rock. She felt the pain and saw a burst of stars inside her head, then everything went black.

*   *   *

Wes and Gibby fought the wind and sleet all the way back from the last line shack on the west range. The place had been in pretty good shape, so all they had to do was drop off the supplies, fix one of the hinges on the door, and close the place up tight.

Sleet hit him full in the face. Wes could tell the storm was going to be a bad one. Even a fellow from down in Texas could see that. He looked forward to getting up to the house and having a hot cup of coffee. His hands and face were numb with cold. Conversation with Gibby was impossible, even if the other man had been given to conversation. Wes hunched down in his jacket.

He pictured Katie in her office. He would talk her into closing her ledger for a while and sitting and talking with him. He had something very important to tell her.

He couldn't say exactly when his feelings for her had changed from admiration to love, but he knew now that there was no doubt that he did love her. He had always thought she was pretty, from the first time he had been able to peel his eyes open after she brought him into her home. Her clear brown eyes and lustrous brown hair had appealed to him from the beginning.

And he admired her spunk, too. Taking on the ranch by herself, and then marrying a man she thought was an outlaw to keep it. She defied the sheriff in Dennison and saved his hide. As soon as he could get his name cleared, he wanted to marry her. Again.

This time he would ask her on bended knee, then buy her a ring. He wanted to be able to remember the ceremony. Wes wanted to adopt Hannah, he wanted both of them to have his name. He would never ask her to leave her ranch to go back to Texas. He had become used to the idea of making his home here, in Montana. Despite the weather, it was fine cattle country.

His thoughts turned to last night, and his body ached for her. He wondered if he could coax her upstairs and into bed in the middle of the day. He wanted to make love to her and watch her. He wanted to see her passion for him in the daylight.

They rode into the barn, and the warm air caressed his face like a welcoming lover. What a relief to be out of the wind. Wes dismounted stiffly, peeled off his gloves, and rubbed his face to wipe away the sleet. Ice had formed on his mustache, tiny crystals embedded in the hair. Katie's mutt, Hamlet, came to him and sat at his feet, leaning against his legs.

Hannibal hurried over to take their horses. "You all see Miz Holman?"

Wes heard the wrangler's question. Alarmed, he swiveled around to face the old man. "Katie's out riding?" He couldn't imagine why she might have gone out in the storm.

"Yup. Left about an hour ago to drive in some stock. Took some of the hands with her before it got so bad. Blew up quicker than she expected, I imagine."

And it was going from bad to worse. "Where'd she go?"

"I heard her tell the fellows to head across the stream to the east range and pry the cows out of those ravines."

She had no business being out in this kind of weather. "I'll need a fresh horse."

Hannibal nodded and went to one of the stalls in the back of the barn.

Gibby looked surprised. "You going after her?"

"You bet I am." Wes wondered why that should surprise the foreman.

"You best not be telling her to come on in. She holds to a lot of pride being able to hang out as long as the last man in weather like this."

Wes listened to what Gibby had to say. "I'll remember that." But it wouldn't stop him from going out and helping her.

Hannibal came back leading a grulla and gestured to the ugly little horse as he spoke. "Don't pay no never mind that she looks like a plug, there's no end to her bottom."

"I don't care what she looks like, if you say she'll last, that's good enough for me." Wes stripped the saddle and bridle off his mount and transferred it to the mousy brown animal in record time.

Gibby removed the saddle from his own horse as he spoke. "Most likely they're on their way back. Got more sense than to stay out in that." He jerked his head in the direction of the barn door.

Wes hoped the old foreman was right. He thanked Hannibal, mounted up, and headed for the door. Hannibal rolled the door back, and the cold wind hit Wes and stole his breath away. He hunched down on the ugly mud-colored horse and headed her toward the east. He had to go on pure instinct, because the sleet was so heavy he couldn't see a hundred yards in front of him. When he got to the stream, he made out three drovers and cattle coming toward him. None of the riders were small enough to be Katie. Between the howling wind and the noisy cattle, he had to wait until he was almost on top of them to shout.

He recognized Olsen. He cupped his hand and hollered at the big drover. "Where's Miz Holman?"

Olsen gestured over his shoulder. "They're back there." Wes raised his hand in a salute and moved past the herd.

After about fifteen minutes, he made out another group of riders driving cattle. Katie was not among them. The animals bawled and complained as they moved with the wind at their backs.

He repeated his question to Wade. "Where's Miz Holman?"

Wade shook his head and cupped his hands and shouted above the wind. "She must be headed back with Jake and Tully."

Wes felt uneasy. Jake and Tully had been riding with Olsen, and Katie wasn't with them. He grabbed the front of Wade's jacket and pulled him close so the young hand could hear him. "Where was she working?"

Wade thought for a moment before answering. "About in the middle of the hills. There's a deep ravine that runs back at an angle to the others."

"Anyone else still out there?" He hoped against hope that someone had remained behind with her.

"Nope. We're bringing up the tail." Wes took in the information and plowed through the wind past the riders.

It seemed to take forever to get to the hills. He headed for what he thought was the middle and prayed he was close to where he would find her. It was going to be difficult to find anyone in this weather. The tracks the drovers had made were already covered up by the sleet and wind.

When he got to the hills he turned east, peering into the wind. The sleet cut at his face. His fear for her safety caused a wave of anger to wash over him. What the hell business did she have to be out here by herself, anyway? Did she think a few more head of cattle—that could probably survive just fine on their own—were worth risking her life for?

He heard the calf before he saw him. The critter was all alone, bawling his head off. The hands must have missed him when they moved the stock.

Wes, his attention on the calf, almost missed Katie's horse. At first, his vision obscured by the sleet, he thought Dynamite was just another cow, further up the ravine. The animal stood with his back to the wind and his head down. The saddle was empty. Wes felt as if someone had punched him in the gut. He tried to concentrate on finding her, and tamp down the feeling of panic that rose like bile in his throat.

"Katie! Katie! Where are you?!" The wind ripped the words out of his mouth.

He urged his horse up the slippery, icy ground of the ravine, and grasped Dynamite's reins. Since he hadn't seen any sign of her on lower ground, he decided to try looking further up the ravine. He left her mount where he was.

He found he had to go slow over the treacherous ground, and his horse had a hard time finding her footing. He called Katie's name, knowing with the howl of the wind she would never hear him. He searched until his mount could go no further. The rocks under foot were covered with ice, and as slippery as glass.

As he turned his mount around, a patch of red caught his eye. He dismounted, and slowly made his way over to where she lay.

The lower half of her face was covered by a bandanna, and her hat was knocked askew, covering the top part of her face. He pulled her hat away and saw the skin on her cheeks showed blue with cold. He pulled his glove off and put his fingers down inside her collar, against her throat. He felt tears of relief form in his eyes when he detected the strong beat of her heart.

He yelled against the wailing wind. "Katie, Katie darlin' wake up." Her eyelids fluttered for a moment, but her eyes drifted closed.

He took off his other glove and felt with both hands along her arms and legs, reassured when he found no broken bones. He could detect nothing amiss through her heavy clothes, and he decided to try and carry her to his horse. He put his gloves back on over his freezing hands.

Wes managed to get his arms under her shoulders and her knees. He lifted her, slipping and sliding on the frozen ground. He twisted his ankle and went down on his knee hard against a rock, sending a jolt of pain up his leg. Ignoring the discomfort, he struggled to his horse. He hoisted her over the saddle on her belly like a sack of grain, and mounted up behind her. Turning her over he pulled her into his lap, opened his jacket and tried to button her up inside. The jacket would not reach around both of them, and he knew if he took it off and put it on her he would freeze. There was no shelter between here and the ranch. He had to settle for wrapping his arms around her.

The sleet had turned to ice, but at least the howling wind was at his back as he rode back to the ranch. Unable to see ten feet ahead of him, he gave the mare her head on the unfamiliar range, hoping that the ugly short-legged horse would be able to find the barn she knew as home. He had no idea how long they rode after they crossed the stream, but finally the dim outline of the house came into view. Katie hadn't moved once since had found her.

17

Wes turned from staring out the window in Katie's room and walked to the side of her bed. He pulled the quilt up and tucked it around her shoulders for the tenth time since he had put her to bed an hour ago. Immediately she began to toss and turn, trying to throw the covering off. She muttered something he couldn't understand, and feebly pushed at the quilt with her hands. Sitting on the mattress, he took her hands in his, feeling her hot dry skin.

"Katie, wake up," he coaxed. She opened her eyes for a moment and squinted at him.

"Leave me alone," she protested. Her voice was a raspy whisper, and she grimaced as she spoke.

He wrung out a cloth in the basin on her bed table, and wiped the hot skin on her face. Sliding an arm under her shoulders, he lifted her limp body gently and coaxed her to drink some water.

She pushed the glass away after a few swallows and muttered, "Hurts. Go away."

"I love you, Katie. You married me and now you're stuck with me. I'm never going away." He didn't know if she heard him. He planned to keep saying those words until he was sure she understood.

He smiled and kissed her forehead, then checked the wound on the back of her head. Consuela had been able to wash away most of the blood before Katie had awakened. The lump had gone down and the gash was a small one.

He had noticed how pale she looked this morning out at the chicken coop, and Consuela said she had complained of a headache yesterday, and had had no appetite. He had to assume the fever came from the same illness that Hannah and Consuela had both suffered. Only Katie's was made worse by her exposure to the freezing weather. He felt lucky she wasn't sicker.

She thrashed around and managed to kick the bed covers down to her waist. Perhaps if he could get her cooled down, she would keep the covers on. He rung the cloth out in the cool water, and started with her forehead, wiping at the hot skin of her face and her neck. He unbuttoned the front of her nightdress and, wringing the cloth out again, he wiped her chest and shoulders, then started over on her face. She calmed a bit, and he pulled the front of her gown together, and covered her lightly. She seemed quieter.

Consuela came to the open door, holding Hannah's hand. The child looked very serious. Wes recognized that look. She was worried about her mother.

He spoke in a quiet voice. "Come in." He motioned for them to come to the side of the bed, and he pulled Hannah into his lap, so she could see Katie.

The child leaned over and reached for her mother with her little hand, patting at the quilt. "Mamma, wake up."

Wes gently took Hannah's hand and held it. "Hannah, your mama needs to rest. We don't want to wake her up."

Hannah's face crumpled and she started to cry. Poor thing, he thought. It must be frightening to her to see her mother sick. She reached for Consuela. The Mexican woman quickly scooped the child up and held her close, patting her back and murmuring to her in Spanish. Then she turned and spoke to Wes. "Senor, do you need anything?"

Wes shook his head. "When Hannah is ready to take a nap, bring her back and she can lie here on the bed with her mother. Hannah, does that sound like a good idea?"

The little girl pulled her head away from Consuela's shoulder and nodded, rubbing at her eyes and hiccuping. Wes could tell Consuela and Hannah still were not feeling well themselves. He wondered if a doctor might be able to help, but realized that even if there was one in Miles City, in this storm they would never be able to fetch him to the ranch. They were going to have to take care of each other by themselves, at least until the weather let up.

Consuela left with Katie's daughter, and Wes wandered back over to the window. The landscape was a blur of white as far as he could see. He wasn't worried about the running of the ranch. Gibby was a very competent foreman and would see to things that needed to be done.

He turned back to the bed and noticed that Katie had pushed the covers off once again. He threw a log on the fire to keep the warmth in the room up, and returned to her side to wipe her down again with the cool cloths.

She tried to push his hands away and kick the covers off. Why couldn't they all just leave her be? She felt as if her skin was too tight and everything that touched her set off feelings so uncomfortable that she wanted nothing except to be left alone. Wes kept rubbing her skin with a cold cloth and setting her nerves on edge. She lapsed into fragments of dreams that were frightening and disjointed. Katherine could not tell what was real and what she imagined in her half sleep.

Her dreams were interrupted frequently when he made her sit up and drink. She tried to tell him of the burning pain in her throat that made swallowing impossible, but she had no voice. The most noise she could make was a faint croak. Her head hurt along with every joint in her body. The aching was unbearable, and every time someone jostled her, she could do nothing but cry. She could feel the tears slipping hotly down her cheeks.

Several times she felt someone on the bed beside her, and knew Hannah spoke to her, but she couldn't get her thoughts together enough to roll over or speak to the child. Voices murmured and swirled around her, but she could make little sense of what was said, and if she tried to listen, the pain in her head became intolerable. All she wanted to do was sleep.

Wes heard a noise, and looked toward the doorway. Katie's daughter stood there, looking frightened and unsure.

He motioned to her to come in, and put a finger to his lips to warn her to be quiet. Katie had just settled into a deep sleep, and he didn't want the child to wake her.

Hannah stopped beside his chair and braced a small hand against his knee as she stood on tiptoe to peer at her mother, then turned to survey Wes with her big eyes. He sat still under the little girl's scrutiny, aware of the trusting way she stood close to him. A protective feeling came over him, and he lifted Hannah into his lap.

She leaned against his chest and whispered while she watched her mother, "You making her take a nap?"

Wes chuckled and put his arm around the little girl. He knew Hannah hated naptime. "Your mama is sick. She needs to rest."

"Are you sitting here to make her stay in bed?" Hannah reached up and touched the corner of his mustache as she asked the question.

Why was he sitting here? He hadn't bothered to think about why he stayed until the child mentioned it. Katie really didn't need him to be there. "I guess I just like being with your mama."

Hannah considered his answer for a moment. "She likes being with you too. She smiles a lot when you come in the house." She touched his mustache again. "Does that get mixed up with your food when you eat?"

Wes laughed quietly and hugged the child. He was going to enjoy watching this little one grow up.

Finally Katherine awoke and felt clear-headed. The sun shone weakly through her bedroom window, and she tried to pull herself up against the pillows, but found she had little strength. She lay back, and closed her eyes. Her throat was sore, but no longer burned with pain, and her head had quit aching quite so badly. Katherine wondered where Wes was. Had he told her he loved her, and that he was going to stay? Had he really said the words? Or was that part of her dream? She wanted to see him, to ask him to tell her again.

Consuela was sitting in the rocking chair from Wes's room, Hannah curled up on her lap. The room was almost dark, and Katherine guessed it must be past suppertime. Hannah was the first to notice that her mother was awake. She scampered off Consuela's lap and leaned against the side of the bed near Katherine's head.

"You feel better, Mama?" The child looked so serious, Katherine had to smile.

Katherine paused for a moment before she spoke. Her voice sounded low and rough from disuse. "Yes, darling girl, I suppose I do."

Consuela stood up as Katherine spoke, and leaned over Hannah to smooth the bed covers up over Katherine. "You rest, senora, Hannah and I will fix you something to eat."

"Before you go, could I have something to drink?" Consuela propped her up and held a glass of water to her lips. The cool liquid tasted wonderful. She drank half a glass, then slumped back against the pillows.

Consuela took Hannah by the hand and led her from the room. Katherine watched them go, and wanted very much to call them back and ask them where Wes was. She missed him and wanted to tell them to bring him here, to her room. But her eyes fluttered closed and she could not seem to summon the energy to call out to them.

Katherine slept a good solid uninterrupted sleep, and when she awoke the next morning she found that although she still felt shaky, a little of her strength had returned. She got up and found her new robe all finished, lying across the end of the bed, and a pair of slippers on the floor. She struggled into the garment, and pushed her cold feet into the slippers. Then she had to sit on the end of the bed for a moment. That little bit of movement had left her exhausted. She rested, and after a few moments, her stomach began to growl, and she decided to head downstairs. She came out of her room and into the hallway. The door to Wes's room was open, and she stood there for a moment, wishing he was there so she could see him. She caught sight of herself in the oval mirror on the washstand, and decided it was just as well he was out working. She looked a fright. Tendrils of hair had come out of her braid and floated wildly around her pale drawn face.

She would have Consuela fill the reservoir in the stove, and heat some water so she might bathe and wash her hair before he came in for the noonday meal. She wanted him to eat here, at the house, and not with the hands in the cookshack. She wanted him to eat with her and sleep with her, and become in fact the husband she had legally made him. The day in Dennison she had chosen him off the gallows and married seemed very long ago, indeed.

Katherine clutched the banister as she made her way downstairs. Halfway down the stairs she sat and rested, leaning her spinning head against the balustrade, sorry that she had attempted the trip. She was much weaker than she had thought.

From where she sat she could see out the windows of the front room. Snow lay over the ground, drifts along the north side of the bunkhouse. It must have snowed all night. When she had been out looking for the cattle, there had been plenty of wind and sleet, but little snow.

Consuela came through the dining room door and spotted her on the stairs. "*Dios mio*, senora, you should not be out of your bed." She hurried up the stairs to where Katherine sat.

She gave the concerned woman a wan smile. "I figured that out for myself halfway down these stairs. Where is Hannah? Is she all right?"

"Si. She is all better and out in the barn helping Senor Hannibal."

Katherine allowed Consuela to take her by the arm and help her back up the stairs and into her bedroom.

She shrugged out of her new robe. "Consuela, thank you for making this robe." She ran her hand over the soft green wool. "When did you have time to sew it?"

"I worked at night, after Hannah had gone to bed."

Katherine felt strangely out of kilter and sat on the side of the bed. "How long have I been sick?"

"It has been two days since Senor Merrick brought you home." Consuela straightened the covers and held them up so Katherine could slide her legs in.

She looked at Consuela, not comprehending. Two days? And Wes had brought her home? She thought back and did not remember what had happened. The last thing she could recall was riding up into a ravine after a calf. She would have Wes tell her what had happened when he came in.

"Consuela, I'm going to rest for a while, then I want to take a bath and wash my hair."

Consuela looked horrified at her statement. "You cannot have a bath yet, senora. You were too sick. You must wait."

Katherine didn't want to wait. Weak as she felt, she had no intention of Wes seeing her as she looked now. "I want to bathe, and I want to be sure Mr. Merrick comes up to the house for supper tonight."

Consuela stood in front of Katherine shaking her head the way she did when Hannah made an unreasonable request. "I don't think Senor Merrick will be back for supper."

Her disappointment that she might not see him today was instantaneous. "Where did he go?"

"He waited until your fever broke and he knew you would be all right. Then he left early today to see the sheriff in Dennison. He told the reason to Senor Gibby."

Katherine sank back against the pillows. "I see. When you go down to the barn to get Hannah, would you tell Hannibal that I would like to see Gibby?"

"Si. You rest now." Consuela tucked the quilt snugly around Katherine and left the room.

Katherine must have slept for hours, because when she awoke, she could tell by the sun that it was late afternoon. How long was it going to be before she got her strength back? Fuzzily she recalled Wes's words. He was staying here in Montana, with her. A thrill shot through her as she thought about being a real wife, having him in her bed every night, and waking up in his arms every morning.

When she got up out of her bed this time she did not feel quite so weak. She was just struggling into her robe when Consuela came into her room.

"I am glad you are awake. Senor Gibby is in the front room. Why do you not climb back into your bed. He can come up to you."

That was probably a very good idea. She should save her strength for later. She was determined to have a bath, no matter what Consuela said.

"Consuela, make sure the reservoir is full." Katherine ignored the woman's look of exasperation. "Is there anything to eat? I'm hungry." That should cheer her up. Consuela firmly believed that once a sick person's appetite returned, they were on the road to recovery.

Consuela's wrinkled old face split in a grin. "Si. I have made you some soup. I will heat it up." She left, and Katherine could hear her instructing Gibby to come upstairs.

Hat in hand, Gibby stood awkwardly in the doorway. "I sure am glad to see you're feeling better, Miss Kate. You sure had us all worried."

"Thanks, Gibby. Come in and sit down. Tell me what I've missed." She motioned him to the rocking chair by her bed. She wondered briefly when the chair had been moved from Wes's room into hers, but her attention went back to her foreman. She wanted to hear about Wes, but felt strangely shy asking about him. Gibby launched into a report.

"We got through the storm all right. Because of the quick thaw the stream has flooded, but that should be down in a day or two. There's still plenty of graze out there for the cattle. Everything else is all right. Patches held on the cookshack roof. Joe doesn't need all them buckets on the floor anymore."

"Consuela told me Wes has gone into town. She said you knew why."

"He got a message from Denty. Sheriff said he had evidence that would help clear his name. He wouldn't leave, though, until he knew you would be all right. Then he borrowed that ugly old mare and went to town."

She loved what Gibby had just told her. The most important thing in the world to Wes was getting his name cleared, and he had delayed going to see Denty for her sake.

"Said he would find out what Denty had and check to see if there was any word from his brother, then probably go straight on to Dennison and see the sheriff there."

If he did all that, she reasoned, he wouldn't be home tonight, but he could be back by tomorrow. Katherine thanked Gibby for the information, and he left to go to supper. Consuela brought up a bowl of soup, and talked her into having her bath in the morning. She had to agree that going to bed with wet hair was not a good idea, and because she was growing very tired, she gave in.

Hannah came and spent an hour with her after supper, and they read books together until Katherine was so tired she sent Hannah off with Consuela to be put to bed, and blew out her own lamp.

In the morning she insisted on her bath after breakfast. Consuela would have put her off for another day, but Katherine wouldn't give in. Her hair smelled, and she needed a bath badly. The session in the copper tub in the kitchen exhausted her, however, and as soon as Consuela had brushed her hair dry by the stove in the kitchen, Katherine went upstairs for a nap.

Consuela came upstairs and woke her. Sheriff Denty was in the parlor to see her. Odd that he would stop by now, she thought, in the middle of the afternoon. Supper wasn't for hours yet. She got up and went downstairs, curious as to why the sheriff was here.

Martin Denty, his pants and boots splattered with mud, stood with his back to her staring out the window. She bit back a comment about his rudeness, coming into her house without wiping his boots. Wes never would have tracked mud into her front room.

She amended her thoughts. Their front room. She wondered when she had lost her fierce hold on her independence. She felt a flush on her cheeks when she suspected it might have occurred in her bed. She was ready to share everything with him. Her ranch, her house, her life. She toyed with the idea of asking Wes to adopt Hannah, and give her his name. It would make them a real family. Much as she wanted to continue thinking on that pleasant subject, she knew she needed to speak to the sheriff.

"Hello, Martin. Would you like a cup of coffee?"

He turned at the sound of her voice. "Sure. You all right, Katherine? You don't look so good."

The man certainly did know how to turn a phrase. "I'm all right. I'll get that coffee." She left the room and returned with a steaming mug.

He took it out of her hand and looked at her intently, making her uncomfortable. "Everything going along here, with the storm and all?"

"Martin, please sit down. Everything's fine." She wished he would just say whatever it was he came here to say. She sat down on one of the overstuffed chairs and motioned to him, filthy pants and all, to sit. Her mother would have been proud of her skills as a hostess, she thought wryly.

"I got some extra hands. I could come and help."

"Thank you, but I don't need any help." No one could annoy her as fast as this man.

"Katherine, I've had a message from the sheriff in Dennison, and I just rode over to tell you." He paused and took a drink from the mug.

Tell her what? A shiver of fear seized her. Had something happened to Wes? Had he been hurt somehow?

"You won't have to bother anymore with that drifter, or that sham of a marriage. Merrick cleared his name, and he's on his way home on the train, to Texas. I brought back the horse he was riding." He motioned toward the barn, and for the first time Katherine noticed the mousy little mare tied to the water trough.

Katherine could only stare at Denty. She felt as if he had punched her in the chest and she couldn't get her breath. He must be wrong. Wes wouldn't just leave, not without saying anything to her. He had feelings for her, didn't he? Or had she made another huge mistake and fallen in love with a man who wouldn't be around when she needed him?

Katherine blinked, not wanting to cry in front of Denty. "When did you get this message?"

"One of the deputies from Dennison came down to pick up a fellow we had in jail who's wanted up there. He brought this." Denty pulled a folded piece of paper from his pocket and handed it to Katherine.

She unfolded the paper with shaking hands and read the unfamiliar handwriting: *Miss Holman, Thank you for everything. W. Merrick.* Numbly she stared at the note. She had never seen his handwriting before. Somehow she imagined it would be better than it was. Then her vision blurred, and a tear dropped on the short, impersonal missive.

How could he leave her like this? How could he walk out of her life without saying good-bye? She vowed never to give her heart again, as she doubled over, the pain of his desertion nearly cutting her in half.

18

Samuel Houston Merrick had no trouble following the directions from Miles City to the Rocking H. He shifted his large frame on the uncomfortable rented saddle. Given more these days to a desk chair, he looked forward to getting off his horse and sampling the hospitality that the owner of the ranch had been extending to his younger brother for the last few weeks.

He chuckled to himself as he paused on the low rise above the shallow valley that sheltered the ranch buildings. Maybe after he met Katherine he could get used to the fact that she was his sister-in-law. He tried to imagine the woman who had caused his brother to marry in such a hurry and under such unusual circumstances. Sam was pleased his little brother was alive and well. He had not endorsed Wes's dangerous pursuit of Jim's killers on his own.

Looking around he could understand why Wes planned to stay in Montana territory. Beautiful cattle country. Before his search for justice Wes wanted only to be a rancher.

Sam had lots of questions for his brother about the way this whole thing had come about. He'd talked to the sheriff in Miles City, but instead of getting a clearer picture, the things the man had said only muddled up the situation. Sam had disliked Denty from the moment he'd walked into the sheriff's office. The man was too slick at evading questions.

Smoke curled from chimneys on both ends of the rambling stone and wood house. Eager to see his brother, and to warm the chill from his bones, Sam urged his horse toward the ranch.

Listlessly Katherine looked up from her desk. A furious barking out front brought her back to the present. In the three days since Wes had left, her emotions had fluctuated wildly between anger and heartache.

Now, she welcomed the blessed numbness that had finally set in. She tried to work on writing an agreement between herself and Gibby, deeding him the ranch and custody of Hannah in case anything happened to her. Never again would she depend on love, she vowed, her burns still too fresh and raw to heal into hope for the future.

Looking out for her daughter's welfare, she hoped the old foreman would accept her proposition. Annoyed by the continued barking, she rose from her chair and walked to the front window to see what had upset Hamlet.

A rider approached on the road from town. The paper dropped from Katherine's lifeless fingers as she watched the broad-shouldered man. It was Wes on that horse, she just knew it was. Vows forgotten, the icy band around her heart shattered, and she felt like singing.

With a shaking hand she opened the front door and stepped out into the sunlight, feeling warm for the first time in a week. Hamlet raced off the porch and ran circles around the unfamiliar horse, barking furiously.

When the man was about even with the bunkhouse, he took off his hat and raised his arm to wipe his forehead on his sleeve. Her elation dissolved like sugar in hot water. The rider was not Wes. By some hopeless coincidence he just looked like Wes. Now that he was closer she noticed his hair was lighter, and had some gray at the temples, and he wasn't as big as Wes.

The pounding in her chest made breathing difficult. It was true, she thought as she watched the man tie his mount to the trough outside the barn and walk toward the house, it was possible to die of a broken heart.

Hamlet followed him up the steps and planted himself between Katherine and the stranger. Eyes wide, she shuddered as she looked at him, feeling as if she were seeing a ghost.

He reached out and took her by the elbow as he spoke. "Are you all right?"

She shook herself out of her trance and pulled her elbow out of his grasp. "Who are you?" She could hear a frantic edge to her whispered words, but she had already guessed the answer to her own question.

The man removed his hat and took a step back. "Sorry, ma'am. I'm Sam Merrick, Wes's brother."

Sam. The lawyer. Wes had mentioned him. Standing out on the cold porch, she remembered her manners. "Won't you come in, Mr. Merrick?" She moved in small jerky steps, and her hand trembled as she gestured for him to follow her.

He looked as if he were about to ask a question when she stopped abruptly and turned to him. "Make yourself comfortable. I'll get you some coffee." She walked away from him without waiting for a response. There could only be one reason Wes had sent him here, and that was to have their marriage dissolved. Childishly she wanted to run upstairs and lock herself in her room and refuse to talk to him.

Instead she squared her shoulders and returned to the parlor with a mug of coffee he accepted gratefully into his cold hands.

"I want to thank you for what you did for my brother. He was darned lucky to have you show up when you did."

She gave him a slight nod, and stood staring into the flames. Unable to prolong her agony any longer, she turned to Wes's brother. "Why did you come here?"

A look of surprise, followed by suspicion, crossed his face. "To see my brother. Where can I find him?"

The bottom seemed to drop out of her stomach. A moment passed before she could stammer out an answer to his question. "He took the train home, to Texas."

He cocked an eyebrow at her, the exact same way Wes did when he didn't believe her. "When?"

"Three days ago." The longest, most painful days of her life.

"May I call you Katherine?" He stared at her intently. She nodded, wondering at his doubtful expression.

"He wired me a week ago and told me he was staying in Montana."

Katherine felt her heart leap. She hadn't dreamed Wes's words when she lay ill. He had told her he was going to stay.

Where could he be, if he wasn't in Texas? She felt a frisson of fear go down her spine. "If he didn't go home, then where is he?"

"I think we need to find out." His look turned back to one of suspicion. "Why did you think I was here?"

Katherine swallowed hard. "You're the lawyer, aren't you?"

He nodded in response to her question.

The words wanted to stick in her throat. She had to force them out. "I thought you were here to see about clearing his name. And getting him an annulment."

Again his eyebrow went up. "What did he say to you before he left?"

She closed her eyes for a moment against the pain when she recalled the day he had left. "He left without speaking to me. I'd been ill. He sent a message for me with the sheriff in Miles City."

"Denty?"

She wondered at his skeptical tone. So he had checked in town before he came to the ranch. "Yes." Where did Sam think Wes was?

"Do you have the message?"

She nodded. She had kept it and read it over and over, as if the pain caused by the impersonal message might help her to love him less. Opening the porcelain box with roses on the cover sitting on the mantle, she pulled out the tattered piece of paper and handed it to him.

As Wes's brother read the note, Hannah came rushing into the parlor. Katherine watched as the little girl stopped in her tracks and stared at Sam.

"Mr. Merrick, this is my daughter, Hannah." Hannah edged behind Katherine's skirt as Sam went down on his haunches until he was eye-level with the child.

"I'm pleased to meet you, Hannah."

Katherine gave her daughter a little nudge. "Me, too." The child responded. "You got his name."

"Wes is Mr. Merrick's brother." Hannah eased out

from behind her mother, keeping contact by grasping a handful of Katherine's skirt.

She looked up at Sam, a hopeful expression on her little face. "Is he coming to supper, too?"

If only, Katherine thought, stroking her daughter's curly hair. "Not tonight, sweetheart. Is supper ready?"

Hannah ducked out from underneath Katherine's hand. "Consuela says almost." She galloped back into the dining room.

Hardly missing a beat, Sam took up his questions. "When Wes wired me he said he had a broken arm. Left or right?"

His interrogations frightened her. Katherine hesitated for a moment as she thought. "His left, but the splint has been off for a while."

"Wes is right-handed. His broken arm wouldn't affect his writing." He glanced back down at the paper in his hand. "What did the sheriff tell you when he gave you this note?"

She wanted to scream at him. Why was he asking all these questions? What did he think had happened to Wes? "He said proof of Wes's innocence had come in, and Wes had decided to go back home."

"Wasn't he tried and sentenced in a place called Dennison?"

"Yes. Why are you asking all these questions?" She heard the note of hysteria in her voice.

Calmly he ignored her fear and continued to speak. "Then why did Sheriff Denty bring you the message?"

"He said a deputy from Dennison brought it down, and Denty told the deputy he would pass it on to me." Katherine knew she was near to tears, and wondered how much more of this agony she could take without screaming in frustration.

Doggedly, he went on. "How well do you know this Denty?"

How well did she know him? Not very, she mused. She had not paid that much attention to him. "Since he moved to town about five years ago to take the job of sheriff. He just bought a ranch close to mine." She pleaded with him, placing her hand on his sleeve. "Please, why are you asking me all these questions?"

He patted her hand, an absentminded gesture that carried some comfort for her. "Katherine, I'm just trying to figure out what's going on here. When I arrived in Miles City today Denty told me he hadn't seen Wes for two weeks." He hesitated for a moment. "You have any idea why Denty would lie?"

She thought about Martin's visit last week, trying to recall his exact words. "He was angry when I married Wes."

"Was Denty courting you?"

She felt her cheeks flush. "Yes, but I wasn't paying him any heed." Fear and hope warred within her. "So you don't think Wes left willingly?"

"I really doubt it." He glanced down at the paper in his hand. "He didn't write this note."

Katherine started at his revelation and grabbed the paper out of his hand, staring at it. "Are you sure?"

"Positive."

Frantically her thoughts jumped around. Where could he be? She had been so ready to assume that she had only dreamed his words when he told her he would stay, or that his feelings for her must have changed. Guilt slammed into her. What if he needed help? She should have sent some of the men after him. Her dismay and sorrow began to ebb, and in their place, fear, frustration, and anger grew, at Denty, and not least of all, at herself.

Sam's voice broke in on her thoughts. "I'm going to ride to Dennison tomorrow and check to see if he's been there. How far is it?"

"About a three-hour ride. I'll take you." She intended to be a part of his search.

"Are you up to a ride like that?" He looked at her with a skeptical expression on his face.

She planted her fists on her hips. "I'm going." She must look worse than she thought.

"We could take a buggy." She could tell he was reluctant to offer this compromise.

"We can ride. It's quicker." She stuck her chin out in a challenge. She wasn't going to give an inch.

"Yes, ma'am." She saw him fight a smile. "I can't wait to see you and my brother together. You're as stubborn as he is."

Katherine felt grateful tears forming in her eyes. "Thank you for coming." Her pain at how much he looked like Wes dissolved. For the first time in a week she felt hopeful about a future with the man she loved.

She spotted Consuela in the dining room, placing food on the table. "Shall we go in to supper?" Sam nodded and offered her his arm. She slid her hand into the crook of his elbow and silently thanked him for the strength his being there gave her.

She needed the little acts of normalcy, like showing a guest in to supper and calling her daughter to a meal, to help her maintain a facade of calm. Sam's comments had frightened her. The more she thought about what he had revealed, the more a sense of dread built in her. She should have realized that the Wes she had grown to know and love would never have left without speaking to her. She should have known immediately that something was wrong. She would have known, too, if she hadn't been so ill, so devastated by his leaving.

Now, as she picked at her food and tried to keep up her end of the conversation, she worried about the length of time Wes had been away. If he hadn't left of his own accord, anything could have happened in the week he'd been gone.

She forced herself to eat as much of the supper Consuela had prepared as she could. She had not had much of an appetite for the last week. Tomorrow she would need her strength.

After supper she showed Sam to the room Wes had used, then put Hannah to bed. Wearily, she decided to turn in early herself. She snuggled into the pillow she had taken from Wes's bed a week ago. The scent of him on the linens comforted her through the long, sleepless night.

The morning dawned clear and cold. The snow had melted, and the mud on the roads had dried enough to make riding easy. Katherine insisted Sam leave his rented mount and take one of her best saddle horses.

Sam pulled the collar of his jacket high up on his neck against the cold. "We'll ride straight into Dennison, and find out what we can."

Katherine nodded in agreement. This was rough country this time of the year, not a good place to get stranded. She pushed a vision of Wes, hurt, from her mind.

Sam asked all kinds of questions about ranching in Montana on the ride, and he talked about his family, Wes's family. She loved hearing about the closeness of the sisters, brothers, and all about the nieces and nephews. The stories didn't stop her from worrying about Wes, but they brought him closer to her.

Holidays must be very special with such a large family, she thought. Sam described trying to fit all the
brothers and sisters around the table, and the fact that
it took four pecan pies to feed the group dessert after
church on Christmas day.

She thought of her last Christmas. Her father had
been bedridden by then. Because of a terrible snow-
storm they had been cut off from town and neighbors.
She had felt so lonely. This year would be different, she
vowed. This year Wes would be there for Christmas.
Consuela would bake and—

Sam's voice jolted her from her thoughts. "We'd better give the horses a rest and some water." A rush of
feelings washed over her. He indicated the exact spot
where she had stopped with Wes on the way home
from Dennison, the time they had ridden there to try to
recover some of his belongings. She remembered the
way he had kissed her that day.

"The ride must be doing you some good. You have
some color in your cheeks." Sam's observation broke in
on her thoughts and caused her to blush even more.

She wanted to keep going, her anxiety gnawing at
her, but she pushed the feelings away. Sam had set a
brisk pace, and pushing the animals straight through
would be cruel.

They dismounted and offered the animals some
water, then to her relief, quickly mounted up and continued on into Dennison.

Katherine led the way to the livery stable where they
left their mounts. Every place she passed reminded her
of Wes, and twisted the painful wires a little tighter
around her heart. They started across the square, chins
drawn down against the cold wind, headed for the sheriff's office.

Sam stopped dead in his tracks when he spotted the scaffold. He took off his hat and gave a low whistle as stood looking at it. "That the one they were going to hang Wes on?"

She nodded, not trusting her voice. Seeing the scaffold for the third time was no easier for Katherine. That dusty summer day he was going to be hanged seemed like so long ago as she stood in the muddy square, her cold hands shoved deep in her pockets.

"An angel must have been smiling on him that day. He's wiggled out of some tight situations before, but this beats all." He gestured to the scaffold, put his hat back on. "Thank you, Katherine."

Katherine's throat tightened up and she couldn't speak. She hoped they found Wes and Sam would soon be able to talk to his brother and find out firsthand what had happened. And then later, she thought with a smile, she would ask Wes herself about the tight situations Sam mentioned.

They crossed the sloppy street and climbed the steps up onto the boardwalk outside the sheriff's office, stomping the mud from their boots. Sam opened the door and stood back to let her enter. She felt another rush of memories when she stepped into the office.

The sheriff of Dennison sat behind his desk, tipped back in his chair with his boots propped on the blotter, reading a newspaper. He glanced up when they entered. A look of recognition, then surprise, crossed his face when he looked at Katherine. Startling, he nearly tipped backward out of his chair.

Just as she was about to turn to Sam to see his reaction to the sheriff's strange behavior, she heard her name bellowed forth from the third cell at the far end of the building. Head swiveling toward the familiar voice, she spotted Wes, arms extended through the bars, waving frantically to her. Her voice catching on a sob, she ran toward him on wobbly knees.

"Wes, Wes!" She threw herself against the cold metal bars and felt his arms come around her. She clung to him for a moment, then pushed back to look at him.

An ugly bruise marred his forehead, and he looked thinner, but he was alive and well. He hadn't left for Texas. She reached through the bars and stroked her hand down his stubbled cheek, not caring why he was in the cell. She had taken care of that once, and she would do it again. "Oh, Wes."

"Katie! Are you ever a sight for sore eyes." He laid his hand over hers and looked into her eyes.

Shoving her arms through the bars and around his waist, she pushed her face up against the cold iron, and kissed him as hard as she could, not caring who was there to see.

She felt Sam come up behind her and Wes let go of her with one arm to shake his brother's extended hand. "Sam, thanks for coming. God, I'm glad to see you two."

Wes let go of his brother's hand and stroked Katherine's face again through the bars. "Are you all right?"

She rubbed her cheek against his hand like a cat might, so happy at his tender touch she felt as if she could purr. "I am now."

The sheriff started shouting, and everyone else joined in. Wes wanted out. Katherine wanted him out. Sam demanded to know what was going on, and the sheriff finally bellowed for all of them to be quiet. The outer door flew open and banged against the wall.

The hullabaloo stopped dead when they saw the two deputies in the open door with drawn guns.

Wes's arms tightened around her, and Sam stepped in between the deputies and Katherine. She turned around within his embrace to better see what was happening.

The sheriff waved his arms at the deputies. "For heaven's sake, put your guns away and get out of here."

One of the deputies pointed at Sam and offered an explanation. "We seen them come in. Thought it was Merrick."

The sheriff shook his head. "You fools. Did you think he was breaking *into* jail?" The deputies shook their heads and looked chagrined, backing out of the office.

The sheriff walked over and kicked the door closed, then he fixed Katherine with a look of frustration. "You ain't dead." His words sounded like an accusation.

Her mouth dropped open and for a moment she wondered if he wanted her to apologize. "You're right." Then she realized that wasn't quite true. She had been dead, in a way, dead inside from the hurt and the longing of having Wes gone.

"I told you she wasn't harmed." Wes's arms tightened around her middle, drawing her back against the iron bars.

The sheriff ignored him. "Denty brought him into town all trussed up and told us he killed you. Showed me a warrant." The sheriff turned from Katherine to Wes. "If you didn't kill her, who did you kill?"

Wes tightened his grip on Katherine and spoke in tense, measured tones. "For the hundredth time, I didn't kill *anyone*!" His voice rose to a roar that threatened to deafen Katherine.

Confused, she spoke over her shoulder to Wes. "Why would Martin tell them you had murdered me?"

He turned her around in his arms so he could speak to her face. "Because he wants you and the Rocking H for himself."

Katherine thought that was about the strangest thing she had ever heard. "Martin's crazy if he thought just because he eliminated you he could step into your place."

Wes smiled, and drew her forward for a tender kiss that left her wanting so much more.

Sam stepped into the conversation, directing his comments to the sheriff, a look of understanding on his handsome features. "And if Wes were accused of any crime, they would hang him here in Dennison on the original charge, without another trial. Right, sheriff?"

"That's right. All we're waitin' on is Judge Casey to get back from Billings and reinstate Merrick's sentence."

"Don't you mean, *were* waiting on?" Sam certainly sounded like an attorney.

The sheriff eyed him with a defensive look. "Who are you?"

"I am Mr. Merrick's lawyer. Are you going to release him, or do I need to get a writ of habeas corpus?"

Katherine was fairly sure by the look on the sheriff's face he had no idea what Sam was talking about. Blustering, he turned to Katherine. "If you're willing to sign a paper saying that he hasn't killed anybody or broken the law, I suppose I can turn him back over to your custody."

As far as Katherine could tell, he hadn't broken anything except her heart, and that was well on its way to being mended as she stood in the circle of his arms.

And she fully intended to take custody of him, permanently.

"You write it, and I'll sign it." Katherine snuggled up against the hard iron of the cell door, wrapped in Wes's arms.

Again he tenderly stroked her face. "I kept thinking about you, how you would think I had left without saying good-bye." He spoke, his frustrations of the past few days evident.

She wondered at his words. Had he been planning to leave Montana, to say good-bye to her all along? "Martin brought a note, signed with your name, saying you were going home." Her voice caught on the last of her words. She wanted to hear him deny that he planned on going back to Texas.

"I'm sorry, darlin'. He told me he had some news. The next thing I knew, I woke up in a cell in Dennison. I told the sheriff and his deputies about a thousand times that you were back at your ranch, safe and sound, but no one would listen. I've been trying for three days to get word to you." She reached up and stroked the yellowing bruise on his forehead, holding back tears.

"Don't cry, Katie, it's over."

Was it over? She couldn't bear to ask. "What about Martin?"

Wes's features hardened. "Sam and I will take care of Denty."

Katherine was about to protest, when Sam interrupted them. "Ready?"

"Oh yes, big brother, I'm ready." Wes let go of her as the sheriff took a ring of keys out of his desk and opened the heavy cell door.

Wes scooped Katherine into his arms and gave her a deep wet kiss that made her toes curl up inside her boots. After he finished kissing her he let go of her with one arm and pulled Sam into the embrace.

Then Wes let go of both of them, grabbed his hat and jacket off the bunk and said, "Let's get out of here."

Katherine walked into the midday sunshine, one Merrick brother on each side of her, leaving the sheriff scratching his head and muttering to himself.

At the livery stable, Wes asked Sam to pay for the rental of a horse. Turning to the wrangler, Sam said, "Charge the horse to the sheriff."

Wes grinned at his brother, wrapping an arm around Katherine's shoulders. He leaned down and whispered in her ear, "Come on, let's go."

As his hands slid around her waist and he helped her to mount, she yearned to be alone with him, longed to have him tell her the words that she feared she had only imagined during a fevered dream, that he loved her and would stay forever, here with her in Montana.

19

Katherine snuggled deep in her jacket against the cold as she rode between Wes and Sam, listening to the brothers' conversation. Breath formed white clouds in front of their mouths in the frigid air as they disagreed on what needed to be done about Denty. Sam wanted to wire Washington for a federal marshal. Wes argued that would take too long and they could take care of the situation themselves. Every few minutes Wes would reach out and touch her on the arm, almost as if he expected her to disappear. Would he touch her like that if he was planning on leaving? She wanted so to ask him, but not here, in front of his brother.

Sam, adamant about turning the situation over to the authorities, suggested an alternative to waiting for a marshal. "We could go back to the sheriff at Dennison, and have him swear out a warrant for Denty's arrest."

Katherine thought that sounded like a pretty good idea, wanting Wes with her, safe at the ranch.

"The sheriff of Dennison is an idiot!" Wes exploded with vehemence.

"Well, little brother, he had you in a cell twice," Sam smiled, winking at Katherine.

Wes waved a hand in dismissal. "Don't give him any credit for that. The first time I was unconscious and all the bastards that killed Jim were dead drunk. One of the deputies told me what happened."

"And the second time?" Katherine could tell by Sam's teasing tone he wasn't going to let go of this subject very easily. She enjoyed the banter between the two men.

Wes looked a little sheepish. "The second time Denty took me by surprise. He sent a message to the ranch saying he had some proof of my innocence. I figured he had received something from you. When I went into town he got the drop on me and put me in a cell."

Sam gestured toward Wes's forehead. "How did you get the bruise?"

Wes brought his hand up and gingerly pressed on the yellowing skin near his temple. "He must have put something in the coffee he gave me with dinner, made me sleep. Bastard must have hit me then. Woke up in that cell in Dennison. At first I thought it was a bad dream."

Katherine could keep still no longer. What Martin had done didn't make sense to her. "But why? Why get rid of you by making up a lie and turning you over to the sheriff in Dennison?"

Sam laughed, but the sound had no humor in it. "To Denty's way of thinking Wes would be hung and Denty would have what he wanted. Lucky for Wes, that judge was out of town."

Katherine considered what he said, then grumbled. "People would have found out I was alive, and Wes was innocent. It still doesn't make much sense."

"And neither does Denty, darlin'." Wes grabbed her hand and pulled her close enough that he could get a kiss, their legs bumping together between their horses.

"Do you think he's crazy?" Katherine mulled over the idea. She had known him a lot longer and he had never acted demented.

"That would be my guess." This time Wes let go of her long enough to pull off his glove with his teeth, then he removed her glove and wrapped his warm hand around her fingers. His eyes locked with hers in an intimate gaze as his thumb made lazy circles on the back of her hand. "He sure doesn't seem to see a clear picture of the way things really are." He brought her hand up to his mouth and kissed her palm, laving her with his tongue, branding her.

Mesmerized, she watched his mouth. Sensation tingled up her arm. Her heart pounded and the part of her that rocked against her saddle went all warm and liquid. She swallowed hard, and looked up, guessing from the look on Wes's face he knew exactly what he was doing to her. He cocked an eyebrow at her. She felt color flame in her cheeks, and glanced over at Sam, who discreetly looked ahead, as if nothing was happening. She tried to pull her hand away and Wes smiled, then let go, handing her her glove.

Katherine forced her mind back to Denty, trying to gain some control over her wayward thoughts. Denty had danced around the idea of marriage to her in the past, but she thought she had been clear that she wasn't interested in his half-hearted proposals. She toyed with the idea that he was crazy.

They were coming up on the spot near the creek where they usually stopped to rest the horses. Tired to the bone, Katherine thought Sam had probably been right when he had said she wasn't well enough to come along. But she was treasuring every moment with Wes, glad she hadn't stayed behind at the ranch.

His voice broke into her thoughts. "You look tired. We'll rest awhile."

Just as she swung her leg clear of her saddle to dismount, a shot rang out. The bullet struck a branch above her head, spitting wood with a loud crack and spooking her horse. The animal reared and twisted, throwing her against his side as she held on. Wes vaulted over the far side of his horse. He yelled at her to get down, which she planned to do as soon as she could get her foot untangled from the stirrup.

Another shot whizzed over her head. She couldn't tell which direction they came from. Just as she got her boot clear of the stirrup, Wes grasped the waistband of her skirt. He hauled her back and pushed her to the ground. Stunned, she felt the air leave her lungs in a whoosh as he covered her with his big body. She struggled for breath.

The shooting stopped. Wes grabbed her arm and yanked her toward a small rise, under the trees. Katherine crawled on all fours, and dove behind the low barrier.

"Who's firing at us?" she gasped, when she had been able to pull enough air into her lungs to talk. She lay flat on her stomach on the ground, flanked by Wes and Sam. They had both had the presence of mind to pull their rifles out of their scabbards, she thought with chagrin. Her gun still stuck up out of its case, her horse too far away in the open now for the weapon to do her any good.

Wes rolled onto his side and checked the magazine in his gun. "If I had to make a guess, I'd have to say it's probably Denty." He propped the gun up between two rocks on the mound of dirt in front of them and scanned the area. "See them, Sam?"

Katherine stuck her head up a mite to look, only to have Wes's large hand push her face down into the dirt. "Katherine, keep down!" He sounded angry.

Katherine realized it was the first time she had ever heard him raise his voice. She spit out some dirt, and rolled her head to the side to glare at him. He was right, of course, but she was still smarting over forgetting to take her gun with her.

Another volley of shots rang out, and Wes and Sam waited for a split second, then they both rose onto their elbows and fired.

"How many?" Wes ejected his spent cartridges and reloaded his gun.

"I count two firing." Sam, busy reloading, didn't look up.

"Did you see them?"

"One. On the other side of the creek, behind that boulder. I couldn't tell where the other shots are coming from."

"I think the other one is to our left of the first guy. You take the right and I'll take the left, on three. One, two, three." Again they shot in unison. In the distance Katherine heard a yelp of pain. Then a bullet exploded into the rock in front of them. Fragments of stone sprayed everywhere. A piece caught her in the forehead, stinging like crazy. When she put her fingers to the spot, she felt blood. Wes continued to fire. She turned to Sam. He lay face down in the dirt.

Katherine screamed, and frantically tried to roll him over so she could see where he'd been hit. Placing a hand on her arm to calm her, Wes reached across her and slid a hand under Sam's chin, turning his head. The bullet that had ricocheted into the rocks had glanced along the side of his head, leaving a nasty-looking furrow oozing red above his ear. Wes gently lowered his brother's head and placed his fingers at Sam's throat.

Wes's breath whispered in her ear. "Doesn't look deep. Probably just knocked him out."

Katherine gulped in air and struggled to calm herself. Wes dabbed at her forehead with his cuff. "You all right?"

Not trusting her voice, she nodded at him, trembling. Fear hung in her middle like a ball of ice.

He surprised her with that slow lazy smile she adored. "Good girl. Hands steady enough to shoot?"

"Y-yes." How could he sound so cool when whoever had them pinned down seemed determined to kill them?

"Take Sam's gun. Stay here with him." He opened her hand and dropped some shells into her palm. "I'll get around behind Denty. I think I killed the other one."

Her eyes flew to his in surprise. "Denty? Did you see him?"

Wes shook his head.

"How do you know it's Denty?"

"Just guessing."

She grasped at his sleeve, frightened for him. "Be careful."

He cupped her face with his hand and gave her a hard quick kiss. "You bet, darlin'. Keep your head down. Don't aim, just fire at those rocks and draw his attention."

As he crawled away from her, she laid the rifle along the edge of the dirt mound that protected her and fired blindly. She drew back to reload. Sam lay still beside her, unconscious. She froze when she heard gunfire, and offered up a quick prayer that Wes had been able to surprise Denty.

As she slipped the last round into the chamber, she heard a rustle in the grass and felt something hard poke into the small of her back. She looked back over her shoulder. Martin Denty stood behind her, dressed in a long, heavy coat, his rifle barrel against her spine.

"Martin." She nearly choked on his name. If Denty was standing there, did that mean he had shot Wes? No, she told herself frantically, there hadn't been enough time. Denty had come up behind her, from the direction opposite the gunfire. That meant there had been more men out there with Denty.

"Katherine," Denty had a bemused look on his face as he pressed the cold metal gun barrel into her back up under her jacket. "I warned you about taking up with that outlaw."

Katherine wanted to argue with him, to tell him Wes was no outlaw, but fear kept her quiet. Denty was about to kill her. She squeezed her eyes closed against her tears, and thought of Hannah growing up without a mother or a father.

Her fingers tightened around the stock of the newly loaded rifle. If she rolled away from him and brought the gun up at the same time, she would have a chance. She shifted slightly to give herself some leverage. Denty must have seen her move, because he took a step over her and his boot came down hard on the rifle, pinning her hand underneath the barrel of the gun. The pain in her fingers made her yelp. Her hand uncurled from the stock, and he kicked the rifle out of her reach. She cradled her injured hand to her chest.

Finally Denty spoke. "Merrick, you come out here where I can see you and drop your rifle, or I shoot her." His tone was still civilized, as if he were asking her to dance.

"I'll kill you. My rifle is aimed at your heart, and your men are dead." Wes's voice came from surprisingly close by, in the trees to her right.

"Drop the gun, Merrick. You might get off a shot, but can you take the chance?" Denty poked her hard, just above the waistband of her skirt, and she gasped, biting her lip to keep from crying out as the cold steel jammed into her spine.

No! she wanted to scream at Wes. She feared Denty would kill him once he dropped his weapon.

She heard the rifle hit the ground. "Hurt her and you die," Wes said.

Denty laughed as if this whole thing was some kind of joke. He eased up on the pressure on her back.

Denty tossed a coil of light rope down in the dirt by Katherine's face. "Take the rope and get up."

Katherine glanced over at Sam as she got to her knees. He lay face down in the dirt beside her. She grabbed for the coil of rope, apparently too slow for Denty's liking. Denty grasped her upper arm and hauled her to her feet, keeping a bruising hold on her.

He motioned to Sam with his rifle. "Who's that?"

She thought fast before she answered his question. "His name was Sam. He was Wes's brother."

Denty took the barrel of the rifle and poked Sam between the shoulder blades. For a breath-stealing moment, Katherine thought the sheriff intended to shoot him in the back.

Apparently convinced that Sam was dead, Denty let him be. He shoved Katherine toward Wes, who stood about twenty yards away. "You're going to tie him up, and if the ropes aren't tight enough, I'll shoot him. Understand?"

Did Denty want Wes tied before he shot him? Why would he do that? Katherine felt the blood rushing in her ears, making her feel light-headed. She nodded and clutched the rope.

Denty motioned to Wes, "Take your shirt and jacket off."

"No!" She spoke before she had even thought about it. The sun was low, and the temperature was dropping fast. If Denty left him outside through the night without his jacket, he would freeze to death. Then she realized, with a horrible sickening feeling, that that was just what Denty intended. Wes had the buttons of his jacket undone and was working on his shirt. He dropped the garments at his feet, never taking his eyes off Denty.

"His death will look like an accident. He froze to death. He's from Texas, and didn't realize how cold it gets up here." Denty sounded as if he was explaining a simple fact to a slow child.

Katherine stared at the deranged sheriff. "No. I won't do it."

Denty trained the rifle on Wes. "Katherine, do as I tell you." She looked into his wild eyes and knew she had no room to bargain.

By the time she got to Wes, her knees were shaking so badly she wondered what was keeping her upright.

Denty picked up Wes's gun and flung it into the underbrush. Then he threw the jacket and the shirt after the gun. "Tie him to this tree." Denty indicated a sapling with a trunk of about six inches in diameter.

Wes obliged by backing up against the tree and sitting on the ground. "Do a good job, darlin'. Just do what he says." His voice held the encouragement she needed to keep her nerve up as she moved around behind him. Denty kept the rifle trained on both of them.

She fumbled with the bindings, her bruised hand making her clumsy. She could already see the goose flesh on Wes's arms from the frigid air.

Her chin quivered, and her eyes were so full of tears she could hardly see to tie the knot. "I'm sorry." She laid a palm on his shoulder.

He turned his head and kissed the back of her hand, his lips soft against her. "Don't worry about me. Try to do what he says and keep yourself safe until I come for you."

There was such confidence in his tone, Katherine felt a small measure of relief.

Denty motioned to her to back away, and she held her breath as he came over to check the job she had done. Apparently satisfied, he motioned toward the horses. "Time to go back. Time to go home."

She didn't move. Home? Would he take her to the Rocking H? Was he that crazy? She prayed he was.

When she didn't move, Denty gripped her elbow and pulled her away, his quiet tones set in an eerie contrast to his rough grasp.

She glanced at Sam's unmoving body and fought down another surge of panic. If Wes couldn't get himself free and Sam didn't wake up, both men would freeze to death. She looked over her shoulder in the gathering twilight and through her tears saw Wes smile at her.

Frantically her mind churned as Denty led her to her horse. He thought he could make this look like an accident. Didn't he know she would tell what happened? And what about the others? Sam was still alive, but

Denty didn't know that. Unless she could get away from the demented man, Sam was the only chance Wes had. She didn't know about the men who had been with Denty, but if they were alive, they knew what had happened. If they were dead, someone would miss them and ask questions, wouldn't they?

Denty was clearly crazy. She would have to play along with him until she could find a chance to get away.

Denty pulled another small coil of rope and a pair of wrist shackles out of his coat pocket.

"Give me your hands." Unwillingly she held her trembling arms out. He snapped the iron bracelets over her wrists, tightening them down as far as they would go. "Grab onto the saddle there," he said, indicating the saddle horn. He lashed her hands to the saddle horn, then grasped her ankle, lifting her foot and placing her boot in the stirrup.

Katherine swung her leg over her mount as she spoke, trying to keep her voice normal and conversational, "Where are we going?"

Denty paused for a moment, then gazed up at her with a look of surprise. "Well, back to our ranch, of course, my dear."

As they rode away Katherine managed to twist around in her saddle and watched until she could no longer see Wes in the shadows of the trees. She closed her eyes and prayed that he would get his bonds untied.

20

After Katherine lost sight of Wes, she concentrated on Denty, hoping he was crazy enough to ride to the Rocking H. He stayed on the main road, evidently unconcerned that they might meet other riders. To her dismay, he took the turnoff to the old Chapman place.

She worked at the knots he had used to tie her shackles to the saddle horn, managing to untie almost half of them. If she freed herself she might be able to jerk her reins out of his hand and outride him to the Rocking H for help. Trying to ignore the panic that gnawed at her, she forced herself to think, to plan. Sam and Wes couldn't last much longer in this cold, and somehow she had to get away and help them.

Soon she could make out the small, deserted-looking house in the darkness. In the daytime she could see her land from here. How desperately she wanted to be there, warm and safe with Wes and Sam.

Denty stopped at the crooked wooden steps leading up to the front porch. The windows looked vacant and dark. There wasn't a living soul around as far as she could tell.

Katherine pushed the swell of fear down and concentrated on the situation at hand. She couldn't count on anyone from the Rocking H coming out to look tonight. If she and Sam did not return, Consuela and Gibby most likely would assume they had decided to stay over in Dennison. And Denty's hired hands weren't around, so there was no one here to appeal to for help.

Katherine sat up a little straighter as Denty dismounted and tied their horses to the porch rail. She was going to have to take care of herself. She wondered if she could catch Denty off guard as he approached her horse and kick him hard enough to stun him. She slipped her booted foot from the stirrup and drew up her knee slightly, ready to strike out at him.

He walked around her horse and approached her from behind. Without a word he grabbed her foot and held it in a firm grip.

"Katherine, get down." His conversational tone did not change.

She dismounted, and waited while he untied the cord attaching her hands to the saddle horn. Then he leaned into her, trapping her against her horse and his soft, fleshy body. She turned her face away and closed her eyes, trying to stay calm. Taking shallow breaths, she played along with him and acted docile, biding her time until she could escape. The temperature must be close to freezing now. How long could Wes survive out there?

To her relief Denty backed away, leaving the cord attached to her manacled wrists. He took her by the elbow to lead her up the sagging, rotten steps. The front door opened on protesting, squealing hinges, and he pushed her into the house. She heard the scurry of some small animal, and shivered at the thought of sharing space with the vermin that had taken up residence here, both two-legged and four-legged.

The smell made her want to gag. He must not have even opened a window since he'd bought the ranch. The walls and roof of the mean place provided no relief from the freezing weather. Surely he wasn't living here.

He released her long enough to light a small glass oil lamp, which revealed how crude the place still was. Neglect and disuse had made it even worse. The only furniture had been left behind by Chapman. To her right, beyond Denty, stood a dry sink that tilted at a bit of an angle, and to her left was an old table with a warped top and two chairs, one with all the rungs on the back broken out. Denty brought the lamp over to her and took her by the elbow once again. "You must be tired from the trip." He was still speaking to her in that calm, solicitous tone that scared her half to death. "You come and go to bed. I'll take care of everything."

She couldn't help but jerk away. It was the word *bed* that did it to her. A horrible thought crossed her mind.

She tried desperately to recover her poise. "Martin, it's so dark. You go ahead and I'll follow the lamp."

His mouth was set in a hard line as he grasped her elbow again, so hard this time she knew she would have a bruise.

His tone was more clipped than before, and his expression was eerie in the feeble light. "Now, Katherine." He propelled her ahead of him toward the dark opening into the other room. She tripped over a warped floorboard and slammed her shoulder into the doorjamb. Please, she prayed, let Wes get away and come and get me. A muffled sob escaped her before she could control her panic.

Martin didn't say a word as he brushed past her through the door. The only furnishing in the second room was a bare iron bed frame, complete with rusty sagging springs. There was one small window set high in the wall, and from the blackness outside, she could tell the moon had not risen yet. The drop to the ground from the windowsill was probably only about five feet, but she doubted she could fit through the small opening.

"Katherine, come here." At the sound of his voice she bolted for the front door. She could hear him pounding after her, bellowing in anger. He hit her from behind and sent her sprawling across the filthy floor. She flung her hands out to break her fall, and felt the manacles tear the skin at her wrists.

Denty flipped her over onto her back and grabbed the front of her jacket, dragging her across the floor into the second room.

He dumped her on the bare bedsprings. Terrified, she scrambled close to the wall.

"Katherine, you're tired. Stay in bed. I'll see to the horses." He leaned across and took hold of the cord dangling from her manacles, tying her tight to the bedstead.

When he left the room she calmed herself enough to realize he didn't mean to join her just then. Heartened by the momentary respite, she eased herself forward on the side of the bed. Katherine frantically twisted her hands in the manacles, trying to reach the knot that lashed her to the bed frame. She succeeded only in cutting into the already lacerated flesh of her wrists.

Exhausted and in pain, she stopped the fruitless struggle with her bonds and pulled her knees up under her chin, resting her cheek on them. She closed her eyes, finding no point in keeping them open. The room was so dark she couldn't see anything.

She shivered in the cold air. Her fingers were numb even with gloves on. She remembered how Wes had taken one of her gloves off when he held her hand. She turned her forehead to her knees and tried to fight back the sob of fear that threatened to erupt from her throat. Had she lost Wes too? Was this God's punishment for breaking His rules? She tried not to give up hope, but she felt so overwhelmed.

Katherine forced herself to plan. If Wes couldn't get to her, she would have to take care of herself. How long would it take Denty to put up the horses? If she could get him to untie her, she might have a chance to overpower him. Then she could get back to Wes before he froze to death. She had known him such a short time, but she knew without doubt that she loved him. He made her laugh, he made her feel like a woman, and she wanted him beside her, day and night. He would be a good father to Hannah, she knew he would.

The thought of Hannah made the lump in her throat grow so that she felt she couldn't breathe. Would Gibby raise her little girl if she was gone? The thoughts of her daughter growing up without a mother were more than Katherine could bear, and she sobbed, pushing her face into her skirt to muffle the sound.

The squeal of the hinges on the front door stopped her crying. Over her shoulder, through the open door, she could see Denty in the dim glow of the lantern. He moved out of her line of sight and she couldn't tell what he was doing from the scraping, scratching noises he made.

The cold of the room seemed to seep through her heavy clothing, and she thought of Wes, tied to that tree with no protection from the night air.

She waited, but for what, she didn't know. Martin Denty seemed to have a plan, but it probably made no sense to anyone but himself. He seemed to think that with Wes out of the way, he could take over her life and join his land to hers. It was crazy, but in his own twisted mind she supposed it made sense.

When Denty reached the bed he took off his long coat and spread it over the bare springs. Then he untied the cord that lashed her wrists to the bed, tugged off her gloves, and tossed them on the floor. For a brief moment, she entertained the thought that perhaps he was letting her go. Her hopefulness did not last very long.

"Katherine, you don't want to fall asleep with your clothes on. Come, I'll prepare you for bed." He chided her in a voice a parent might use with a disobedient child.

She tried not to give in to hysterics. She had to pretend to go along with the charade.

Trembling, she managed to say, "Martin, I really am having difficulty with these." She held her manacled wrists up toward him.

Denty studied her face, then he looked at the manacles. His serene composure slipped for one brief second, and his voice was harsh when he replied, "Katherine, you will get used to them, believe me. This is necessary."

She tried to keep heart, but wondered if she had a chance to get away still encumbered as she was.

"Lie down, my dear, and rest."

She obeyed, not wanting to alarm him or put him more on guard while she waited for her chance to get away. Awkwardly she tried to stretch out on the bed frame. The old springs creaked and shifted as she moved over them. She scooted until she had her back up against the wall, as far away from him as she could get. Gingerly she lay on her side, her hands held awkwardly out in front of her. She closed her eyes briefly and prayed for deliverance, then opened them and watched him.

Stiffly he lay down beside her. Katherine figured he must have put his rifle on the floor by the bed. The springs groaned and dipped as he rolled toward her. She had nowhere to go to get away from him.

He grabbed the cord still tied to her manacles, and used it to pull her hands up against the front of his trousers. She recoiled in horror, but he jerked the cord to bring her hands back to him.

"Touch me, Katherine. Take me in your beautiful hands." He continued to pull on the cord and as she resisted, the metal of the manacles bit deeply into her wrists. Bile rose up in her throat and threatened to choke her as she tried to pull away.

She could feel the slick warmth of her own blood where it flowed over her cold skin. She knew if she did what he wanted, she could stop the awful pain. Even that could not make her touch him. She silently vowed that her hands would fall off before she gave him any pleasure.

He groaned and moved closer, rubbing himself against the backs of her shaking hands. Then he began to make little mewing sounds like a small hurt animal.

Katherine's fear turned to disgust and anger. Finally she managed to pull free of his slack grasp and made it to the end of the bed before her skirt caught on a loose coil of metal spring.

Denty reared up behind her, his sobs turning into a roar, and grabbed her leg just above her knee in a punishing grip. Katherine screamed at him and swung her manacled hands so that the chain connecting her wrists struck him in the face. He lunged at her and the bed frame tipped, pitching them both to the floor. Katherine scrambled to her feet. Denty had his legs pinned under him, tangled in the springs. He placed his hands on the edge of the bed frame to hoist himself up.

In a flash Katherine knew she could not outrun him. A dam of fear and hatred broke loose inside her for what he had done to them all. She flipped the chain that connected her hands together over his head and pulled hard, bringing the chain against his neck, under his chin. Then she pulled as hard as she could, choking him. He made an awful gurgling sound in his throat as his hands clawed at her. Then Denty worked his hands up under the chain, forcing it away from his throat. He flipped the chain up over his head and shoved her back.

She landed hard on her bottom on the floor. Denty loomed over her. A voice shouted her name. Denty reached down, then stopped, and turned his head toward the door.

Wes was alive, and he had come to save her from this horrible nightmare.

Denty grabbed his rifle, knocking over the lamp. He ran out the door as the glass chimney shattered. A sheet of oil and flame spread across the old dry floorboards, blocking her only escape from the room.

As she scrambled out of the way of the fire, she tripped over Denty's coat. She heard the front door open, and men's voices yelling. A single gunshot rang out.

Smoke filled the room. She tried to beat out the flames with the coat. She heard Wes's voice calling to her, and felt a surge of relief. She opened her mouth to answer him, but sucked in a lung full of smoke and strangled on her reply.

Blinded, she smothered as much of the flames as she could with the coat. Then she ran over the smoldering wool, through the open door, and into the front room. She collided with someone, and in her frenzy, she thought it was Denty. She flailed with the chain, trying to free herself from the grip he had on her arms.

"Katie, Katie!"

Finally Wes's voice penetrated her hysteria, and she collapsed in his arms, coughing and choking.

Wes gripped her firmly around the waist and led her onto the porch. There, blocking the front steps, Martin Denty lay face down on the dry, splintery wood, a pool of blood spreading from under his body.

She stopped and looked down at the man who had almost succeeded in killing them all, and a huge shudder shook her.

Gently Wes lifted her over Denty's still form and set her down in the yard. She bent over at the waist, hands on her knees, and sucked in fresh air as Wes held her shoulders.

Sam sat on the ground, his head cradled in his hands. A bandanna was tied across his forehead under his hat. He groaned and looked up to give Katherine a rueful smile.

"Sam, are you all right?" The words came out raspy from her smoke-filled throat.

Wes turned her and drew her into his arms.

"Oh, Katie girl. Are you all right?" He whispered the words against her hair as he ran his hands up and down her back.

"Now I am." She clung to him, reveling in his warmth and vitality. "I was so frightened. All I could think of was you tied to that tree in the freezing cold." Katherine cursed the manacles that still bound her wrists, wanting to put her arms around him. Hooking her hands into his waistband, she laid her head on his chest, absorbing his solid strength.

Wes rocked her gently in his arms, his face buried in her hair as he spoke. "I was afraid I'd lost you." His words rumbled against her ear as he echoed her own thoughts. He drew back from her and cupped her head between his hands, staring intently into her eyes. "I love you. Marry me." He brushed his warm lips over hers.

When he asked like that, Katherine thought, he could have anything he wanted. She laughed through her tears, giddy with relief. "We are married."

"Let's do it again. I want a ceremony I can remember." He ran his hands up and down her arms. "I want Consuela and Hannah to be there. And Gibby and the hands. And the neighbors. And pictures. And a photograph of us on our wedding day." He reminded her of a child talking about Christmas.

Katherine laughed at his ramblings, then sobered. "Everyone knows we're married. What will they think if we do it again?" The scandal of Hannah's birth had not lost its sting. She would do almost anything to avoid more gossip.

His expression became serious. "They'll think I love you so much I wanted to marry you twice."

Her chest tightened so with emotion that she had to whisper, "Oh, Wes. I love you." She grabbed two handfuls of jacket and hugged him as fiercely as she could wearing manacles and a chain. "Never leave me. Promise. Never."

"Not in this lifetime, Katie girl, never in this lifetime." He kissed her again, a hard possessive kiss that left her lips throbbing.

A groan from Sam brought their attention back to the situation at hand. Katherine could feel heat on her back. The rear of the old cabin was fully engulfed in flame. Wes, his arm around her waist, moved over to where his brother still sat. "Sam, come on, get up. We need to move back."

He slid a hand under his brother's forearm, and helped him to his feet. Wes walked Sam and Katherine away from the house, and eased both of them to the ground. He walked back to the house and up the steps, grabbed Denty's body by the back of his coat, and dragged it out into the yard. Then he fished around in the dead man's pockets and found the key to the manacles Katherine wore.

He sat down beside her. Gently he removed the manacles from her wrists, then pulled her into his arms. As Katherine relaxed, she began to notice the things around her. The fire had spread into the front room. Part of the roof collapsed in a huge shower of sparks.

Katherine tipped her head up and watched Wes in the glowing firelight, struck by what a calm, competent person he was. He saw what needed to be done, and went ahead and did the job. He gave her one of his grins, and kissed her. She felt her insides melt.

She must have had a guardian angel looking out for her the day she decided to ride into Dennison and pick someone off the gallows to get herself married.

He held her against him for a long time, and she put her hands around his waist and lay her head on his chest, listening to the strong, true beat of his heart.

Katherine tipped her head back and looked up into his blue eyes. "I love you, Wes Merrick."

No longer could she imagine living on the Rocking H without him.

Gently he lowered his head and softly kissed her lips, then drew her close again. She heard his words as they rumbled up from his broad chest. "And I love you, Katie Merrick, forever. Marry me."

She laughed at his single-minded persistence. He didn't sound as if he planned to give up on the idea of getting married again.

He cocked an eyebrow and waited.

She wanted to convince him so they could avoid gossip and just go back to the ranch and live as man and wife, so she tried again. "You're still not sure it was legal? Ask Judge Casey." She had the certificate in her desk drawer.

He brushed a kiss across her forehead. "Is that the memory you want of our wedding day? Getting married to an unconscious stranger in a sheriff's office while a hanging was going on?" He bent his head and kissed her on the ear.

Katherine felt a flutter of need and bent her head to give him easier access to her neck, where he nibbled on her earlobe. "Perhaps it did lack a bit of romance." She trembled and held on tighter to his waist.

"I want to remember our wedding day, with friends and flowers, and a cake. And Hannah." He worked his way around to her mouth, and gave her a kiss that was all lips and tongue, promising of things to come.

If a wedding was this important to him, she thought through a haze of need, she could ignore what people might think. "Just try leaving Hannah out. She loves a party." Her voice sounded breathy, as if she had just run all the way here.

He leaned back and grinned at her, looking very pleased that she had finally agreed to marry him again. "And I want to adopt Hannah. I want her name to be Merrick, too. Then I want to have a dozen more children. Our children."

She just smiled at his comment. He wanted a dozen? Maybe she'd check back with him after they had had three or four. He had no idea what it was like to raise a child.

"We can talk about children later." Katherine pulled away from him, embarrassed about the way she was acting in front of Wes's brother, glad he couldn't read her thoughts. She wanted to drag her husband into the trees and start on the next generation of Merricks right now.

Nestled against his chest, she watched, mesmerized, as flames licked out the front door. The small front windows of the little cabin blew out with popping sounds. Hot air warmed their faces. Flames roared up through holes the fire had created in the porch overhang. With a tremendous crash and another huge shower of sparks, the rest of the roof collapsed in on itself, and two of the walls followed.

The three of them turned at the sound of hooves on the road. Gibby, Tully, and Wade rode into the yard, their faces taking on a devilish look in the reflected orange light of the fire. Their mounts whinnied and danced in fright.

"What the hell happened here? We heard a shot and could see the flames from the bunkhouse." Gibby looked at Katherine, Wes, and Sam, then glanced over at Denty's body.

Wes spoke up. "First I want to get Katie home. I'll explain it all when we get back to the ranch. Wade, we left two horses about a quarter mile back by the stream. Get them for us."

Wade nodded and spurred his horse into a gallop.

"Tully, there are two more horses in the barn. Saddle them and bring them out."

Tully touched the brim of his hat and wheeled around toward the rickety looking outbuilding.

Suddenly the excitement of the night waned, and Katherine felt drained. She slumped against Wes, lacking the strength to sit up straight. She sighed at his tenderness, and leaned into him, welcoming the strength and warmth of his embrace.

21

Katherine sat at her dressing table, looking into the oval mirror as she poked tiny silk flowers into the mass of curls gathered at her neck. Snow lay a foot deep on the ground, and there were no live blossoms in all of the Montana territory. She didn't really care. Her wedding would be special without real flowers.

Hannah scrambled up onto the bench beside her and peered into the mirror at their reflection as Katherine fastened her mother's opals on her ears. "We are pretty, Mama."

"Yes, we are, darling girl." Katherine tucked a flower into her daughter's curls. The child smelled of soap and vanilla. She must have been helping Consuela frost the cake.

"Wes is going to be my papa, and Sam told me to call him Uncle. Can I?"

"Of course, darling." Tears welled up in her eyes.

"Are you crying, Mama?" Hannah patted the back of her mother's hand where it rested on the crisp lace runner atop the table.

"Good tears, Hannah, only good tears." Katherine wiped at her eyes and hugged her daughter. Hannah wore a dress of pale yellow silk made from the same yardage as her own gown, the fabric she had purchased the day she and Wes had gone into Dennison.

"Gibby and Hannibal and Wes are downstairs, and they have on white shirts." Hannah fiddled with a bottle of perfume as she spoke.

"Today is very special, so they wanted to get dressed up." Katherine took the bottle out of Hannah's little hands and removed the stopper. She dabbed a drop of perfume behind each of the child's ears, then did the same to herself. "Now we smell as good as we look." She put the perfume down and surveyed her hair and dress, adjusting the ruffles at the cuff of her long sleeves so that they covered the bandages on her wrists. "I think we're ready."

Hannah held her wrist to her nose and sniffed noisily. "Is Wes going to marry us right now?"

Katherine smiled at the way her child phrased her question. In a way he was marrying both of them, because from this day Hannah would carry his name, too. "Yes, darling girl, he is."

"Then the party?"

"Then the party. Shall we go?" Katherine took her daughter by the hand and walked out her bedroom door. She paused at the door to Wes's room. All his things lay folded neatly on his bed, ready to move into her room. She felt her body go warm and dewy at the thought of waking up in his arms every morning. Hannah tugged on her hand to get her moving.

Katherine and Hannah stopped at the head of the stairs. Hannah spotted Hannibal and Gibby down in the front room, and let go of her mother's hand to hurry and join her friends.

Wes waited near the bottom of the stairs. He turned when he heard Hannah's shoes come clattering down. Katherine stood on the landing, watching him. Lordy but she looked beautiful. He started up the stairs at the same time she started down, her yellow silk dress shimmering, the flounces at the hem dancing as she held the skirt so she could descend. He took her hand and felt it tremble as he tucked it in the crook of his arm.

Bending toward her, he smelled the fragrance of lavender. Tenderly he kissed her cheek, then whispered into her hair, "I love you."

She turned her face up to him for another kiss. "And I love you. Forever, with all my heart."

In that instant, he knew in his heart that marrying Katherine was the best thing he had ever done.

Together they started down the stairs, full of love and hopes and dreams, headed for their new life together.

Author's note

Some of the towns of the American West, like the fictitious town of Dennison, Montana, adopted laws that originated in England allowing a spinster to claim a condemned man on the theory that the prisoner might be saved by the love and influence of a good woman.

Let HarperMonogram Sweep You Away!

Sooner or Later by **Debbie Macomber**
Twelve million copies of her books in print. Letty Madden asks a soldier of fortune to help her find her brother in Central America, but Murphy's price is high—one night with the demure postmistress. Letty accepts and Murphy realizes that protecting his heart may prove to be his most difficult mission of all.

A Hidden Magic by **Terri Lynn Wilhelm**
Ghost romance. When Cicely Honeysett sells Griffin Tyrrell her family's estate, she forgets to tell him about the mischievous ghost that has made Cranwick Abbey his own. At odds with the unwelcoming spirit, Griffin yearns for Cicely—a heavenly creature who will share his bed instead of trying to chase him from it.

Queen of My Heart by **Donna Valentino**
Time travel romance. Dante Trevani escapes from an unwanted betrothal in Tudor England by traveling through time to 19th-century Arizona and beautiful Gloriana Carlisle. When he realizes his fiancée is destined to be the Queen of England, Dante must choose between returning to the past or staying with the queen of his heart.

Montana Morning by **Jill Limber**
Debut novel. To find a husband and claim her family's ranch in the Montana Territory, Katherine Holman marries Wes Merrick and saves him from the hangman's noose. Wes refuses to ride off into the sunset, however, and instead tries to turn a marriage of convenience into a match made in heaven.

And in case you missed last month's selections . . .

Chances Are by **Robin Lee Hatcher**
Over three million copies of her books in print. Her young daughter's illness forces traveling actress Faith Butler to take a job at the Jagged R Ranch working for Drake Rutledge. Passions rise when the beautiful thespian is drawn to her rugged employer and the forbidden pleasure of his touch.

Mystic Moon by Patricia Simpson

"One of the premier writers of supernatural romance."—Romantic Times. A brush with death changes Carter Greyson's life and irrevocably links him to an endangered Indian tribe. Dr. Arielle Scott, who is intrigued by the mysterious Carter, shares this destiny—a destiny that will lead them both to the magic of lasting love.

Just a Miracle by Zita Christian

When dashing Jake Darrow brings his medicine show to Coventry, Montana, pharmacist Brenna McAuley wants nothing to do with him. But it's only a matter of time before Brenna discovers that romance is just what the doctor ordered.

Raven's Bride by Lynn Kerstan

When Glenys Shea robbed the reclusive Earl of Ravensby, she never expected to steal his heart instead of his gold. Now the earl's prisoner, the charming thief must prove her innocence—and her love.

Escape to Romance
and
WIN A YEAR OF ROMANCE!

Ten lucky winners will receive a free year of romance—*more than 30 free books*. Every book HarperMonogram publishes in 1997 will be delivered directly to your doorstep if you are one of the ten winners drawn at random.

Harper Monogram

FOR THE FINEST IN
WESTERN HISTORICAL ROMANCE

THE MARRYING KIND by Sharon Ihle

Liberty Ann Justice has no time for the silver-tongued stranger she believes is trying to destroy her father's Wyoming newspaper. Donovan isn't about to let a little misunderstanding hinder his pursuit of happiness, or his pursuit of the tempestuous vixen who has him hungering for her sweet love.

HONEYSUCKLE DeVINE by Susan Macias

To collect her inheritance, Laura Cannon needs to join Jesse Travers's cattle drive—and become his wife. The match is only temporary, but long days on the trail lead to nights filled with fiery passion.

TEXAS LONESOME by Alice Duncan

In 1890s San Francisco, Emily von Plotz gives advice to the lovelorn in her weekly newspaper column. A reader who calls himself "Texas Lonesome" seems to be the man for her, but wealthy rancher Will Tate is more than willing to show her who the real expert is in matters of the heart.

RECKLESS DESTINY by Teresa Southwick

Believing that Arizona Territory is no place for a lady, Captain Kane Carrington sent proper easterner Cady Tanner packing. Now the winsome schoolteacher is back, and ready to teach Captain Carrington a lesson in love.